HOMECOMING
Homicide

KELLY BRAKENHOFF

Also By Kelly Brakenhoff

Cassandra Sato Mysteries
Dead End (Short Story)
Death by Dissertation
Dead Week
Dead of Winter Break
Scavenger Haunt (Short Story)
Death 101: Extra Credit
Halloween Hustle (Novella)
Primary Source (Short Story)
Homecoming Homicide

Duke the Deaf Dog ASL Series
Picture books
Never Mind
Farts Make Noise
My Dawg Koa
Sometimes I Like the Quiet
Duke the Deaf Dog Workbooks Ages 3-5/Ages 6-9
Chapter books
I Belong Here
It's My Story
Take Your Shot
IEPs R4U and Me / Teacher Guide Workbook

Previously in *Death 101: Extra Credit...*

Cassandra Sato, Morton College's perpetually over-caffeinated VP of Student Affairs, is still knee-deep in drama and mayhem. Her latest honor? "Queen of Doom"—a nickname gifted by her students, with love, fear, and no filter.

In Book Four, she's juggling faculty feuds, budget black holes, and a campus theater production with more sword fights than common sense. While pushing for better emergency alerts for Deaf students, Cassandra stumbles into another mystery full of suspicious paperwork, awkward suspensions, and secrets hiding in plain sight.

When her colleague and friend Professor Shannon Bryant ends up in hot water (because of course he does), Cassandra jumps in to clear his name. She uncovers shady dealings, navigates office politics like a pro, and proves she may not be ready to run a college quite yet, but she's definitely ready to go to bat for her people.

Meanwhile, her parents are visiting from Hawai'i with plenty of opinions and zero chill about her romantic life. They also manage to completely spoil her dog Murphy, who still isn't sure how he feels about his new human. Cassandra is also sorting through big feelings about her late fiancé, her maybe-boyfriend Marcus, and whether she'll ever feel truly at home in the land of snow shovels and potlucks.

Somewhere in the middle of all the chaos, she starts to realize something big: this job is more than a stepping stone. It's a chance to make real change for the students and the college community. It's about life and living—even when the course catalog says Death 101 and doom is apparently part of the uniform.

By the end, there's a new president at Morton, Shannon is back where he belongs, and she's reminded—again—that peace and quiet around here usually means something weird is about to happen.

One chapter ends, another begins. And Cassandra Sato is ready.

Probably.

For Lori Ideta and her mother, Evelyn,
whose stories shaped the heartbeat of this one.

Hawaiian Terms Glossary

*M*OST OF THE HAWAIIAN *words appearing in this series can be guessed from the context of the sentences. But if you ever get stumped, check back to this page and confirm the meaning of the word. These terms are used in everyday life and conversations in Hawaiʻi where Cassandra Sato was born and raised.*

ʻĀINA: the land; often used with reverence, reflecting deep cultural and spiritual connection to place

ALOHA: hello, goodbye, and love or affection

CHICKEN SKIN: Hawaiian-style goosebumps. The kind you get from eerie stories, beautiful music, or moments that hit you right in the heart

DA KINE: the word you use when you don't know the word, whatsit, that thing

HAOLE: a white person, a foreigner, a tourist, a person not from Hawaiʻi or Polynesia

HAUPIA: a traditional Hawaiian coconut milk pudding, often served at luaus

HULA: a type of dance of Hawaiʻi

KEIKI: children

KUPUNA: elder or ancestor who is respected for wisdom, guidance, and life experience.

MANAPUA: Delicious food with origins from China (char siu bao). Usually sweet & sour pork wrapped in a steamed slightly sweet bun, but it can be made with a variety of fillings

MUSUBI: Spam musubi is a popular food in Hawaiʻi and typically consists of spam, rice, nori, and shoyu (soy sauce)

MANA: a sacred word from native Hawaiian culture meaning the spiritual energy of power and strength

MAHALO: thank you, gratitude, respect

MENEHUNES: (men-neh-HOO-nay) are shy, mischievous legendary creatures

'OHANA: family

'ONO: delicious food, tasty (also the name of a type of fish)

PAU: finished, done

SHISHI: local slang for "pee." Used by kids and adults alike. If someone says they need to shishi, just point them to the bathroom and don't ask questions

STINK EYE: death glare. The silent art of side-eyeing someone so hard they feel it in their soul. Used by aunties, toddlers, and grumpy uncles across the islands

TUTU: grandma

WĀHINE: female or woman

Chapter One

CASSANDRA SATO STEPPED INTO the Duke Kahanamoku hotel lobby with a plan, a clipboard, and the naïve belief that everything would go smoothly.

Which, in hindsight, was adorable considering nothing with Morton College had gone smoothly since her first day as Vice President for Student Affairs.

"I can't believe you grew up here, Dr. Sato," Logan Dunn said, dropping his backpack with a heavy thud on the expansive travertine floor before sprinting after his classmates.

A chaotic tower of suitcases and carry-ons teetered near the concierge desk, abandoned as the students rushed outside to take in the view.

"I can't believe she left paradise for Nebraska," quipped Ethan Miller. "I mean, who in their right mind does that?"

Who indeed?

Cassandra allowed herself a small smile at their wide-eyed enthusiasm. Their participation in the Honolulu PastForward conference would earn them elective credit hours, and for some, this was their first time on a plane, their first glimpse of the ocean. Their excitement was contagious and not even a little bit quiet.

She passed the front desk, where a glossy sign on an easel greeted them in bold vintage lettering:

WELCOME TO PASTFORWARD: HAWAI'I UNFORGOTTEN

A FIELD SCHOOL IN HISTORICAL RECKONING

LOST RECORDS. SILENT WITNESSES. UNANSWERED QUESTIONS.

GO BEYOND TEXTBOOKS AND TACKLE THE STORIES HISTORY LEFT UNFIN-ISHED OR DELIBERATELY ERASED. THROUGH PRIMARY SOURCES, IMMERSIVE VR, AND ORAL NARRATIVES, YOU'LL RE-INVESTIGATE CASES THAT SHAPED COMMUNITIES AND CHALLENGED THE OFFICIAL RECORD.

BRING YOUR CURIOSITY, CRITICAL THINKING, AND CAFFEINE. YOU'LL NEED ALL THREE.

THE PAST ISN'T DEAD. IT'S JUST WAITING FOR SOMEONE TO LISTEN.

Cassandra paused, her gaze catching the moody description clearly written by a group of well-meaning grad students. Overdone? Absolutely. But probably not wrong.

Moments later, she stepped onto the lanai facing Waikīkī beach, inhaling the familiar scent of saltwater and sunscreen.

Ivy Olson snapped photos with her phone. "You guys saw the Past-Forward rumors, right? Everyone's saying this year's mystery challenge is deep-dive worthy." She lowered her voice, "There's a whole thread online claiming it has WWII wartime spies, encrypted love letters, the works."

Logan added, "My cousin did New Orleans. She said it was ninety percent ghost stories and ten percent dodging hexes from wizard wannabes."

Every year PastForward picked a new city, a new unsolved case, and invited students to play historian-slash-detective-slash-time traveler. Ghost-jazz murders in New Orleans, Prohibition bootleggers under a Chicago preschool. This year's mystery happened to be in her backyard.

Cassandra shifted her tote bag, nodding. "My former professor, Dr. Nakano, runs Hawai'i Unforgotten. If he helped design this year's challenge, expect drama. He never does anything halfway."

Ivy grinned. "Honestly, I'm here for it. True crime, high stakes, postcard views. What's not to love?"

Cassandra stepped farther out, letting the view fill her vision. The air wrapped around her, thick and familiar like a warm hug. Unmistakably home. The ocean breeze brushed her cheek, teasing her with the kind of homecoming that whispered, *You could stay. You belong here.*

Then her phone buzzed.

Reality. Nebraska.

With a sigh, she pulled it from her pocket. Marcus Fischer. Her boyfriend of several months and lately, a source of emotional whiplash thanks to Fran Morrison, the new college president, and the shared ghosts of their service in Iraq.

She braced for impact.

The din of tourists and excited students faded as she answered.

"You don't happen to know anything about construction near the student center, do you?" Marcus's voice was tight.

Cassandra frowned. "Construction? No. Why?"

"There's a crew out there unloading equipment. Looks like something major. I wasn't informed."

Her fingers gripped the phone tighter. Marcus ran Facilities. If dirt was moving, he should've signed off first.

"I haven't heard a thing," she said. "Maybe it's something Fran or the board fast-tracked? You know how things have been since she moved in."

Marcus let out a long exhale. "That's what I figured. Still annoying not to be looped in."

Cassandra nodded, even though he couldn't see it. Fran had barely warmed the seat as college president, and already she was making power plays.

"If you think it's serious, you should push back," Cassandra said.

"I will. Just wanted to make sure it didn't sneak through while you were still interim."

"Nope. Not on my watch," she said. "Let me know what you find out."

"Will do."

Cassandra slid her phone into her pocket, taking one last glance at the ocean before heading back inside to the students milling near the luggage. No matter how far she traveled, Morton College found ways to pull her back.

She scanned the lobby, nudging her focus back to the plan.

"We've got the opening dinner in an hour," Cassandra said, holding out a stack of room keys. "Go ahead and drop your bags, get settled if you need to, and meet back here in 45."

Ethan took his key with a grin. "Did you see the swimming pool has three levels?"

Diego, who'd probably try to surf a tsunami if given the chance, was already plotting his escape. "I don't need to eat. Let's hop in quick on our way to the room."

Of course. Nothing said higher education like multilevel chlorinated bliss.

Cassandra felt her pulse throb in her temple. She opened her mouth to rein them in—

"Last one upstairs sleeps on the couch. And it won't be me!" Brandon Nguyen darted into the elevator, barely glancing back.

The odds of everyone making it to dinner on time without getting lost, sidetracked, or accidentally joining a ukulele jam session? Slim to zilch.

While the students clattered upstairs, Cassandra turned back toward the beach. The familiar shape of Diamond Head crater anchored the far end of Waikīkī, steady as ever. Between the hotel's meticulously landscaped property and the shoreline, people of every shape, size, and SPF level soaked up the late-afternoon sun.

Well, except for the lobster-colored man wrestling with a rogue beach umbrella. Cassandra smirked. Tourists.

"Auntie Cassandra, did you see the ocean?" Tony O'Brien bounced on his toes like the Pacific might vanish if he blinked.

"Seen it a few times, buddy," Cassandra said, ruffling his curly red hair.

He was eleven, relentlessly curious, and currently winning his long-running campaign for Favorite Non-Blood Relative.

His mom, Meg, the trip's co-chaperone, stood nearby reviewing the itinerary. Technically, she was here to interpret for their Deaf student. Realistically, this was a full-circle trip.

They hadn't planned on coming. Meg had been very pregnant when Cassandra organized the conference visit, and traveling with a newborn ranked somewhere above wrestling an octopus on her personal challenge scale.

Then Cassandra's mom had deployed her full grandma powers and offered their family home in Waipahu.

"The O'Briens lived at Schofield for five years," Michiko had said, "that makes them *'ohana*. And 'ohana doesn't sleep in a hotel." She was hand to chest like the idea physically pained her. "What would the neighbors say? I open my home to strangers, but not my daughter's best friend? Might as well hang a sign outside that says Michiko Sato has no aloha spirit."

Meg had wisely surrendered. Resistance was futile.

Connor O'Brien stood near the lobby doors, baby Olivia snugly velcroed to his chest in a wrap, rocking gently in full Vacation Dad mode. He still carried himself like the Army man he was—rigid posture, calm intensity—but today his mission appeared to be "don't drop the pacifier."

Cassandra smiled. This family. This island. These people reminded her who she was underneath the spreadsheets and crisis emails.

She exhaled, letting Nebraska slide off her shoulders.

By some miracle, most of the students assembled in the lobby alcove on time.

Lexi Wagner, social butterfly and pre-law hopeful, was mid-rant about sunscreen conspiracies. "I'm just saying, if the FDA can't agree on reef-safe formulas, how are we supposed to trust anything?"

Maria Gonzales, whose energy registered at a much more sustainable wattage, quietly studied the conference app like there would be a pop quiz later. "I wonder what the most bizarre virtual reality booth will have."

"I heard one shows drones flying over secret jungle communes," Lexi said, eyes bright. "If it turns out to be shirtless hermits doing CrossFit, I'm deleting the app."

Cassandra suppressed a laugh. So much for an academic mindset.

Lance Erickson leaned against a column, arms crossed, taking in the scene. When Diego and Ethan strolled in with wet hair and guilty grins, Lance arched a brow and signed something quick and dry.

Meg glanced up from her phone just in time to catch it. "He says we've officially entered the 'questionable decisions' portion of the field trip."

Cassandra rolled her eyes and signed, *And we've been here less than three hours.*

Lance grinned and gave her a mock salute.

Ethan and Diego flopped into leather chairs with no shame, just as Cassandra began the group welcome and formal intros.

She gestured to her left. "This is Meg O'Brien, our team's ASL interpreter and my right hand this week."

Meg gave a warm wave, already scanning the group like someone who'd run logistics in a war zone. Which, at a community college, she basically had.

"She and I have worked together for years," Cassandra continued. "She knows how to keep me organized and how to keep you out of trouble. Or at least document it clearly."

A ripple of laughter spread through the students, but Meg barely smirked—already mid-interpretation for Lance.

"And in case you were wondering," Cassandra added, "yes, she brought her family along. No, her baby will not be attending the keynote lecture. Unless we need a better guest speaker."

Tony grinned and gave a thumbs-up from the sidelines.

Cassandra folded her hands and slipped into syllabus mode. "You all earned your spot on this trip by proposing solid poster topics that linked Nebraska and Hawai'i. You'll present them this week, attend sessions, and take notes like your GPA depends on it. Because it kind of does."

She caught the side-eye from Diego and returned it with a raised eyebrow. No one warned them field trips came with homework.

"And yes, there will be a reflection paper when we're back in Carson," she added. "But you'll be fine. Just pay attention and try staying semi-conscious during the panel discussions."

"Wait, this is graded?" Ethan stage-whispered to Diego.

Ignoring the hecklers, Cassandra adopted her best museum field trip voice: firm but not hovering. "Alright, team. Let's walk over together. Dinner's at the conference center, and I'd like us seated before the welcome remarks start."

She paused, letting her voice carry above the shuffle of backpacks and sneakers. "This is a real conference, not a beach vacation. You're presenting. You're learning. And you're solving a historical murder in your free time. So, you know... welcome to the liberal arts dream."

They fell into step behind her, amped on post-travel energy and the promise of free buffet shrimp.

Students in matching aloha shirts stood at every doorway, directing attendees toward exhibition areas, meeting rooms, and the buffet dinner. The cheerful, "Aloha! Welcome to Honolulu," in their lilting local voices were balm to Cassandra's jet-lagged senses.

Dignitaries in elegant lei chatted in small groups and the air buzzed with a mix of academia, tourism, and something indefinably Hawaiian.

As Cassandra walked past the booths, familiar accents caught her ear.

"Hey braddah, been long time, eh," one man said, clasping another's hand in a handshake-half-hug.

As they neared a brightly lit display, Lexi grabbed Maria's arm. "Check out the 'Lava Surfing Extravaganza!' You can surf molten lava down an erupting volcano."

"Sign me up," Ethan said, scanning the QR code. "It says if you wipe out, you don't just get wet, you get pixelated into digital smoke!"

Then Diego pointed toward a darker booth with moody lighting and vintage signage. "Is that the VR murder mystery?" he asked, squinting. "The one with the cash prize?"

Cassandra followed his gaze. A towering banner loomed over the booth, its red letters stylized like dripping blood:

WHO WAS THE MĀNOA MARAUDER?

She nodded. "Every PastForward Conference builds the mystery around a real unsolved case. This one's from right here in Honolulu."

Maria and Ivy posed for a selfie in front of the backdrop: a blown-up photo of early 1900s Honolulu, all wooden storefronts and horse-drawn carriages.

Ivy read the placard. "They added more VR this year, and the prize money's doubled."

A slow, electric thrill ran through Cassandra. A cold case. A historic mansion. Solved through archives, analysis, and a little bit of storytelling. She could already picture the immersive VR, the clunky digitized photo scans, the familiar musty scent of microfilm rooms. Her students were going to love this.

Then Maria pointed to the display. "Did they base that map on something real, or just create it for the virtual reality game?"

"They pulled it from a 1909 fire insurance survey," Ivy said, not missing a beat. "I saw the digitized version on the PastForward site last week. It's pretty detailed."

Cassandra's smile faltered. The other cities had moonshine and haunted diaries. Honolulu had scars. A cold case, real victims, and a silence that hadn't faded. This was her island, her history.

"Dude," Diego Ramirez whispered, snapping a photo. "This is sick."

Was it right to turn tragedy into a scavenger hunt? She'd agreed to lead this trip to connect students with real history. Not gamify cultural trauma.

No pressure, she thought grimly. *Just solve a century-old mystery without offending an entire state.*

Before she could spiral further, she glanced at her watch. Duty first.

"Alright, team," she said, corralling the group with a half-turn, "keynote starts in ten. Let's be on time and look like we belong here."

As they moved past the exhibits, Cassandra felt the tug.

The aloha shirts, the slack key guitar playing over the speakers, even the faint, smoky smell of teriyaki BBQ all hit her like a wave. The ocean was just steps away. She could hear it beneath the noise, feel its pulse in the humidity, in her skin. In her blood.

Surfing had always been more than a hobby. It was the drop, the pull, the pure freedom of sliding across a wall of water. She'd told herself she didn't need it anymore.

And yet... standing here now, she ached for it.

For a split second, she let herself wonder: *What if she stayed? What if she never went back?*

Then her gaze snagged once more on the blood-red banner.

Who was the Mānoa Marauder?

A shiver traced her spine.

She had a feeling she was about to find out.

Chapter Two

C ASSANDRA LEANED BACK IN her chair, her stomach uncomfortably full from a dinner of BBQ chicken, sticky rice, and haupia dessert. She regretted clearing her plate, but the tastes of home were impossible to resist.

The ballroom lights dimmed. She sat straighter in her seat as the emcee introduced one of the conference sponsors and cued up the video for *Hawai'i Unforgotten* on the ballroom's big screen.

A swell of slack key guitar filled the air, followed by sweeping drone footage of modern-day Pearl Harbor, Waikīkī, and Diamond Head. Then the tone shifted. Lush green peaks beyond the Pali lookout gave way to grainy black-and-white photos: Queen Lili'uokalani, her royal family, her people.

The contrast hit hard. What O'ahu had been, and what it had become.

The voiceover spoke of land lost, languages silenced, communities displaced. A century's worth of struggle distilled into two and a half minutes. Cassandra felt every word, less like nostalgia, more like reckoning. Hawai'i Unforgotten's mission was clear: bring justice to overlooked histories.

As the last notes faded, pride stirred in her chest. PastForward never opened with dry itineraries or tech demos. They grounded you first in place and people so the whole week felt personal. Whether you came for presentations, VR simulations, or the Cold Case Challenge, you couldn't ignore the history breathing through it all.

When the lights came up, the emcee returned to the mic. "Please welcome this year's keynote speaker and our Cold Case Challenge host, Dr. Richard Nakano."

He looked older, yes. His hair was more salt than pepper, his face a little leaner, but the passionate voice was the same. He wove Hawai'i's past and present into a single unfinished story: colonization, resistance, sovereignty, identity. And somehow, despite the weight of it all, he made it feel hopeful.

Even her students had stopped fidgeting by the end.

As the lights brightened, the screen behind him flickered to a new montage: weathered gravestones, stacks of aging police files, the ornate gates of Iolani Palace, and an aerial view of homes nestled in the Mānoa Valley.

The emcee stepped forward with a clipboard. "This year's teams have been matched to investigative sites across O'ahu: the Honolulu Police Station, Iolani Palace, the State Archives, a plantation estate in Mānoa, and a warehouse district once famous for smuggling and scandal."

A ripple of excitement moved through the crowd.

Dr. Nakano smiled faintly. "Each site holds a piece of the puzzle. Will you put them together and crack a hundred-year-old case? Teams have been assigned field locations based on your survey responses and academic focus."

Cassandra clapped with the rest, but a quiet thought lingered. *Nakano knew exactly how to shape a moment.* Maybe that was leadership. Or maybe it was something else entirely.

"Before we begin, I want to thank the folks who made this year's immersive experience possible." He gestured toward a small group seated near the stage. "Our planning committee includes Nathaniel Oliver, whose family graciously granted us access to their ancestral estate—" a smattering of polite applause followed—"along with reps from the City Clerk's Office, the Mānoa Agricultural Research Station, and the HPD's digital archives. You'll see their fingerprints all over this week's events."

A few others, an eager grad student in cat-eye glasses, a local museum rep in a sharp aloha shirt, waved awkwardly from their seats.

As Dr. Nakano stepped down from the podium, Cassandra joined the line to greet him, her program booklet curling under her grip.

His face lit up the moment he saw her. "Cassandra Sato! Or should I say Dr. Sato?" He emphasized the title with a smile. "Is it true you moved to the mainland?"

He still had that gift, the way he made students feel seen, like the smartest person in the room might be you.

She grinned. "Nebraska. I brought a small group of Morton College students to the conference."

"Nebraska," he repeated, adjusting his glasses. "Their women's volleyball team is always top-notch."

"They are amazing athletes, sir." She laughed.

"Tell me," he smiled thoughtfully, "Are your students as relentless as you were?"

She smiled, a little caught off guard, but in a good way. He remembered.

"You always tackled the messy stuff head-on," she added. "It's been years, but I still think about your seminar on Hawaiian sovereignty."

"How fortunate," he said smoothly, "we're placing your team at the Mānoa Plantation House."

Her eyebrows lifted. "The coffee estate?"

His smile didn't waver. "I thought it might resonate with your students' range of backgrounds. Some stories ask to be remembered by the right voices."

He let the statement settle, then added with a wink, "And I expect Morton College will give the others a run for their money."

Cassandra hesitated, reading something deeper beneath his words.

"You know," he said, shifting his tone, "tough topics often hide the most truth. People are multilayered. History is too."

Cassandra wanted to stay longer. Ask more. But the line behind her was growing, and it wasn't her moment anymore.

She tucked the program into her tote and rejoined Meg and the students, weaving through the crowd of buzzing academics and over-stimulated undergrads. Everyone seemed energized except Cassandra, who was still replaying Nakano's words in her head.

People are multilayered. History is too.

Which, unfortunately, also applied to rival administrators.

Just ahead, a group in matching forest green polo shirts moved confidently toward the registration desk. Cassandra spotted their leader instantly. Kalia Chun.

Of course, Kalia's team would have coordinated uniforms. Cassandra suppressed a smirk.

Kalia hadn't noticed her yet, which was fine by Cassandra. The last thing she needed was an early run-in with Miss Private School Perfect.

Meg, seeing where Cassandra's attention had drifted, leaned in with a low chuckle. "Looks like the polo brigade is here. Bet she's got a minute-by-minute spreadsheet of their itinerary."

Cassandra rolled her eyes. "She probably wrote her own phone app."

They shared a quiet laugh before heading to the group check-in table, but the sight of Kalia's team chafed. Small things turned competitive around her. Big things got messy.

And if this year's mystery turned out to be as dark as the rumors said, Cassandra had no doubt Kalia would find a way to treat the whole thing like a season finale episode of The Amazing Race.

Jet lag was doing battle with adrenaline, and Cassandra had downed a diet soda at dinner in a doomed attempt to level out. Her students were running on island buzz and shave ice, scattering to the lava surfing booth and pool decks.

Cassandra's phone vibrated. Ten texts from her mother. So much for easing in gently.

She and Meg made their way across the convention center to the hotel lanai, passing actors dressed as vintage TV icons posing for selfies near a tiki torch-lined stage. A faux Magnum P.I., complete with mustache and Detroit Tigers cap, cheesed it up with a group of tourists, while a man in a floral blazer recreated the iconic Brady Bunch Hawaiian vacation episode, waving a tiki idol in the air like it might actually summon a curse.

Soon Cassandra heard a familiar voice. "Tom Selleck is here! Do you see? I've met him!"

Cassandra sighed, already bracing.

Family legend included many sightings of Tom Selleck during his *Magnum P.I.* years. The most unforgettable? When her mother had cornered the poor man at the dry cleaners for a ten-minute conversation.

Behind her mother, the rest of the Sato family trailed along: her nephews skipping on their gangly legs, her father smiling placidly, and her younger sisters exchanging embarrassed looks.

She's doing it again.

"Aloha, Mom," Cassandra said, half-laughing, half-mortified. "Mr. Selleck can probably hear you."

Kathy, her middle sister, added, "Everyone can hear you, Mom."

Sure enough, heads turned in their direction, witnessing the family reunion. Cassandra and Meg hugged each one in turn, pecking them on the cheek.

Being smothered in hugs and noise was overwhelming, but comforting in a way Nebraska never quite managed. These people were her foundation.

"I thought we were meeting on the hotel lanai," Cassandra held up her phone containing multiple texts confirming their plans.

Her youngest sister, Sarah, held her toddler Diana and shrugged. "Mom couldn't sit still. She was too excited to see the prodigal daughter."

They side-hugged and Cassandra smiled at Diana.

"Aloha, sweetie. Can auntie hold you?" She held out her arms in invitation, but Diana turned her head away and buried her face in her mother's shoulder.

"She's having a shy day. Wait thirty minutes, and she'll probably bawl when I want to take her home later."

The nephews weren't shy. They hugged her tightly at waist-level.

"Eh, braddahs! You went get so tall already?" She marveled, slipping into her local accent.

They'd each grown several inches. And that was the tangible proof she'd been away an entire year.

"Keoni and Leilani aren't here?" she asked, referring to their brother and sister-in-law.

Kathy's lips pressed together and the subtle head shake was a signal not to ask more questions in front of everyone.

What was that all about?

"Wait, was this guy around when you were a kid?" Sarah asked their dad as they passed the closed Mānoa Marauder exhibit. "I remember reading about it in school, but I didn't realize they never caught anyone."

Ken Sato chuckled and ran a hand through the gray buzz cut hair on his head. "Eh, now. Raising three daughters get me many gray hairs, but that guy was from 1910! How old you tink I am?"

As they continued walking, Cassandra noted unusual silence and turned back looking for her mother. Mama stood toes to the Marauder exhibit banner, leaning forward examining the black and white photos in the advertisement.

When she felt Cassandra watching, she broke away, nonchalant mask firmly in place. She hustled to catch up, her short legs working double-time.

"Must be Mai Tai time, eh?" Mama said as she passed by, taking her place at the front of their family.

Since when did her mother drink Mai Tai's? Cassandra's gaze bored into the back of her mother's head. Apparently more things had changed this past year besides her nephews' growth spurts.

"How's my grand-dog, Murphy?" Her mother asked. "You didn't give him up to a shelter did you?"

"Mom! How could you think such a thing? I promised I'd take care of him. We've come to an understanding. He stopped making shishi all over my house, and I only pet him when he asks for it. Andy Summers volunteered to dog-sit while I'm gone."

"Andy Summers, eh?" Her mom's eyes twinkled. "Good with animals. Nice arms. You could do worse."

"Okay, wow. Don't make this weird."

"I'll bake some doggie treats you can bring home from his tutu. I crocheted him a little sweater for the winter, too."

When her mom turned to face forward again, Cassandra rolled her eyes so far back she nearly bumped into her sister.

She muttered to Sarah, "You would not believe the way she spoiled that picky dog."

"You're kidding, right? She's like that on steroids when it comes to the grandkids. Every day is special at Tutu's house."

After hugs, small talk, and a barrage of family selfies near the hotel entrance, her parents and sisters headed home, content with the brief reunion. Except her mom, who was still grumbling about how the "real" Magnum wouldn't have had such skinny legs. It had taken three people and a firm reality check to convince her the man in the Detroit Tigers cap was an actor.

The goodbyes finally over, Cassandra met up with Meg and Jocelyn on the beach. They'd already staked out three chairs near the shoreline, the ocean doing its quiet work as the noise of the day melted away.

Jocelyn, her childhood best friend, lounged with her feet buried in the sand, wind tugging at her curls, laughing and sipping wine like they'd never spent a day apart.

"So. Dr. Nakano. Still lighting academic fires wherever he goes?"

"Some things never change." Cassandra said.

"He's got a reputation," Jocelyn went on. "Brilliant, impossible, totally magnetic. Half his students left our class ready to start a revolution. The other half transferred to geology."

Meg snorted. "The best professors make people uncomfortable."

Cassandra nodded, watching the horizon. "He made us see history differently. Not just names and dates but power. Who got to tell the story, and who got erased."

"But?" Jocelyn asked, catching the pause.

"I don't know," Cassandra said after a beat. "Something about tonight felt... curated."

"Dramatic curated, or manipulative curated?"

She let that hang. "Let's just say I forgot how good he is at steering the narrative."

The waves lapped at the shore as the conversation paused.

"Okay, your turn," Cassandra said, nudging Jocelyn with her foot. "You lasted, what, a year in Florida before coming back? Spill."

"The summer heat. The winter snowbirds. The snakes," Jocelyn said. "I thought surviving a tsunami was bad, but Florida has rattlers. Literal ones."

Meg's eyes widened. "No freaking way."

"The job was great. Florida had the labs, the tech, the career ladder. Coral Gables gave me a research team and a fancy USDA badge. But..."

"But?" Cassandra prompted.

"They have beaches and Mickey Mouse, but it's not home. I was studying genetic markers in endangered avocados while sweating through every piece of clothing I owned."

Meg winced. "Florida is the armpit of the tropics. No offense."

"None taken. Then this position opened at the USDA field station here, tied to native crop preservation and community science outreach. I start in two weeks."

"That sounds... perfect for you," Cassandra said.

"It is. It's science, but connecting culture and local agriculture. I'm still a nerd. Just a nerd in rubber boots now."

"With a hot boyfriend?" Cassandra teased.

"Not just that. Although Jeff is spicy-hot and carries heavy things without being asked, so."

"Well, if he makes you this happy," Cassandra said, "I'm rooting for him."

"I don't know. Maybe this time I got it right. New guy, new job, new me."

"And Jeff?" Meg asked, waggling her eyebrows.

"From Hilo, actually. We both moved halfway around the world just to meet the boy and girl next door."

Cassandra mock-gasped. "You're a walking Hallmark movie."

"If Hallmark had centipedes and avocado gene sequencing."

They all laughed, and Cassandra let it settle before adding, "Actually, I could use another adult on deck. Want to help out this week?"

Jocelyn tilted her head. "With what? I'm not teaching anymore, remember?"

"Exactly. You've got local knowledge and a healthy amount of skepticism."

"You're asking me to join your Scooby Doo gang?"

"Honorary team wrangler. Scooby snacks optional."

Jocelyn grinned. "Count me in."

Cassandra exhaled into the hush, warmed by the reunion. Peace like this was probably on a timer.

"Tomorrow, it's all conference and competition," she murmured, "like academic Survivor with less sleep and more whining."

"Then rest up," Meg said. "We'll need our fearless leader at full power."

"Whatever happens," Jocelyn said, "we've got your back."

And just like that, vacation was over.

Chapter Three

B Y MORNING, THE RESORT had traded vacation vibes for academic hustle. Adrenaline and curiosity had kept most students up past midnight, but now they reappeared jet-lagged, caffeine-fueled, and ready to compete. From her hotel window, Cassandra spotted clusters gathering outside the conference center, tote bags slung over shoulders, iced lattes in hand. In the middle of it all, a guy in an aloha shirt dished out swag bags like candy on Halloween.

She stood at the mirror, blending her makeup with methodical precision. Her inbox was already full, her phone pinging with schedule updates, and the Mānoa Marauder exhibit, allegedly "not open yet," had somehow been unlocked overnight.

She slipped into a lightweight pantsuit, grabbed a fruit and granola parfait from the café downstairs, and headed to the conference center.

Outside the opening session, her students huddled in a group, energy bouncing between them like static.

"Anyone else wake up before sunrise?" Lexi yawned, hitching her bag higher on her shoulder. "My body clock is still on Nebraska time."

"Same," Brandon muttered, juggling a coffee and a project folder. "Or maybe I just couldn't sleep knowing we're up against MIT's robotics demo."

Diego clapped a hand on his shoulder. "Dude, our project is cooler. Way more heart."

Lexi smirked. "If by 'cool' you mean historical data about Hawaiian migrants in Nebraska, then sure. Super chill."

"We're profiling the jobs they held, the communities they built, the challenges they faced." Brandon added, "It's history that's been overlooked."

"Sure thing. But really I just want the resume boost, a tan, and a few phone numbers." Ethan wiggled his eyebrows. "Not necessarily in that order."

Lance and Logan joined them, signing back and forth as Meg interpreted.

We researched the history of cattle and pineapple exchanges between Hawai'i and Nebraska, Lance signed. *I hope we get to see a real pineapple farm while we're here.*

Maria and Ivy arrived last, flipping through notes.

"Our project compares Native Hawaiian and Midwestern Native American culture during the pioneer era," Ivy explained. "We're looking at shared struggles, colonization, and how these communities adapted to change."

Cassandra listened, nodding with pride. People often dismissed kids who grew up in the technology age, but these students were using data to uncover histories that shaped the present, giving voice to stories often overlooked.

She glanced at her watch. Still time to grab her own caffeine before the morning sessions began.

As the students broke off into smaller conversations, she wandered toward the open-air lanai, letting the warm breeze wash over her. From here, she had a perfect view of the waves rolling in, early-morning joggers cutting across the beach, the golden light making everything feel like a memory.

It still felt like home, no matter how long she'd been away.

With a quiet sigh, she turned toward the coffee kiosk, filing into the short line. The scent of Kona coffee mingled with the sweetness of fresh plumeria and grilled breakfast meats from a nearby buffet. She scrolled through emails, mentally preparing for the day ahead.

Then, just as she reached for her coffee order, a flurry of movement caught her attention. Ethan, Diego, and Brandon rounded the corner, their faces flushed with urgency.

"Dr. Sato, there's been a mix-up!" Diego blurted, skidding to a halt. "They put us in the room next to the MIT robotics demo. We're gonna get drowned out."

"Who's gonna sit through a history lecture about Hawaiian migrants when they've got sexy robots next door?" Ethan groaned. "We're doomed."

Brandon rubbed his forehead. "We worked so hard for this. No one's going to hear a word we say."

Cassandra assessed the situation with calm, unflustered precision. Venue conflicts, sound bleed, bad timing. She'd seen worse.

"Let me take care of it," she said, striding toward the conference coordinator's desk. Years of event management had prepared her for moments like this.

Within minutes, she returned, a reassuring smile on her face, and three warm malasadas from a pink Leonard's Bakery box in hand.

"It's settled," she said, handing them each a pastry. "You've been moved to the larger auditorium across the hall. Better acoustics, better seating, and a better chance of upstaging the robots."

Diego blinked. "Wait... we got an upgrade?"

Cassandra winked. "Think of it that way."

Ethan exhaled dramatically. "Okay, you're a genius."

"Take a breath, guys," she added. "I've seen the work you put in. Your research matters. Get your room set up, run through your opening, and shake off the jitters."

For a moment, the students said nothing, their mouths full of cinnamon-sugar perfection. Then, as one, they groaned in delight.

"Thank you, Dr. Sato," Brandon mumbled through a mouthful.

Diego gave her a quick side hug, balancing his malasada in the other hand. "I wonder if Leonard's would let me franchise a food truck and bring these delicious puffs of joy to Nebraska. I'd be a millionaire."

He wasn't wrong.

"If you convince them," Cassandra said, "I'll be your best customer."

If she hurried, Cassandra could still grab a seat in the back for the opening session. Scanning the food table as she passed, her eyes landed on an empty tray where the Spam musubi had been. Too late.

Hadn't had a fresh one in a year. Hadn't realized how much she'd missed them, either.

Note to self: *Get here earlier tomorrow!*

Cassandra took a sip of her coffee, then checked the room number again just to be sure. The digitizing archives session was one of the few things on her schedule that didn't involve putting out fires. Just her, her notes, and no responsibilities beyond listening.

She never made it through the door.

"Well, well, look who's back."

Cassandra turned, already recognizing the voice before she saw the perfectly curated ensemble.

Kalia Chun.

Once a colleague at O'ahu State, now the queen of Kualoa College's PR machine. Kalia had gone to prep school, floated through admin jobs on family connections, and spent most of her early career sniping at Cassandra and Jocelyn while taking credit for their work.

The other woman stood a few feet away, her hibiscus-print dress the kind that wasn't pulled off a tourist rack, and the delicate shell necklace at her throat glinting under the soft lighting. Everything about her looked expensive, deliberate, and designed to remind Cassandra exactly where she stood.

Cassandra forced a polite smile. "Kalia. It's been a while."

Kalia tilted her head, a slow, assessing glance sweeping over Cassandra's outfit. Not outright rude. Just enough to make a point. "I heard you traded in paradise for, what, cornfields?"

Cassandra's smile didn't waver. "Nebraska, yeah. It's different but fulfilling."

Kalia sipped her iced coffee, her expression unreadable. "Interesting choice." She let the words hang for a moment before adding, "I suppose it must be quite... grounding."

There it was. The barb beneath the silk.

Cassandra said nothing, letting Kalia have her moment.

The silence only seemed to amuse her. "At Kualoa, we've been fortunate to secure some amazing grants. Incredible what you can do when you've got the right resources." Her gaze flicked, just briefly, to Cassandra's several-year-old pantsuit and wedge sandals.

The implication landed. Kalia walked through doors Cassandra had to break down.

Cassandra refused to take the bait. "Yes, I imagine it makes a difference when someone hands them to you."

Kalia's smile tightened, just enough to show she'd felt that one.

"How's Jocelyn?" Kalia asked casually, stirring her iced coffee with an air of detached interest. "I heard she came crawling back. O'ahu State is desperate, maybe they'd take her back."

The woman in question materialized at Cassandra's side, effortlessly sliding into the conversation like she'd been there all along. Draped in a breezy maxi dress, her hair in waves that looked effortlessly undone, she was the opposite of Kalia in every way.

Jocelyn took a slow sip of her drink, her expression amused. "Desperate? You're funny, Kalia."

Cassandra exhaled, a quiet laugh under her breath. Of course Jocelyn would show up now.

Jocelyn eyed Kalia, her grin sharpening. "For the record, I'm not crawling anywhere. I just started at the USDA's new field station doing local crop preservation and science outreach. Pretty sure that beats adjuncting for O'ahu State again."

Kalia's brow twitched, but she covered it with a knowing smile aimed at Cassandra. "Well, best of luck. I'm sure your team will... do its best."

And with that, she turned, her heels clicking softly against the tile as she disappeared into the crowd.

Jocelyn watched her go, shaking her head. "Same Kalia, different year."

Cassandra waited a couple of seconds, letting the tension settle before exhaling through her nose. "Yeah. But public school grit beats designer dresses any day."

Jocelyn tipped her cup in agreement. "And I'd take rubber boots and seed vaults over campus drama anytime."

They clinked their coffee cups together and headed inside.

The students arrived at the Mānoa Marauder display with a mix of excitement and relief now that the poster presentations were done.

"You all crushed it," Cassandra said. "We've earned a break. After our virtual reality session, you'll have some free time before dinner."

"Calling dibs on a poolside nap." Lexi said, already stretching.

"I won't be able to sleep," Maria said, practically bouncing. "I want to solve this thing!"

The booth was buzzing. Cassandra led the group through the crowd past tall black-and-white banners promising: *Travel Back to Honolulu, 1910. Who Was the Mānoa Marauder?*

Five VR stations lined the back wall, each occupied by students spinning, pointing, or reaching into a history only they could see. The banners showcased plantation homes, coffee harvests, constables on horseback, and grainy portraits of Queen Liliʻuokalani in her elegant 1887 London gown and Duke Kahanamoku surfing.

Ethan, Diego, Ivy, Maria, and Meg grabbed VR headsets as the next round began.

"Welcome, time travelers!" said a guide in a straw boater and vintage vest. "The year is 1910. The Territory of Hawai'i is just fifteen years old. And the Mānoa Marauder murders have rocked a community already on edge."

He swept a hand toward the banners. "Native Hawaiians were being displaced. Sugar barons, missionaries, and political newcomers were reshaping the islands. Immigrants from Japan, China, Portugal, and the Philippines worked long hours in fields and mills often in brutal conditions."

He let that hang before adding, "Four victims. No convictions. A city divided by class, race, and power. And a killer who vanished without a trace."

Cassandra caught sight of the speaker and blinked. "Andrew Gloria?"

The young man turned, face brightening instantly. "Dr. Sato!"

She hadn't seen him in over a year. "Last I checked, you were all about biology."

"I was," he said, laughing. "Until that tsunami evacuation. Remember that?"

She nodded, the memory flashing: panicked students, muddy floors, soggy office equipment.

"Yeah, that pretty much flipped everything. I realized I was more into the stories behind the science. I traded microscopes for microfilm."

She laughed. "I always knew you had a flair for drama."

Andrew shrugged. "This exhibit's the best of both the research and theater worlds."

Ethan let out an exaggerated groan. "I just got chased by the chickens. Again."

A stumble sent him bumping into a wall and nearly toppling his VR stand.

Andrew pressed a button on his earpiece. "You're fine. Back up two steps and avoid the poultry."

"Not the chickens!" squawked a yellow-headed parrot from a perch nearby, causing the surrounding students to crack up.

Cassandra blinked. "Wait, is that your bird?"

Andrew sighed. "That's Skipper. He came with the apartment and refuses to pay rent."

The screen behind them lit up with an image of the Oliver estate. An actress in period costume appeared, holding a microphone.

"The first death was ruled an accident. Jean Oliver, sister to the estate owner, reportedly fell from a second-story balcony. No foul play was suspected.

Then came Hana Nakamura, the family's seamstress, found dead under suspicious circumstances. Rumors surfaced about missing royal artifacts. The estate's gardener, Manuel Reyes, was questioned but never charged.

When Reyes turned up dead weeks later, plantation owner, Edward Oliver, offered a $500 reward for the killer's apprehension. It went unclaimed.

Months later Mary Pauahi, a young Hawaiian woman, was found buried in a shallow grave on the edge of downtown Honolulu.

As for suspects, the list was short: A housekeeper who knew all the victims. A groundskeeper rumored to have been infatuated with Miss Oliver. Or a shadowy bogeyman "marauder" the national press was all too eager to invent.

Four victims. Four suspects. No convictions. Until now?"

Next Dr. Nakano appeared on screen, flanked by museum display cases. "This isn't a game," he said. "What you hold are pieces of someone's story. Respect the voices. Consider the cost of silence. Uncover the truth."

Who was the Mānoa Marauder? flashed on the screen in bold red text. *Solve the mystery. Win $10,000.*

"Each team has their own set of materials," Andrew said enthusiastically. ""Use the VR to explore, then dig deeper with documents and interviews. Your case theory has to hold up."

Cassandra's arms tingled. Still reward money on the line, after all these years? She rubbed the back of her neck.

"Okay," she said, trying to sound casual. "Let's see what we're up against."

Fifteen minutes later, it was her group's turn. Cassandra adjusted the headset straps and the exhibit hall vanished.

A breeze lifted her hair. She stood near the shore, surrounded by terraced fields. Taro plants glistened in flooded paddies. Rows of rice and coffee flanked narrow irrigation ditches. In the distance, a woman in a plaid shirt crossed a narrow plank bridge, a woven basket balanced on her hip.

Waikīkī, before the crowds. Before the concrete.

Birdsong filtered in through her earpiece. Water trickled behind her. She stepped forward, gravel crunching underfoot, wind hissing through tall trees. A horse-drawn carriage clattered past on a nearby dirt road, the driver tipping his cap like she belonged.

The landscape shifted. Now she stood on Honolulu Harbor's old wooden docks. Sugar crates and molasses barrels lined the planks. Men in suspenders barked orders as they loaded a steamship. Nearby, a poster flapped in the wind: *Territory of Hawai'i Welcomes You!* A line of women waited near the telegraph office, skirts swaying, parasols shading paper-wrapped parcels. Through the customs window, Cassandra spotted a portrait of Queen Lili'uokalani, her gaze steady and unmistakably regal.

Next came Mānoa Valley, 1910. Nothing like the quaint present day properties. This place stretched for acres. Coffee fields rolling down the hillsides, workers bent over in taro patches near a trickling stream, chickens scratching the dirt near a row of cookhouses.

Inside now. A richly appointed study. Carved koa desk. Stained-glass windows casting amber light across ledgers and a half-full inkwell. A phonograph spun softly in the background. On the far wall, a painted portrait—three figures frozen in formal posture. Cassandra stepped closer, but the details blurred before she could make out their faces.

Another cut. A group stood outside the estate kitchen. Staff in pressed uniforms. Some smiling. Everyone looked tired. She searched their faces, wondering about their lives, their loyalties, their secrets.

The reel jumped again.

A young woman stood on church steps, arms raised in mid-speech. Silent film. Behind her: Kūpa'a Nā Wāhine. *Women Stand Firm*. Cassandra leaned in. Whoever she was, she looked bold. Unafraid.

A voice slid into her ear, calm and low:

"In 1910, the Territory of Hawai'i was a crossroads of ambition. Royalists, missionaries, suffragists, and businessmen fought to shape the future. The Oliver estate stood at the center—prosperous, political, and deeply divided."

One last image. A hallway of artifacts: sewing needles, a sugar scale, legal papers under glass. An open journal beside a cracked inkwell. A yellowed envelope peeked out from beneath a ledger. Cassandra reached toward it.

Darkness.

The screen went blank. Just like that, it was over.

Cassandra pulled the headset off slowly, her skin damp, hairline prickled with sweat. She stilled for a moment, adjusting to the lighting, and glanced around.

Jocelyn looked dazed, like she'd been yanked out of a dream mid-sentence. Lexi already had her phone out, thumbs flying as she muttered something to her neighbor about colonialism and bad lighting. A few students took off their headsets and gave polite nods like they'd just watched a documentary on PBS.

Cassandra didn't move.

The whole thing had lasted under fifteen minutes, but the past had sunk into her skin like humidity. It hadn't felt like history. It had felt like memory.

The students regrouped near the booth, buzzing with excitement. A volunteer handed Cassandra a stack of packets, each stamped with the Hawai'i Unforgotten logo.

"Each team gets the core document set. Take a look and start forming your theory."

Lexi tore into hers like it was Christmas morning. "Whoa. This is straight out of *CSI: Hawai'i*. Look at these grainy old photos!"

"No one's auditioning you for Netflix," Logan said, already paging through a witness statement. "There's ten grand on the line, remember?"

Maria didn't look up. "The VR was amazing, but these," she tapped a faded map, "...make it feel real."

Cassandra glanced around. Other teams huddled in corners, some whispering like they had state secrets, others throwing out wild theories.

"An East Coast team thinks the whole thing was a smuggling cover-up," Ethan muttered, squinting at a historical map of the city. "A California group swears it's cult-related. NYU's betting on an insurance scam."

Brandon raised an eyebrow. "No one can even agree on what actually happened."

"That's what makes it fun," Lexi said, already scribbling notes. "It's a historical dumpster fire."

"We got assigned the Oliver estate," Cassandra reminded them. "Former coffee plantation. That's your research location."

Lexi groaned. "Seriously? A plantation?"

Brandon nodded slowly. "So we got the spooky coffee farm because someone saw Nebraska on our forms and assumed we'd be ag experts?"

Diego shrugged. "To be fair, we did drive our tractors to high school on the last day."

"Speak for yourselves," said Maria. "I'm from San Diego."

"Take the rest of the afternoon to go over the packet," Cassandra said, warm but firm. "We've got a quiet space reserved in the morning. Come ready to work, and bring your weirdest theories."

A short while later, she joined them on the pool deck, dressed in lightweight capris, a linen shirt shielding her from the sun. She dragged a chair into the shade and leaned back, letting the murmur of student chatter roll over her like waves.

"I can't stop thinking about those victims," Lexi said, sitting cross-legged beside Ivy. "The only one anyone seemed to care about was the heiress."

"Some things never change," Maria muttered, her voice tight.

Diego stretched out in a neon swim suit, sunglasses covering his eyes. "Ten bucks says it was the housekeeper. Probably bumped off the others to protect the royal jewels."

"You're wrong," Brandon said, glancing around like a spy. He lowered his voice. "It was a man. Three of the victims were strangled. Women don't strangle people. My bet's on the groundskeeper. Or the estate owner because he had access to everything. Maybe he was chasing treasure."

Ethan stretched and stood, revealing a dark farmer's tan, his torso a full ten shades lighter than his arms and face. "I investigate better with a cold beer. I'm heading to the pool bar. Might consult with the UCLA gals and see if they noticed anything we didn't."

Then, with all the grace of a wounded manatee, he executed a belly flop and swam toward a group of tanned, fit women with various shades of blonde hair.

Diego stood with a snort. "Guess I'd better go supervise before he leaks all our secret theories."

Cassandra watched them go, torn between amusement and the faint tickle of worry. She didn't have time to finish the thought.

"They're just here for the sun and the social life," Maria said, her tone flat. "I need that prize money."

Cassandra turned, hearing the edge in her voice. "I know how hard you've worked," she said gently. "But don't burn yourself out. Sometimes taking a step back is the best way to move forward."

Maria nodded, her expression softening. "Thanks, Dr. Sato. I'll try."

Cassandra gave her shoulder a quick squeeze, then leaned back again, watching the sun ease toward the horizon.

Tomorrow would bring more presentations, interviews, and the first real steps into the case. For now, she let the quiet linger.

The game had begun.

Chapter Four

CASSANDRA STEPPED OUT OF the sun into the blissfully cool café. No tote bags, no badge scanners, no lava surfing booths in sight. Just ceiling fans spinning like lazy helicopters and the air thick with espresso and guava syrup.

Jocelyn was already at a bistro table, sipping something frothy. "Jet lag looks good on you."

Cassandra dropped into the seat. "I'm running on four hotel pillow options, none of them comfortable, and zero REM cycles. I need a caffeine IV."

Jocelyn slid a cup across the table. "Raspberry-hazelnut mocha. Waikīkī's trending flavor of the month."

Cassandra took a sip, then blinked. "This tastes like dessert. Did you get this off a child's menu?"

"You're welcome," Jocelyn said, unfazed. "So, how was day one?"

"Only one meltdown during MIT's robot demo. We lost our breakout room to them, but no fistfights broke out, ...so it counts as a win?"

She pulled the thick Hawai'i Unforgotten packet from her tote. "The VR experience was intense. They even added sounds. It all felt so immersive. But when I saw Mānoa and the large homes, it really hit me. It felt personal."

Jocelyn tilted her head. "You okay?"

Cassandra paused, her fingers tracing the mission statement on the envelope: *To uncover the hidden truths of Hawai'i's past, restore the voices of those silenced by history, and ensure that cultural heritage is remembered, not erased.*

She nodded. "I think Nakano gave us more than a research prompt. There's murder, class tension, old money, everything. We might actually be chasing something real."

"Figures," Jocelyn said. "You always had a thing for dusty secrets and drama."

Cassandra smirked. "Better than that phase where I had a thing for vampire novels and bubble tea. C'mon, the others are meeting us in the back."

The café's back room was more of a repurposed storage area with kitschy posters of hula dancers, a framed vintage Spam ad, and a busted lava lamp in the corner. Two bistro tables, and a huge sectional sofa filled the floor, and a water cooler rounded out the décor.

Lexi was already sprawled on the couch, sandals off, thumbing through her packet. Lance leaned against a windowsill, tossing bits of granola to a pigeon perched just outside.

The others were glued to their phones, barely noticing anything else.

Jocelyn raised a brow. "What is this, a startup office?"

Lexi smiled without looking up. "More like a detective agency with a hydration station."

Cassandra dropped the packet on the nearest table. "Alright, detectives. Let's see what Hawai'i Unforgotten thinks we should find."

Inside were scans of newspaper clippings, a brief bio on each of the four 1910 victims, the official police theory: isolated tragedies, no proven connection. Public records of the Mānoa Marauder case, including death certificates and crime scene reports. There were website links to video oral histories, anthropology policies, and interviews with descendants of prominent historical families of the time.

Ethan tossed his packet on the coffee table and leaned back on the couch. "They're burying us under all this information. How are we supposed to sort out what's important? We aren't here for a month, just a week. Maybe we just skip the competition, rent a car, and visit the pineapple plantation. I want to try a Dole whip before I go back to Nebraska corn."

Across the room, Lance grinned and made a double finger-gun gesture, then signed, *Same*.

Maria had already organized her packet with sticky flags and post-it notes layered like armor. "You really aren't interested in a share of ten thousand dollars? Too bad. We are dividing the work between all of us. Then getting frozen desserts."

She handed Ethan a clipped stack of documents. "You take the official materials about the overview and historic Honolulu. I can do the public records. Ivy?"

Ivy reached over and picked the next paper clipped stack. "I've got the crime scene reports."

"And I set up a Trello board," Maria added, tapping her tablet screen. "We'll sort everything into categories: historical context, possible motives, death details, weird inconsistencies, and things we can't explain yet.'"

"Color-coded?" Cassandra asked.

"Obviously."

Lance added, *I labeled one column 'Hunches That Sound Dumb But Might Be Brilliant Later.'*

Cassandra asked, "What about a timeline?"

"Already building it," Maria said. "We'll log every clue and event as we go. Anything out of place gets tagged. If the pattern's there, we'll find it."

The rest of them divided the other papers and started flipping through. It was quiet for all of 45 seconds before Andrew Gloria strode through the doorway, earbuds in, head down. When he looked up and spotted Cassandra, his face lit up.

"Dr. Sato!" he said. "Didn't expect to find you here."

"Hey Andrew," she said, genuinely pleased. "Doing recon?"

"Against my will. My thesis advisor volun-told me to serve as a team resource. Give tips and hints. I'm basically her minion." He grinned. "I brought backup."

A loud squawk made several students jump. "Watch out for the tsunami! Got any test answers?"

Jocelyn doubled over laughing. "I love your bird."

Andrew shrugged. "Skipper's an acquired taste. Like bitter melon or conspiracy theories."

"Want to help us dig?"

"For ten percent of the prize?" he asked, sliding into a seat.

"Best we can offer is wild guesses and moral support. Take it or leave it," Cassandra said, arching an eyebrow.

Andrew held up a folder. "Deal. Also, this is from Dr. Nakano. The other teams got digital files, but he wanted you to have the hard copies."

Cassandra blinked but took them without comment. It wasn't unusual. Not really.

Inside were black-and-white estate maps, faded ledger scans, and a brittle pamphlet titled *Mānoa Agricultural Holdings, 1909.*

Diego whistled. "They really didn't want this stuff circulating."

"Or they didn't think anyone would take it seriously," Ivy muttered.

The team got back to work.

Jocelyn cleared her throat, reading from a newspaper article. "Here we go. 'Heiress Found Dead at Mānoa Home.' Authorities ruled it a fall from the second-floor balcony. Staff reported she was alone. Family declined to comment."

Ivy leaned over to read. "A fall? That's it? No coroner's report? No witnesses?"

"Edward Oliver didn't think so," Logan added, pointing to another article. "He told reporters the gardener was the only one on duty that night. Everyone else was already in their cabins."

Lexi wrinkled her nose. "That's kind of shady."

Jocelyn kept scanning. "There's more. Edward didn't just suspect the gardener. He flat-out accused him. Said the guy was acting weird after they found the body."

Cassandra said, "If it was just an accident... why be so fast to blame someone?"

Logan ran his finger down the paper. "Two days later: 'Groundskeeper Questioned in Oliver Death.' Says he may have had... quote... 'unspoken affections.'"

Lexi squinted. "So the story is what? Forbidden love?"

"Or convenient scapegoat," Jocelyn muttered.

Maria looked up from her notes. "And then the gardener turns up dead. Strangled. No witnesses, no arrest."

Brandon exhaled. "That escalated fast."

"Feathers of justice!" Skipper cried, flapping once.

For a moment, no one said anything.

"A love triangle?" Lexi asked. "Or maybe... I don't know. Maybe the gardener saw something."

"Or someone thought he did," Ivy added.

Logan read aloud: "'Unusual Nighttime Digging at the Oliver Estate Raises Eyebrows.' Someone started excavating a few months after Jean's death."

"Looking for buried secrets?" Cassandra mused.

"Or trying to hide them," Andrew added.

Jocelyn handed her a paper. "Here's another one. 'Missing: Local Seamstress Hana Nakamura Disappears from Oliver Estate.' That's your mom's family name, right?"

Cassandra nodded, frowning.

Jocelyn's tone softened. "You know, my great-tutu used to talk about working in Manoa. She mentioned your Gran and her sister a few times."

Cassandra's eyes widened. "Wait, really? I knew Gran was a cook for a big house, but no one ever talked about an auntie," Cassandra admitted. "It's like she got erased."

Jocelyn tilted her head, thoughtful. "Maybe not erased. Just filed away where no one wanted to look too closely."

Cassandra said, voice low. "I'll ask my mom. Could be my family."

Everyone went quiet.

Cassandra stared at the page, the silence thick around them. Whatever this was, it ran deeper than any classroom case study.

Lexi leaned in. "First the heiress. Then a seamstress. That's not a coincidence."

Andrew squinted at a colorful poster of the King Kamehameha statue covered up to his neck in lei. "Okay, hear me out. What if this wasn't just murder? What if it was an inheritance heist gone wrong?"

Diego perked up. "Like a forged will? Hidden documents? Maybe Jean Oliver found something and someone panicked."

Lexi flipped a page dramatically. "Or Jean was in love with the gardener, and the family disapproved, so they staged her death and framed him."

"Then why kill Hana?" Maria asked.

Lexi shrugged. "Collateral damage. Maybe she knew too much."

Logan raised an eyebrow. "Or Hana was the brains behind the operation. Seamstress by day, whistleblower by night."

"I'm not ruling out secret societies," Ethan added. "It's suspicious how four people died in one year and nobody talks about it."

Andrew nodded. "It's a classic pattern. Power. Property. Suppressed scandal. Jean was progressive, an activist involved in women's suffrage. Maybe she went too far and upset the wrong people."

Diego snapped his fingers. "Or buried treasure. Gold bars. A forbidden love letter that could bring down the monarchy."

Cassandra pinched the bridge of her nose. "C'mon back folks. Let's focus."

Ivy beamed. "We're solving a conspiracy."

"Or inventing one," Maria said dryly.

"Sometimes it's the same thing," Diego added, grinning.

Lexi's grin faded slightly. "Okay but... we're not going to solve all four murders from 1910, right?"

Andrew said, "We're not CSI: Waikīkī. No DNA. No ballistics."

Maria tapped her pen. "What if we don't need to solve them all? What if just *one* is the key?"

Logan leaned forward. "Like a wedge. One provable lie could unravel the whole story."

Cassandra tapped Jean Oliver's newspaper clipping. "She's the most visible. If someone needed her death to *look* accidental, that's a risk. They might've left a crack."

Maria nodded. "If we find that crack maybe in the map or the estate records, we might expose the rest."

Lexi added, "Then we're not chasing ghosts. We're chasing proof of a cover-up."

Andrew raised his notepad. "We've got leads. And a parrot. We're unstoppable."

"Feathers of justice!" Skipper yelled, flapping dramatically.

Cassandra smiled despite herself.

Jocelyn gave a crooked grin. "So, what's the plan, Nancy Drew?"

She rubbed her temple and began packing up, the beginnings of a headache forming. "You've all done great work today. Let's meet in the hotel lobby after lunch. The estate visit's next."

The past wasn't buried.

It had just been waiting.

Chapter Five

THE VAN DOORS CREAKED open and Cassandra stepped out first, scanning the quiet hush of Mānoa Valley: green, misty, and somehow just minutes away from the beach. Behind her, students stretched and adjusted backpacks, their chatter fading as she led them down a winding stone path flanked by vibrant tropical gardens. When they rounded the final bend, the Mānoa plantation house rose into view, stately and serene. A tour guide waited on the shaded veranda, waving with cheerful energy.

Her smile widened as she recognized Cassandra and Jocelyn.

"Angela Bachman!" Cassandra called. The last time she'd seen the blonde former student, they'd been fleeing a tsunami with a contraband dorm cat and five panicked undergrads.

"Dr. Sato, Professor Kaneshiro," Angela grinned, "As you can see, I prefer higher ground now." She adjusted the name badge clipped neatly to her shirt. "No joke, I got lucky landing this internship. It's competitive and tons of history majors apply. But Mr. Oliver's been a great mentor. He really values people who work hard."

Cassandra blinked. That didn't sound like the same Angela who once refused to leave a sixth-floor bathroom without her cat. Maybe she'd just grown up.

She gestured toward the sprawling estate behind her. "Welcome to the Mānoa Plantation House. Let's check out some cool history."

Angela led the group through the entrance, her voice bright and engaging. The house exuded old-world charm, from the polished koa wood floors to the high, airy ceilings edged in decorative moldings.

Sunlight filtered through stained-glass windows, casting jewel-toned patterns on the walls.

Cassandra spotted details she'd missed in the VR headset version like wood grain, soft creaks, the faint scent of lemon polish. The colors were richer in person, the air warmer. Everything felt more real here, less curated.

The first room they entered was the parlor, where heavy, dark wood furniture sat atop a patterned Persian rug. Above the grand fireplace hung a portrait of Edward and Maggie Oliver, the estate's original owners, his expression smug, hers unreadable. Edward's hand rested on his wife's shoulder; the other clutched a small wooden box, angled toward the viewer like a trophy.

Angela gestured toward the painting. "The Olivers moved here in the 1890s, around the time Queen Lili'uokalani was forced to abdicate. Edward supported annexation. Maggie ran the household. She was famous for her parties, always with the biggest guest list, the best dress code."

Cassandra let her gaze linger on Edward's face a moment longer, then shifted to the fireplace mantel, where a black-and-white photograph leaned against a vase like an afterthought.

Jean Oliver.

The young woman stood on a raised platform in a white linen dress, pleated at the waist, and a broad straw hat that cast half her face in shadow. Behind her, a banner stretched across the wall: VOTES FOR WOMEN. She was mid-speech. Eyes focused, mouth slightly open, one gloved hand curled into a fist.

"Jean Oliver, Edward's younger sister," Angela said. "She got herself in the papers for pushing women's suffrage in the islands before it was trendy."

Cassandra moved closer. Jean wasn't a young debutante posing for a beau. She was confident. She also looked like trouble.

In the dining room, crystal chandeliers sparkled over a long table set with fine china. Angela waved a hand toward the sideboard, where silver serving trays gleamed like museum pieces.

"Everything here was top-tier in its day, and it still holds value. The Olivers were basically influencers before branding was a thing. They understood the power of presentation."

Angela's voice was smooth, but Cassandra caught the note of ambition tucked beneath it.

"We're trying to understand how different groups lived and worked during this era," she said.

Angela gave a polished shrug. "Sure. History's all about perspective. One person's family home is another person's cautionary tale."

She glided through the room like a brand ambassador, skipping past anything uncomfortable with professional ease.

Cassandra remembered the Angela who once hyperventilated in a stairwell clutching a cat like a life raft. This version wore confidence like perfume and seemed to know exactly which parts of the past would sell best to a guided tour.

"We're specifically researching the Mānoa Marauder case," Cassandra added. "Trying to match what we see here to the records from Hawai'i Unforgotten."

Angela's smile thinned. "Oh, *them*. Good publicity team. A little dramatic, though. Dr. Nakano stirs things up more than he solves. But hey, drama moves headlines."

Cassandra returned the smile, cool and even. "Balance is everything."

Jocelyn leaned in as they left the dining room. "Remind me, wasn't she the one who cried over a vending machine and a feral cat?"

Cassandra didn't look back, "People change."

"Yeah," Jocelyn said. "Some of them just get shinier packaging."

When Angela next led them to the kitchen, it felt like they'd used Hermione Grainger's time turner and landed squarely in the twenty-first century. Restaurant-grade stainless steel appliances gleamed under recessed lighting, the modern countertops stretching where old prep tables once stood.

Angela pointed to the massive brick fireplace, now housing a six-burner stove. "This is the only original part left. Back in the day they used to dry herbs here. Now it's a catering dream."

From there, they passed into a sunroom bump out where windows lined one entire wall and half the ceiling. Tropical plants filled the narrow corridor, green and glossy, as if the garden had tried to sneak inside and almost succeeded.

"Most Mānoa homes don't have A/C," Angela explained. "The valley cools off at night. That's why the bedrooms are upstairs. The family still lives in part of the house, so not everything's open to the public."

Cassandra let the group move ahead. She lingered by the garden wall, inhaling the moist, earthy air and letting the silence settle.

Then her gaze drifted to the opposite wall, a gallery of framed photos and heirlooms stretching nearly the full length of the hall, a curated timeline of the Oliver family's wealth and image.

It reminded her of the wall at her parents' house: faded family photos from Japan, her siblings in Halloween costumes, school portraits with crooked bangs and missing teeth. Ordinary memories.

These images, though, told a different kind of story. Iconic posters showed Waikīkī before the hotels. Old wooden ships docked at the Aloha Tower.

A small photograph caught her eye. Maggie Oliver seated near a sunlit window, flanked by other women and several servants, all focused on their needlework. Two Japanese teenage girls stood close together in the background. They might have been sisters or twins, their dark hair pulled into identical twists. One clutched a small cloth doll. Both wore uncertain half-smiles, like they hadn't yet decided if the camera was friend or foe.

Farther down the line, she spotted a larger group photo, one she'd first seen in the VR exhibit. Everyone wore lei, suggesting a celebration. The Oliver women sat in prim dresses and straw hats, posed center-stage. Men in suits and bowties stood behind them, Edward Oliver among them, boot perched on a stack of burlap sacks printed with the estate logo, his smug expression practically daring the viewer to question him.

Household staff flanked the group: Japanese, Hawaiian, Chinese, Filipino. Their best clothes couldn't mask the rigid posture, the careful distance.

Cassandra stared at the image, the injustice of it pulsing behind her ribs. Men like Edward Oliver hadn't just hosted garden parties. They'd helped steal a kingdom.

Underneath, someone had handwritten the names of the twenty-plus people in careful script. Cassandra scanned the list. Oliver. Ybarra. Reyes. Then two names that made her freeze:

Hana and Aiko Nakamura.

The same Nakamura from the newspaper article Jocelyn had found. Chicken skin crept up her arms. She took a quick photo and texted her mom: "Any chance your great-grandma's last name was Nakamura?"

Then she stood back and stared at the photo again. A hundred years gone, and still the questions lingered.

Could this connection be more than coincidence?

She caught up with the group inside one of the bedrooms, where the air felt stale. Glass-front cabinets held museum-quality artifacts. Period furniture stood polished and precise. Every object looked staged, but not quite lifeless.

"According to the stories," Angela was saying. "Maggie Oliver was celebrating their first big coffee shipment to the mainland. The estate had upgraded to a mechanical pulper and drying beds, so they were finally able to export at scale."

The students listened intently, and even Cassandra found herself intrigued.

Angela continued, "Rumor has it the party was thrown together last minute, and Maggie was so thrilled she made all the servants dress up and handed out lei to everyone, something she usually reserved for family."

She paused, lowering her voice just enough to draw the students in. "Here's the fun part. Supposedly, one of the young housemaids was so shy about having her picture taken that she hid behind the others when the photographer showed up. Back then, some people believed cameras could steal your soul. Poor thing had never been photographed before and refused to go near a camera for years afterward."

"When I first started here, I figured all the ghost stories were, like, tourist bait," Angela said with a light laugh. "But now? I think most legends are just history with better marketing."

Cassandra hung back near the doorway, arms crossed. If this internship was truly competitive, how had Angela ended up giving the tours?

Angela gestured toward the velvet ropes. "I mean, it makes you think. In every story, someone's the villain. But maybe it's not who people expect."

Cassandra frowned at her offhand delivery. "That depends on who's telling the story."

Angela shrugged, still chipper. "Exactly. History's basically whoever had the microphone and knew how to work a crowd."

"Or whoever had something to hide."

Angela blinked, then offered a quick smile, like she wasn't sure if that was a compliment or a warning. "Yeah... totally."

Cassandra's watch vibrated. Her mom had replied in her usual staccato manner, "Yah, so what? Us and hundreds of families on the island."

She typed back, "I just wondered. We saw a news article yesterday that a Hana Nakamura had been a victim of the Mānoa Marauder and then her name was on a photo in the house tour. Interesting, eh?"

"Aren't you working?" Her mom asked.

Wow, she expected a little more excitement from her mom. *Fine.* Cassandra would follow up with her more later in person.

Finally they assembled on a small landing area in front of a closed wooden door that Cassandra assumed was another bedroom. Angela waited with one hand on the doorknob until their group hushed expectantly.

"And... according to local legends, this is where the ghosts live." She opened the door with a tour-guide flourish.

Inside, the room looked like a Disney movie set fit for a princess: lace-covered bed, gilded mirrors, flowered wallpaper, and velvet throw pillows fluffed to perfection.

Cassandra's youngest sister Sarah would've loved it. Cassandra hated the froufrou on principle.

"This was Jean Oliver's private suite," Angela continued. "She was only twenty-two when she died, and her body was found right below these windows." Her voice dropped. "Some say she fell. Others say she was pushed. The official report called it an accident, but there were whispers about a secret lover... possibly the gardener."

Cassandra crossed her arms, eyeing the windows. She'd heard versions of this story since childhood, mostly whispered at slumber parties. But now, standing here, it didn't feel like campfire gossip. It felt... intimate.

Angela stepped deeper into the room. "And Jean wasn't the only one. Staff disappeared. Some called the land cursed. Some still do."

She's good at this, Cassandra thought. These stories had floated around for decades. But something about her delivery grated now. It felt too slick, too rehearsed, like tragedy had become a stage prop.

Near the bed, Cassandra spotted a small writing table with a neatly stacked pile of suffrage pamphlets beside a leather-bound journal. The edges were worn, but the pages looked mostly empty. A ribbon marked the third or fourth page.

She reached for it but stopped. Too personal. And besides, the packets from Hawai'i Unforgotten had included a few scans in Jean's careful, looping script, wondering whether anyone would listen to her if she spoke out against her brother's dealings. No dates, no names. Just uncertainty and frustration. It wasn't much, but it was enough to sting.

The room smelled like lavender and lemon polish, a hauntingly calm combination. A breeze stirred the curtains, as if the house itself exhaled.

If Hana Nakamura really was part of Cassandra's family, this cold case was unfinished business.

Watching Angela pad the tour with ghost stories and glamorize the Oliver legacy without offering historical context made Cassandra's jaw tighten. No mention of land loss. No hint of the shift from Hawaiian rulers to American governors. Just lavish parties and wealthy families with polished silver and tragic heiresses.

Cassandra let her irritation fade as they turned toward the Hawaiian quilts on display. Bright blocks of color, from deep reds to ocean blues and golden yellows, were draped across a four-poster bed, folded neatly on a cedar trunk, one hung like a tapestry on the wall. The patterns were bold, the stitches delicate.

She slowed. Ginger blossoms, breadfruit, hibiscus. Each one was art, and each one carried a story. Her fingers itched to examine the seams and tension, judging the craftsmanship like her mother had taught her. She could lose hours in this room without even noticing.

Jocelyn nudged her and lifted the edge of an _Ulu_ quilt from a rack, revealing an embroidered block on the back, presumably with the names of its creators. "Eh, Cass, what if one of these was made by your great-great auntie?"

The thought sent a chill down Cassandra's spine. Discreetly, she started checking other quilts, her eyes skimming the corners for the name Nakamura. Maybe the sisters had worked on these together?

Cassandra gently lifted the edge of an ocean-blue quilt, her fingers tracing the intricate patterns of ginger leaves. The stitching was so fine, it almost felt alive under her touch. She flipped the corner, her breath catching as she spotted the name _H. Nakamura_ stitched in delicate script.

"Jocelyn," she whispered, her voice tight. "This one has it."

Jocelyn turned, holding up another quilt. "So does this. Cass, what are the odds?"

Her mind raced. How many more were there in the house? She wanted to gather them all up, take them home, archive every detail. Maybe her mother could petition one of the Olivers to buy one back.

Before she could say more, Jocelyn's fingers brushed against something beneath the fabric. "Hold on. There's...a pocket here." Her voice was low, trembling with excitement.

"Yeah, isn't that cool? A few of the quilts I looked at had those too." Cassandra shrugged. "Maybe that's where ladies slipped a handkerchief or small fan?"

Angela's voice rang out from the doorway, bright and oblivious. "Let's move outside to tour the beautiful garden designed by Maggie Oliver herself. It was restored several years ago and is maintained by a local heritage garden club of volunteers."

Cassandra hissed, "Joce' we can talk about it more later. C'mon, they're going outside, eh?"

But Jocelyn wasn't listening. She ran her fingers along the quilt again, slower this time, like she was reading it by touch.

Her frown deepened. After a few seconds of searching, she carefully pulled out a folded paper yellowed with age, brittle at the edges.

The parchment crackled in the hush between them.

Cassandra's breath caught. People didn't tuck away grocery lists with this much care. Whatever it was, someone wanted it lost and found by the right person.

Jocelyn unfolded it gently, her hands steady despite the tension between them.

They exchanged wide-eyed looks. The moment felt like something out of *The Goonies*.

Rough, hand-drawn lines. Faint symbols. A map.

Cassandra's pulse jumped as her eyes traced the uneven circles and cryptic markings. The lines wobbled, the symbols were faint, but someone had drawn this on purpose.

Cassandra whispered, "Why would someone hide a map in a quilt?"

Before Jocelyn could answer, a voice cut through the quiet.

"Yo! There you are—" Lexi leaned in the doorway.

Cassandra shot her pinky out to Jocelyn, who instantly hooked hers around it. Quick shake. Pact sealed.

"Didn't y'all hear us leave?"

"Sorry, we got distracted," Cassandra said, flashing a smile. "Go on, we're coming."

Lexi raised an eyebrow at them. "I swear, you two act like you're hosting *Antiques Roadshow: Plantation Edition.*"

Cassandra bit back a laugh, as Jocelyn smirked.

Normally, she'd fire off a snarky comeback, but the map was all she could think about. As they stepped into the sunshine and followed the others into the garden, she adjusted her sunglasses, trying to clear her head.

Someone had drawn that map, folded it away, and stitched it into the fabric of history. Not for safety. For survival.

And whatever they were protecting still hadn't been found.

Chapter Six

"YOU JUST SHOW UP, no call ahead, like we just sitting home nothing to do? Where da kids you supposed to be chaperoning, eh?" Mama Sato's tone was peeved, but still she pulled out a pitcher of filtered water and filled glasses for Cassandra and Jocelyn.

They sat at the scuffed wooden table with six chairs. Cassandra absently straightened the corner of the placemat she'd used during countless childhood meals. As always, the surface was spotlessly clean, but close inspection showed signs of wear and tear.

"They don't need us. This afternoon they're taking surfing lessons, then tonight is a beach party behind the hotel."

Except for one upgrade to modern cabinets while Cassandra was in high school and several refreshes of the glossy white paint on every wall, the spacious eat-in kitchen was the same as she remembered growing up with Keoni, Kathy, and Sarah.

"You oughta teach 'em surfing. Way better than those Waikīkī guys hustling beginners for one wave," Mom said, sliding a plate of still-warm white chocolate macadamia nut cookies onto the table like it was part of the lecture.

Cassandra and Jocelyn's gazes met, then quickly looked away. Clearly her mother had been prepared for them stopping by unannounced.

"I gave my board to Keoni before I moved. I think Leilani or one of the boys uses it now, Mom." A teeny pang hit her heart as she said it. Whether it came from not being able to surf during this trip or from having limited free time to spend with her nephews, Cassandra didn't stop to examine it too closely.

She nodded her chin at Jocelyn as a signal for her to start.

Jocelyn bit off half a cookie and moaned a little. "Auntie Michiko, these cookies were always my favorite. You da best."

While her mom was smugly taking in the compliment, Jocelyn hit her with the real reason they'd come for the visit. "Auntie, did Cassandra tell you we toured a Mānoa plantation house with the students this morning? So interesting, ya?"

Cassandra nodded on cue, and shoved a cookie in her mouth before she could blurt something out and mess up the moment.

"Seriously, beautiful antiques," Jocelyn said, playing it up. "Tons of history. And so many quilts. Some even had the seamstresses' names stitched on the back."

She gave Cassandra a pointed look. "Pretty sure we saw Nakamura on a few. Wasn't that your tutu's last name?"

The pleasant expression slid off her mother's face and a cold mask dropped over it instead. "Why you girls gotta keep digging in the past? Some t'ings are betta left forgotten."

Cassandra pulled out the chair next to her and helped ease her mother into it. She stubbornly crossed her arms and glared at them for several heartbeats.

Gently covering her mother's hand, Cassandra said, "Was that your great auntie who was murdered way back in the day? A tragic victim of the Mānoa Marauder. Why didn't you ever say anything?"

Mom's lips pressed flat like she was counting inside her head. Her eyes darted from Jocelyn's concerned face to meet Cassandra's firm gaze.

The time had come for answers. Her mother wasn't the only stubborn one in the family. Cassandra waited.

"That's why!" Mom yanked her hand away like she'd been stung. "My tutu, Aiko, she got treated bad after the mess with her sister. People said all kine crazy stuff. Like she went killed that rich girl, or that she was doing secret bad stuff on the side. The Marauder was in the papers all the time. Nobody ever get caught."

A red flush crept up her cheeks as she revealed her memories.

"And the shame? It stuck to us. So my family, we had to move on. Couldn't let the next generation carry that kind of weight, yeah?"

By the end of her confession, tears rimmed her eyes.

Jocelyn jumped up to grab a box of tissues. Cassandra's eyes were teary too. "Mom, Auntie was a victim. Great Granny was a victim. Your whole family lost someone special. How awful that you never got closure."

Jocelyn squeezed Cassandra's arm under the table, a silent *let her breathe* signal.

Cassandra took a sip of water, nodding. "I get it, Mom. Really. But isn't there anything left from those days? Anything Tutu Aiko kept that belonged to her sister?"

Her mother hesitated, gripping her tissue. "Not much."

Cassandra waited, sensing the crack in the wall she'd spent years trying to climb over.

"Some trinkets, a couple quilts, one of her old brooches, maybe a cloth doll stitched from scraps."

Cassandra blinked. "I don't remember a tub of family keepsakes?"

Mom shrugged. "Tutu Aiko said her sister hand-stitched them. Real delicate work."

A flicker of curiosity ran down Cassandra's spine, but she let it pass. They had bigger mysteries to solve.

Into this emotional scene walked Cassandra's father, Ken. At first he stepped past them, oblivious. He opened the fridge and pulled out a can of sparkling water, popped it open, and drank deeply. Sweat dampened his hairline and formed a dark circle on the back of his t-shirt.

Moments later, he must have noticed the silence, which was highly unusual when his kitchen was full of women. He turned, frowning. "What trouble you stirring up now, eh?"

Her mother dabbed at her eyes and sat straighter.

He pinned Cassandra with a concerned glare. "It's that Mānoa Marauder cold case isn't it?"

How did he know that? When Cassandra opened her mouth to speak, he said, "I saw da kine booth at the conference yesterday. What, you t'ink I don't know you would jump right in da middle without considering how your mother would feel?"

She was about to protest that it was the students leading this investigation and they were doing it for the prize money, but Dad said, "Don't go digging too deep, eh? Remember what happened last time you got too curious?"

Her lips shut abruptly as her gaze caught sight of Jocelyn's brother, Pono, a uniformed HPD officer, leaning casually in the doorway.

Great. How long had he been listening?

"Still dragging my baby sister into trouble, eh Cass? Poking your nose where it doesn't belong?"

Guess he'd been there long enough. Cassandra responded with a smirk more in line with her inner twelve-year-old than the accomplished woman she had become. "You'd know better than anyone, eh Pono?"

At least she didn't stick out her tongue, too.

Her father ignored all the latent tension in the room and returned to the back yard with his orchids.

"Anyway," Mom said, standing abruptly, "if you girls are done digging up ghosts, I gotta clean the bathroom."

That bathroom was cleaner than most surgical rooms. Cassandra sighed. Typical.

Pono helped himself to a cookie and took the chair vacated by her mother. "Joce' said something about needing my forensic advice? You've been here, what two days? Already need help covering up the evidence. Who'd you kill?" He chuckled.

Jocelyn rolled her eyes and shoved his arm, making crumbs fall all over the table. "C'mon, braddah. Can you just stop with the jokes? This is serious business. Cassandra wants to solve the cold case mystery of the Mānoa Marauder. One of the victims was her mother's great aunt."

Michael "Pono" Kaneshiro and Keoni, Cassandra's older brother, had been inseparable growing up. Their moms made crafts in the living room while the kids ran wild in the yard. Cassandra and Jocelyn playing dress-up, the boys building obstacle courses with sticks and overturned buckets.

She hadn't seen Pono in over a year, and now he looked exactly the same: neat haircut, HPD shirt tucked in like he'd just left roll call. Always sturdy, always steady. He carried himself with the kind of quiet authority that came from years of showing up and doing the job. She'd had a dumb crush on him for about ten minutes in eighth grade, but thankfully her taste had evolved.

Jocelyn pulled out a gallon-sized baggie containing the map and cut to the chase. "We acquired this old map and wanted your help. Are there fingerprints on it? How old is it? Could it be from the early 1900s? We think it might be a map of the old plantation before they sold off some of the parcels."

He swallowed the last bite of his cookie and gently lifted the map. "You just happened to find a hundred-year-old map. Do not tell me how you got this." He placed it on the table. "I could check for fingerprints, but the odds of identifying anyone from 1910 are basically nonexistent. I've got a light we could try to see if there are other markings on the paper. "

Cassandra and Jocelyn exchanged glances and nodded. "Our first clue!" Jocelyn said.

Pono folded his arms across his chest and sat back. "Okay, say this is a real map from the plantation. So what?"

Cassandra said, "Wasn't it fairly common in those times for white settlers to take land that belonged to the *ali'i* ruling class of Hawaiians? It looks like someone was trying to mark important spots on the property. Maybe former holy shrine places? Or... there were always rumors of people stealing treasures. What if someone hid royal artifacts and made a map for where to find them later?"

"That's a lot of what ifs," Pono said.

Considering her parents' thoughts on her involvement in anything crime-related, Cassandra slid the map closer to Pono. "Please just test it with whatever means you have."

"Lemme get my tools from the trunk of the car."

Shortly he came back and set a black tool bag on the extra chair.

Jocelyn tapped the table thoughtfully. "You know, the conference handed out some old police reports from the case. Do you think there might be more in the department archives? Maybe something the students could dig through? Sometimes fresh eyes catch things that got overlooked back then."

Pono made a face. "If they're a hundred years old, you'll be lucky if they're legible. Paper was bad, ink was worse, and half the notes were written in shorthand nobody uses anymore. Some files just vanished without explanation. Budget cuts, 'missing evidence,' you name it."

Two sharp knocks sounded on the front door and a voice sing-songed, "Aloha, Michiko-san..." Soon Jocelyn's mother appeared in the kitchen and pointed an arthritic finger at Pono. "Michael Pono, I thought that was your car outside. You're not getting these girls into trouble again, are you?"

Ope. Their mother only used both his names when she was scolding him. Cassandra smirked.

Jocelyn's foot quietly scooted the chair with the tool bag out of view under the table.

Pono swiped the map off the table and tucked it behind his back. "Not this time, Mommy. I'm just here to help."

"Pono's helping us stay *out* of trouble, Auntie," Cassandra added with a laugh, glancing at Jocelyn, who nodded in agreement.

Her mother appeared from the back hallway, dressed in baggy blue cropped pants and a fresh printed tunic with her pocketbook slung over her arm. "*Ohayou*, Yumi! I'm ready." She seemed inclined to rush out of the house, but Yumiko Kaneshiro wasn't having it.

"What you kids cooking up now, eh?"

"Just doing some research on an old mystery," Jocelyn said. "You remember the Mānoa Marauder? Well it turns out one of the victims was Auntie Michiko's great aunt. Small world, yah? They never caught the guy."

"My uncle always thought it was someone who worked there," Yumi said, "but they never could prove it. Uncle always said it was a cover up."

"Your uncle was a police officer?" It was the first Cassandra had ever heard of it.

"Made it to detective," Pono said proudly. "He was my idol growing up."

Cassandra's mom fiddled with the clasp on her purse and looked generally uncomfortable with the conversation. "I want to get to the market before the tomato guy sells out of all the Hamakuas. Your father likes those in his breakfast sandwich."

Yumiko linked her arm with Michiko's. "You smarty pants girls, figure it out with all the fancy tech stuffs." The two strutted off to the market like teenagers heading to the mall.

Pono pulled out a small UV flashlight from his bag, clicked it on, and shined it over the map. The paper glowed faintly, dust motes dancing under the light.

"Most old documents have some kind of damage," he murmured, angling the beam. "But sometimes..."

The kitchen clock ticked while he slowly moved the light over the map.

Not great at sitting still, Cassandra used the bathroom and transferred a load of wash to the dryer. She folded the towels neatly for her parents and placed them in the closet.

Folding laundry always calmed her nerves, a quiet ritual in the midst of the day's chaos. The danger might have been more than a hundred years in the past, but her mother's discomfort lingered in her thoughts.

When she returned to the kitchen, Pono and Jocelyn gazed at her with identical excited expressions. "Check this out, Cass."

He pointed out more markings and symbols that had once been clear but had faded over time. Using the UV light, they were able to see the lines better. "This one looks like an old well maybe with these squiggly lines. Over here, away from the house this one could be a burial site?"

"It aligns with these Xs and circles," Cassandra tried to hide the rising excitement in her voice.

He paused. Then frowned.

"What?" Cassandra leaned closer, her breath hitching.

"Look at that," Jocelyn whispered, pointing to the faint, slanted script appearing near the edge of the map. The ink had faded, barely visible to the naked eye.

Pono adjusted the angle. "That's handwriting."

The letters were thin, careful. Cassandra traced them lightly with her finger, as if feeling them would help her process what she was seeing.

It wasn't a note. Not instructions. Just a name.

A single, delicate signature scrawled in the bottom corner of the map.

Jean Oliver?

Cassandra's breath caught.

Jocelyn whispered, "Jean Oliver drew this map."

Pono tapped the edge of the map. "If she made this, and her death was ruled an accident, then either the cops missed something huge or they didn't want to see it. We'll never get DNA from a century ago, and fingerprints are long gone. All that's left are the lies people told." He clicked off the light, expression unreadable. "You sure you want to keep chasing ghosts, Cass?"

Her heart pounded. "Yes," she said. "Now more than ever."

Pono's phone pinged, and he glanced at it with a sigh. "I gotta get back to the office and deal with today's crimes."

Cassandra smirked. "And yet, here you are, always getting roped into our nonsense."

Jocelyn added with a grin, "Admit it, you'd miss us if we didn't keep life interesting."

He packed up his toolkit, chuckling. "Interesting, sure. Trouble? Always. I'll see what I can dig up. Just don't let this get out of hand, yeah?"

Cassandra's voice was calm but firm. "Thanks, Pono. And don't worry, we've got this."

"That's what your brother said before trying to build a zip line off our roof." He grabbed his bag and shook his head. "If you end up on the news, don't use my real name."

By the time Cassandra and Jocelyn joined the students on the hotel lanai, the beach party was well under way. In one corner framed by palm trees, a three-piece band played local covers. A tiki bar served fruity drinks with umbrellas in fake coconut cups, and college students from the conference stood in groups throughout the pool decks and chairs.

Cassandra found Ivy, Lexi, and Maria relaxing on chaise lounges drinking bottled water. "Aloha wāhine, howzit? You went try the surfing lessons today?"

At first the girls stared with blank expressions at Cassandra like they didn't recognize her. She looked down at her gym shorts, flip flops which were called *rubba slippahs*, Honolulu Fun Run t-shirt, and realized maybe the students weren't quite expecting "local girl Cassandra" instead of "Dr. Sato."

She cleared her throat and tried again, "Hello ladies, was your afternoon fun?"

Maria was the first to recover. "Erm..., hello Dr. Sato. I couldn't stand up on the surfboard, so I just went boogie boarding. It was fun though. We all got a little sunburned." She showed the pink lines on her shoulder from where her swimsuit top straps were.

Lexi pulled up the bottom of her shirt revealing a sharply defined hand-print that was the only light-skinned thing on her sunburned back. She said, "Pro tip: don't ever ask Ethan to put sunscreen on your back." She shook her head in disgust. "I can't move."

Cassandra reached in her bag for the aloe sun repair cream. "I got your back."

Jocelyn laughed out loud. "Good one, Cass."

Cassandra settled into the chair next to Maria. "We had a good day too, minus the uh, sun situation. Jocelyn and I made some headway on the Mānoa Marauder investigation. It's a pretty complex case. I can see why the prize money is so high."

Lexi looked up from rubbing the cream onto her shoulders. "What did you find out?"

Jocelyn leaned in, voice dropping to a whisper. "We uncovered an old map at the plantation house. My brother used a UV light on it and turns out it has hidden symbols. Like someone meant to hide the truth in plain sight."

Ivy's eyes widened. "Like treasure?"

"Maybe," Cassandra said. "But it could be evidence or a warning. Either way, someone wanted it hidden."

Maria sat up straighter. "If we figure this out, do you think it could actually rewrite what people know about the Mānoa Marauder?"

"It's possible. Hawai'i Unforgotten wants to expose the truth behind these cases. What we find could give closure to families or even reclaim pieces of history that were lost."

Jocelyn tapped the edge of the table. "And there was one more thing. Near the edge of the map, we found a handwritten name. Jean Oliver. It was faint, but clear enough under the UV light."

Maria frowned. "Jean Oliver? The rich girl who died?"

"Yeah," Cassandra confirmed, meeting Jocelyn's gaze. "Which means Jean knew something. Maybe something dangerous. What if her death wasn't just tragic, but intentional?"

Ivy's fingers drummed excitedly on the table. "Do we need to check for more hidden markings? Maybe there's a pattern on the map we're missing."

"Or what about the places?" Maria added. "Did any of them show up in the VR session?"

"Great questions!" Cassandra said, "Let's jot them down for tomorrow. Fresh eyes always help." She glanced at Jocelyn. "We'll cross-check these spots against old police notes, VR scenes, and estate maps. If something lines up, we've got a lead."

"I'm in," Lexi said, wincing as she gingerly touched her arm. "Just as long as it doesn't involve any more surfing."

Cassandra chuckled. "No surfing needed. Just some old-fashioned sleuthing. We're going to need all of your sharp eyes and quick minds on this. If we're lucky, this map could be the key to solving the murders and uncovering a part of Hawaii's history that's been buried for a long time."

"Count us in," Maria said, nodding. "We're ready."

Cassandra smiled. "Good. Tomorrow morning we'll regroup and start digging into those records. The past buried the truth once. Let's make sure it doesn't happen again."

As the evening breeze carried the scent of salt and plumeria, Cassandra leaned back and watched her students chatter about the cold case. The soft strumming of an Israel K. cover mingled with laughter and the rhythmic crash of waves. She counted her blessings: engaged students, home, a puzzle to solve, and the joy of this moment.

It really was a wonderful world.

Chapter Seven

T HE EARLY MORNING SUN filtered through the gauzy curtains of Cassandra's hotel room, casting soft shadows across the floor. Already showered and dressed, she moved through her usual yoga sequence. Stretch, breathe, center. No matter how chaotic the day ahead, this was her reset button.

Her breath slowed. The mat warmed beneath her hands. She let the silence settle.

When she finally straightened from her final pose, the calm fractured just slightly. Her gaze drifted toward the desk, where the quilt map lay folded beside her notebook.

Namaste, now back to murder.

The landmarks, the signature, those curious symbols. Someone had risked everything to preserve those secrets. Now it was their turn to find out why.

She checked the time. Still early. Good.

Cassandra grabbed her phone and typed a quick message in the group chat.

Predictably, replies started pinging almost instantly: groans, memes, and one skull emoji from Andrew. But they'd show up. That was what mattered.

Downstairs, Jocelyn arrived carrying two coffees. Cassandra accepted hers gratefully and did a quick mental headcount. Some students looked more awake than others, but curiosity had won the fight against the snooze button. The group had energy and focus, and that was enough.

"Alright," she said, slinging her bag over her shoulder. "Another day in paradise. At least the archives room has windows. We can still see the palm trees."

A few sleepy chuckles followed as they stepped outside into the humid morning. The walk was short, with the scent of damp greenery in the air and distant traffic humming along the main road.

The Hawai'i State Library's grand columns on the stucco facade greeted them like sentries. Tourists lingered beneath the shady portico, sipping water and arguing over who packed sunscreen. Inside, the cool air smelled of old paper and leather.

Cassandra and Jocelyn led the group straight to the microfilm archives. "All right, detectives. Time to get our hands dusty. I assume you all read the essay Dr. Nakano included about Hawaiian cultural burial practices and symbols?"

Ivy and Maria nodded. Everyone else broke eye contact and studied their shoelaces.

Cassandra let out a frustrated sigh. "Fine. Since you ladies are the only ones who came prepared, you can finish synthesizing what we know and drafting the investigation questions. The rest of us are hitting the microfilm."

Jocelyn flopped into a chair beside a reel machine. "Let the cranking begin."

Cassandra noted the fascinated stares on the students' faces. "You folks act like you see a Velociraptor," she chuckled. "Let me introduce you to microfilm. Back in the *Jurassic Park* days, before you could snap a photo of anything you wanted to remember with your smartphone, they used to employ a small army of people in this department to scan printed newspapers, journals, and documents and store them in a room-sized computer."

Cassandra loaded a reel of microfilm onto the machine, unwound the film, fed it under the glass, and onto the empty spool on the right side. The others leaned in as Cassandra began scanning the *Evening Bulletin* from 1910. The articles blurred across the screen. "Look for anything about the Mānoa Marauder, or other unsolved murders around that time."

The students grabbed a couple of reels and huddled around the remaining machines. At first, Cassandra was distracted by their comical attempts to figure out the old technology, but soon they were scanning headlines and digitized police reports like microfilm experts.

Cassandra watched them with quiet satisfaction. Lance moved with quiet precision, sorting files and tagging patterns. Maria scanned quickly, eyes flicking between documents as she connected ideas others might miss. Even Diego, who usually chased action over academics, had settled in with a police file, eyebrows furrowed in concentration.

Chasing a century-old mystery with a crew who could barely remember to reapply sunscreen. What could possibly go wrong?

Still, Cassandra couldn't let them forget the stakes. That map was both history and a warning. And if her aunt really had died protecting it, they weren't just playing detective. Not anymore.

They'd worked for barely ten minutes when a familiar voice squawked across the room. "Let's go Hardy Boys! Find the clues."

Jocelyn blinked, startled. Cassandra smiled before she even looked.

Andrew entered with a cracker in one hand and Skipper perched on his shoulder.

"Aloha, campers," he said. "Ready to solve a cold case?"

The guys fist-bumped him as he joined their table. Ethan raised his fist toward Skipper's tiny foot, but the bird lifted his beak with obvious disapproval.

"Find the clues," Skipper repeated, flapping once.

Andrew settled in with the crew and pulled out his notes.

Meg arrived later, her normally wavy red hair tighter with humidity, dark circles under her eyes betrayed by the concealer she'd swiped on. She still looked better than most of the students, Cassandra noted.

"Traffic was awful," Meg groaned, dropping into a chair beside Cassandra. "If Connor hadn't been with me, I'd still be crawling through Aiea. Carpool lane saved us."

"Everything going okay at my parents' place?" Cassandra whispered.

Meg brightened. "Oh, they're lovely. Your mom keeps feeding me, and I caught your dad rocking Olivia in that old wooden chair. He's a total marshmallow."

Cassandra's breath hitched. Her family's wooden rocker had held generations of tiny Sato babies. A tangible piece of family history, smoothed by time and care. The thought of it now felt like a hollow ache, a reminder of choices made and dreams she'd quietly let drift away.

She exhaled and forced a light tone. "Mom's been trying to feed people like it's her life's mission since before I was born."

Meg wasn't fooled. She gave Cassandra's arm a small squeeze. "I know you and Fischer aren't exactly seeing eye to eye lately, but give it time. I really feel you've got 'mother energy' waiting to be unleashed."

Cassandra handed Meg a takeout coffee cup. "You sure that's not 'Best Auntie Ever' energy? Sleep deprivation might be messing with your radar."

Meg took a slow sip of her coffee, her expression distant. "You know when Tony was born, I thought I was prepared. But then he showed up, and I realized how much I didn't know. You think you're in control of your life until suddenly, you're holding this tiny person, and they become the only thing that matters."

She met Cassandra's gaze, a knowing softness in her voice. "You might not have a baby of your own, but you've spent years nurturing your students and your career. Even this investigation. Don't underestimate the power of spiritual motherhood."

Before Cassandra could respond, a guy in a Stanford T-shirt leaned back in his chair and said, "So the bird is the secret weapon?" He and his three buddies sprawled around a research pod like they owned the place. "I mean, when you can't find anything helpful on your own turf, why not invade someone else's?"

Lexi inhaled sharply. "Wow. Subtle."

He grinned. "No shade. We get it. You hit a dead end in Mānoa and figured out the original investigation was too primitive to piece together a proper timeline, let alone profile a serial killer."

Lexi didn't miss a beat. "Library's public, isn't it?"

A blond guy with Patagonia vest energy gave an indulgent shrug. "Of course. *Mi research casa es su research casa.* We already have a working theory, but if you enjoy squinting at 1910 microfilm, have at it."

Brandon bristled. "Hey man, we're just using all the tools available. Especially since some teams seem to be getting bonus features."

He smirked. "Sounds like a you problem. We didn't write the game rules. We're just playing smart."

Cassandra, nearby, pretended to focus on her notes but was already side-eying Jocelyn.

Jocelyn leaned closer, voice low. "Little ironic, huh? Us accusing anyone of extra help?"

Cassandra sighed through her nose. "Let's just call it... balanced redistribution."

They weren't wrong. Morton's team was poking around off-site. But it still grated.

Another Stanford bro who had the vibe of a guy who wrote LinkedIn posts about hustle culture, added, "It's about perspective. Smuggling rings, secret tunnels. If you understand the economic power structures of early 20th-century Hawai'i, everything starts to click. It's all right there. Just... not obvious."

Ivy frowned. "So you think the Marauder was what, a front for organized crime?"

"Exactly." Vest Guy tapped his temple. "Think bigger. Smuggling. Political leverage. Blackmail. A cover story built on selective newspaper leaks and a conveniently dead socialite."

Lexi rolled her eyes. "And you know this because your AI said so?"

"Superior methodology," LinkedIn Guy smiled, all dimples and ego. "We're running an AI probability model on case data. Should have results by dinner."

Maria slapped her notebook closed. "Well, please save us all a seat at your Nobel Prize party."

The bros packed up in synchronized ease, laptops snapped shut, water bottles collected like they were wrapping a product demo.

Patagonia Vest Guy chuckled. "See you at the finish line."

"Front row," Lexi's smile didn't waver, "just to watch your algorithm implode."

Silence stretched as the Stanford team strolled off, infuriatingly relaxed, like they'd already won.

Cassandra rubbed her forehead. "Shake it off, folks. We have work to do."

"Yeah," Lexi muttered as she turned back to her notes. "And they have a TED Talk to prep."

Cassandra had just unclenched her jaw when another voice piped up behind her. "Well, well. The Midwest dream team at work."

Cassandra looked up just in time to see Kalia Chun strut through the archives, her team trailing behind like color-coordinated ducklings. Their matching lanyards, leather-bound portfolios, and effortless happiness made jealousy throb in her temple.

Today, Kalia's sleeveless blouse and kapa print skirt were unmistakably Kealopiko. Tasteful, expensive, and perfectly calculated. Like everything Kalia did.

"Kalia," Cassandra murmured, not proud of her feelings. Naturally, she lashed out with cool sarcasm. "Come to do some real research?"

"Thanks, but no." Kalia's smirk didn't budge. "We just wrapped up in the restricted reading room. Our field site is the Iolani Palace, remember?" She swept a polished nail through the air. "This is more of a... courtesy visit."

"Of course," Cassandra said smoothly. "Be sure to grab a souvenir on your way out. Something to commemorate your academic detour."

Jocelyn muttered, "They lucky I don't have my rubba slippah handy."

Lexi leaned over. "Do I want to know what that means?"

Jocelyn grinned. "Ask Cassandra's mom."

"Now we're off to brunch with some trustees," Kalia said breezily, then added as she turned, "Amazing what people will share over guava pancakes." She drifted away, team in tow, their soft laughter trailing like expensive perfume.

Ivy looked sideways at Cassandra. "Should we be having brunch with advisors too?"

"Not unless you're in the club," Jocelyn muttered. "They specialize in curated access."

Then Brandon scowled. "They seriously have an advantage, don't they? How are we supposed to compete?"

Cassandra straightened. This was exactly the kind of doubt Stanford—and now Kalia—wanted to plant.

"Connections and tools help. But they don't guarantee success." Her gaze swept over the students. "Trust me, I've seen Kalia in action before. She'll cut corners if she can. That's not our style."

Maria frowned. "Still. The bros got ChatGPT. Kualoa's got brunch. And we've got... dust and optimism."

Jocelyn grinned. "Don't knock the optimism. That's how underdogs win."

"Good," Ethan said. "Because I don't think I could survive guava pancakes with local trustees."

Cassandra chuckled, feeling the tension ease. "Focus on what we can control. We have evidence they haven't seen."

Lexi stretched, cracking her knuckles. "Well, if they're gonna use their fancy connections, then we should use what we've got." She smirked. "And what we've got is me."

Cassandra raised an eyebrow. "Oh no."

"Oh yes," Lexi said. "Those prep school snobs aren't the only ones who can work the system. Give me five minutes."

Cassandra watched with mild amusement as Lexi strolled up to the information desk, her confidence radiating like a magic spell.

A young library assistant, caught mid-stack with a pile of books, looked up, clearly unprepared for the whirlwind about to hit him.

Cassandra exhaled, already bracing for impact. Elle Woods strikes again.

Leaning in slightly, Lexi dropped her voice into the kind of sugary tone that could turn molten lava to syrup. "I was wondering if there might be any special files tucked away somewhere. You know, the really interesting stuff."

The assistant blinked, his resolve visibly faltering under the full force of Lexi's charm. "Uh, we have some restricted archives, but I'm not really supposed to let—"

Lexi tilted her head just so, her smile as dazzling as the midday sun. Cassandra couldn't make out her exact words, but her lipreading skills caught something about "huge help" and "it'd mean so much."

And like a haupia square left too long in the sun, the assistant melted. Mumbling something about making an exception, he disappeared into the back. Moments later, he returned with a thin stack of dusty files, whispering instructions to Lexi as though they were swapping state secrets.

Lexi's smile softened as she accepted the files, her tone honeyed. "You're the best. Thanks a million."

As she sashayed back to the group, files in hand and victorious grin firmly in place, Cassandra raised an eyebrow. "I don't know whether to be impressed or afraid."

Lexi gave a casual shrug. "Just using my natural gifts."

Cassandra suppressed a laugh. Lexi was wasted on this group. She could run a multinational corporation—or plan the perfect heist—if the mood struck her.

A short while later, Lance banged on the table once to get their attention, then signed while Meg interpreted his ASL into spoken English. *Jean Oliver's death was ruled an accident at the time, but I think the three other murders point to a pattern.*

Logan frowned. "Okay following your logic, I see how the seamstress and the gardener's deaths are connected to Jean Oliver's. But how does this Mary Pauahi lady fit in? She didn't work on the estate."

Lance signed slowly, *If Jean's death wasn't an accident, then someone needed it to look like one. That's not a panicked mistake. That's a cover-up. And if it was a cover-up, then who benefited?"*

Ivy wrinkled her nose. "Just to be clear, the gardener and the groundskeeper were two different dudes, right?"

"Right," Maria confirmed, flipping through a report. "The gardener, Manuel Reyes, was one of the victims. And this says they questioned Daniel Ybarra, the groundskeeper, about Jean Oliver and Hana Nakamura. There were even rumors that Daniel and Jean had a thing, but why would he kill Hana too? Did she find out something and threaten to expose them? It's like a Hawaiian *Downton Abbey*, but messier."

Ivy smirked. "Pretty sure *Downton* didn't have a serial killer subplot. This is more like a true-crime podcast. But yeah, how did a wealthy socialite and two servants die on the same property, and nobody got charged?"

Jocelyn shrugged. "Depends on the circumstances. Maybe the truth was worse than letting the case go cold. Maybe someone powerful needed this buried."

Maria pointed at her screen. "Check this. Land transfer tied to the Oliver estate. Lawyer's name is typed, but the signature line's blank. No date either."

"Sloppy," Cassandra muttered. "For a family obsessed with appearances."

"Or intentional," Logan said. "A missing signature buys you deniability."

Andrew tapped a handwritten stack of papers. "The police reports are a mess. Half of this is just sketchy statements from 'informants.' Half the leads dead-end. The press went full circus with wild theories. No wonder they pinned it on Ybarra early."

Diego skimmed an article. "One guy even confessed. Turns out he was working in Waianae at the time. Completely made-up."

Lexi, still holding one of the restricted archive folders, slid a yellowed page across the table. "Check this out: Hana Nakamura's death certificate. Except the date doesn't match the newspaper obituary. It's off by three days. No witnesses listed."

Cassandra studied the document carefully.

Ivy dove for her notes, messily hunting through pages until she held one up triumphantly. "Here's the one from our official packet. With the same date as the newspaper obituary."

Cassandra skimmed the page. Marital status was single, cause of death: asphyxiation, occupation was seamstress. Survivors and funeral details were blank.

Maria blinked. "So either the certificate was forged... or the obituary was wrong."

Jocelyn muttered, "Wrong date, missing witness, unsigned deed. These people were either hiding something or unbelievably sloppy."

Cassandra frowned. "Maybe both."

Logan stood excitedly. "And if Jean was silenced, maybe Hana was next. Maybe that's the pattern."

Jocelyn looked up. "Okay, but let's bring it in. We've got a map with Jean Oliver's signature, stitched into a quilt by Hana, hidden for a hundred years. It was a warning."

Cassandra nodded. "Agreed. And if Hana was helping Jean, and Jean ended up dead, that's motive for cover-up. Not melodrama. Think intent, not Netflix."

Lexi flipped through her notes. "Right. We've been thinking of Hana as a bystander. But what if she was the protector?"

Diego nodded. "She worked in the sewing room. If someone needed a secret kept safe, she's exactly who they'd trust."

Maria's voice dropped. "And if Hana was murdered because of that map, Aiko would've been smart to keep quiet. That's why it sat hidden for a century."

Cassandra's chest tightened. Jean's delicate signature. Hana's quiet loyalty. A secret stitched into fabric and folded into silence.

And now, a century later, they were finally listening.

Jocelyn scanned her screen. "Here's a blip from 1925. Police reopened the well during the Marauder case."

Logan frowned. "Why the well?"

"Who knows?" Jocelyn shrugged. "Workers said it was *kapu*... taboo. Ghost stories, red water after storms, whispers at night. The usual creep factor."

Maria rolled her eyes. "So, legend, not evidence."

"Exactly," Cassandra said. "It doesn't help us solve the murders, but it tells us the estate was a magnet for rumors. Maybe for a reason."

Jocelyn nodded. "And in 1940, another historian asked to see original property records. Within weeks, police came back. Quietly."

Ivy raised an eyebrow. "Still nothing found?"

"Nothing reported," Jocelyn said. "But that part of the land was renovated in the early 2000s. Garden paths. Tour brochures. Nice, tidy distraction."

Lexi muttered, "Convenient timing."

Lance pointed to a screen. He signed, *We need all three maps. 1910 layout. Jean's hand-drawn version. And the current parcel records. That's how we see what's missing.*

Cassandra opened a third window and pulled up the current property database. She overlaid it first with the 1910 map, aligning by the old creek bed. Then, layer by layer, she added Jean's version.

As the maps aligned, the differences popped into view—whole sections that had vanished from the modern layout.

"Wait, this parcel here," Maria pointed. "It's not on the public record anymore."

"Exactly," Cassandra murmured. "Jean's map shows it labeled with an X. That section might've been reserved for someone."

Logan leaned in. "And if the Olivers forged a fake sale or buried the deed—"

"Then this wasn't just murder," Jocelyn said. "It was theft. Systemic, long-term theft."

Ivy looked sick. "You think Jean knew and tried to fix it?"

"Or at least expose it," Cassandra said. "Which would give someone motive to shut her up."

Lexi sat back. "So now what? Go back and dig through the rose bushes with a shovel?"

Cassandra's eyes narrowed on the overlapping lot lines. "First, we confirm the landmarks. If any of Jean's symbols line up with those blocked out sections of land, we'll know where to look. And what the Olivers were trying to erase."

Lexi grinned. "You mean officially, or are we going full *National Treasure?*"

Cassandra sighed. "Let's call it... stages."

Jocelyn gave her a side-eye. "You're absolutely sneaking back there."

Cassandra took a slow sip of coffee. "I never said that."

They bent over the maps again, tracing creek bends and boundary markers, the urgency thickening. For the first time, it wasn't just about proving what happened.

It was about recovering what was taken.

Ivy checked her phone and winced. "Panel starts in less than an hour."

"Alright," Cassandra said. "After *The Ethics of Historical Preservation* panel, we split up. Some to the VR exhibit, the rest to the plantation. Let's see what's been rewritten, and what's just been paved over."

Andrew raised a brow. "But PastForward is a legit contest. They wouldn't just leave stuff out. Right?"

Cassandra met his eyes. "People don't build games to tell the whole truth. They build them to win."

He didn't respond right away. Then quietly: "I'm working a shift at the VR booth. I'll poke around."

"Good," Cassandra said. "Let's keep digging. The past may be buried, but it didn't disappear."

As they packed up, Lexi waved at her library crush, who nearly tripped over a rolling cart trying to wave back.

Cassandra smiled. Some things never changed.

Her fingertips hovered over the photo of the quilt, where Hana Nakamura's stitched signature marked the place she had hidden Jean's map. A thread between them that hadn't frayed.

And now it was their job to pull it.

Chapter Eight

B Y LATE AFTERNOON, CASSANDRA'S group arrived at the Oliver estate and checked in at the front desk. They clustered together, toting their drawstring bags and still buzzing from the morning's archive discoveries.

Cassandra figured she'd be doing most of the interpreting for Lance, since Diego's sign language was limited to what he called "soccer insults," and Maria could only fingerspell her name. The rest, they'd patch together with phones and patience.

Fortunately, Angela wasn't on duty today. Instead, Mahina, a silver-haired volunteer with the calm patience of someone who'd seen every kind of tourist, manned the check-in. She looked up as they approached and smiled knowingly.

"Ah, more curious minds," she said, eyes twinkling as she spotted their Honolulu PastForward bags. "Dis contest got every team thinkin' they da one gonna crack da case."

Diego grinned. "That obvious?"

Mahina patted his arm like an indulgent auntie. "You da third group today asking 'bout da old stories. But dis land been picked over more than a mango tree in July."

Cassandra caught the amused look Mahina gave her. A subtle *you too, huh?*

Undeterred, Maria leaned in. "We're actually looking into the old well. Some workers used to say it was haunted, right?"

Mahina didn't react right away. She just gave a thoughtful *hmm*. "Da well. Funny place for start. Most folks come asking 'bout da Oliver girl or da murders."

Lance raised his brows. He signed, *So we're asking better questions?*

Mahina chuckled. "Depends what kine answers you like get."

Diego tried again. "You've been around a long time. Hear anything from older workers or caretakers?"

Mahina's gaze slid toward the back grove. "Da well is da well. But da creek... my tūtū used to say no walk there after sundown. Workers would go around even if it mean adding time. Some say they hear voices. Some saw shadows that vanish when you look again."

Maria leaned in. "You mean ghosts?"

Mahina shrugged. "Some say wind. Some say da land remembers."

Diego grinned. "So... did *you* ever see anything?"

Her look could curdle milk. "Boy, you tink I gonna say? Dat's da kine stories you don't go chasing."

Cassandra finally spoke. "What do you believe?"

Mahina's smile was quiet and knowing. "I believe da stories that stay. Dey get long legs. Dey survive." She clapped her hands softly. "You folks got forty-five minutes. Better use 'em."

As she turned back to her crossword puzzle, the group hesitated a beat.

"*Kupuna,*" Cassandra murmured.

Logan raised an eyebrow. "Huh?"

"It means elder," she said. "Someone with wisdom, experience. Their stories carry weight."

Maria sighed. "So basically, she told us a ghost story and didn't help at all."

Cassandra smiled faintly. "No, she gave us what we needed. We just don't know what it is yet."

Logan exchanged a look with Brandon. "We'll check the main floor again. Maybe the VR tour skipped something useful."

Meanwhile, Cassandra led Lance, Maria, and Diego outside to find landmarks from their research.

The trail behind the house was narrow and overgrown, half-swallowed by banana trees and palms. They moved in single file, dodging vines and branches until they reached a low stone table, half-hidden under tangled foliage.

Cassandra glanced over her shoulder. "This way."

They stepped into the grove, and she spread a printed copy of the historical map across the table's uneven surface. Using the house as their anchor, the group began tracing the layout: a crooked garden, a worn footpath, and the tree line marking where the creek ran.

She scanned the overgrown yard sprawled before them. Mahina hadn't really answered their questions, she'd steered them. Away from the well. Toward the creek. That meant something.

If there was a secret buried out here, it was probably hiding under something with thorns.

Lance signed, *Where do we start?*

Maria wiped her brow. "You know, the more we sweat through this yard, the more I question why the other teams were mad we got assigned here."

Cassandra sighed. "Yeah. Everyone wanted this site, but Dr. Nakano gave it to us."

Diego arched an eyebrow. "Not that I'm complaining, but why?"

"Officially? Because our research profile fit the field site."

Maria snorted. "Right. Because the team from Nebraska must be farming experts."

Cassandra hesitated. Nakano had a habit of guiding outcomes, always just subtle enough to maintain plausible deniability. He hadn't said anything specific, but Kalia's team still acted like this case belonged to them.

"He likes to stack the deck," Cassandra said, adjusting her tote. "We just don't know if it's in our favor or not."

She hated how he stayed just far enough removed to seem objective. Trusting his motives felt like a gamble she wasn't sure she could afford.

Lance signed, *You think he's guiding the results?*

That's what we need to figure out, she signed back.

Speaking and signing, Cassandra said, "Do any of these Xs on the map line up with fenced off sections? Flower beds? Or maybe that old shed?"

Half a football field away, the shed looked like it had been built at the turn of the twentieth century and abandoned ever since. Plantation-style roofline, peeling paint, and slatted walls had long since given up the fight against Hawaii's humidity.

It was the kind of place that begged to be left alone. So of course, that's where they headed, Diego's long legs striding effortlessly across the lawn.

Up close, it was even worse. The perfect place to store a century of secrets or an army of centipedes the size of sneakers.

"Seriously, if Dr. Nakano wants us to win," Maria wrinkled her nose, "couldn't he have assigned us a hotel ballroom instead of a glorified spider cave?"

Diego's voice floated out from inside the shed. "Maybe he wants us to dig up something no one else will."

Cassandra followed him inside, undeterred by the faint chemical smell wafting from within. "Or maybe this is his version of a character-building exercise."

The interior was surprisingly tidy, organized even. Shelves lined the walls, stocked with bottles of fertilizer, gardening tools, and stacks of empty pots. High up, near the narrow windows, a row of orchids thrived in delicate shades of white, purple, and yellow. Someone clearly had a green thumb.

Smells like science class, Lance signed, examining containers lining the shelves.

"Please don't touch anything labeled flammable," Cassandra said, while wrinkling her nose.

Lance opened a cabinet, revealing a pile of rusty shovels in the corner.

For a moment, Diego's eyes lit up. "Aha! A clue—" He picked up one of the shovels and then frowned. "Never mind. Just your average murder implements."

Cassandra squinted. "Let's hope they're for gardening, not burying evidence."

Maria remained in the doorway, poised to hop out at the first sign of an insect. "The orchids are impressive, though. Whoever runs this place cares about the landscaping."

Diego replaced the shovel, brushing off his hands like he'd done his duty as a budding detective. "So, no unmarked graves or holy sites. Yet."

Cassandra checked her watch. Thirty minutes until closing. The elderly volunteer at the front desk, Mahina, seemed more interested in her crossword puzzle than enforcing rules, but Cassandra wasn't about to risk an incident. Getting caught snooping off-limits on a college-sponsored trip wasn't a box she wanted checked on her performance review.

She scanned the surrounding area for signs of other staff or tourists. "Alright, folks. Let's move before anyone decides we look suspicious."

Cassandra glanced at the map. The well was the next logical place to check, but Diego pointed toward the tree-line near the property boundary. A few of the map's Xs and circles clustered in that area.

"Fine, let's check it out," she said, tucking the map into her bag.

The group followed a narrow path into the trees, a soft Kona wind rustling through the dense vegetation. Cassandra inhaled deeply, savoring the tropical scent Nebraska could never provide.

A banyan tree massive enough to be much older than a hundred years loomed where one of the larger Xs sat on the map. Its sprawling roots twisted and curled into natural crevices that seemed perfect for hiding something.

Maria ran her fingers over the bark. "If the contest was just an organized game, you'd think we'd see clues here somewhere."

Lance poked around between the huge roots and ducked into holes and crevices near the trunk.

Cassandra scanned the area. The whole Mānoa Marauder challenge felt a little staged, like a made-for-VR scavenger hunt. But the experience was invaluable, and the students were engaged in Hawaiian history and culture in a way they never would be with a textbook.

Still, impatience tugged at her. Was there anything new to find in a hundred-year-old cold case?

The creek gurgled several feet below the path, its rocky bed glinting in the filtered sunlight. Hiking down looked like a recipe for wet shoes or a twisted ankle, so they stayed put, taking in the view of the lush valley stretching toward the mountains.

Growing up, Cassandra had often hiked the trail winding all the way up to Mānoa Falls, its waters tumbling down a 150-foot drop. Maybe she should've taken the students on that adventure instead of chasing prize money and reopening old family wounds.

A man's voice startled her from her thoughts. "Lost, are we?"

She let out a startled "Yeep!" and whipped around. A forty-ish man, his silver-blond hair almost white against a deep tan, lounged in a wooden chair tucked into a seating nook behind them. The vegetation camouflaged it so well they could've strolled right past him unnoticed.

He looked like he owned the place, his presence unsettling. Beside him, a crystal glass sat on a small table, the ice inside melting.

Quick-thinking Diego stepped forward. "Isn't this part of the tour? The creek is pretty cool."

The man stood, unfolding his limbs in a motion that seemed both deliberate and unsteady. Cassandra's gaze flicked to his empty glass. Day drinking, huh?

"Try again," the man said, his smooth voice betraying no hint of a local accent. "Are you with those true-crime idiots? Ever since that ridiculous Unforgotten group dreamed up this competition, we've had trespassers at all hours. If you're supposed to be on the home tour, head back to the house. Otherwise, get off my land before I lose my patience."

Ignoring every red flag, Diego pressed on, "You're Mr. Oliver, right? Are you saying the Mānoa Marauder isn't real, and the conference organizers just made it up? What about the police investigations and the property searches?"

Cassandra groaned inwardly. *Diego, read the room.*

The man's expression hardened, and his long legs brought him within arm's length in just a few strides.

"Nathaniel Oliver, the third. Olivers have owned this land since the territory days. I never should've let Nakano convince me this was about nostalgia for simpler times. He's leading you on a merry chase at my expense. This is your only warning. Stay out of my business." The man towered over them, his blue eyes glaring at Diego and Lance.

He pretty much ignored her, which was fine with Cassandra.

"My private security shoots first and ask questions later. If I were you, I'd leave now and not even consider coming back after sunset."

He's a colonial Lucius Malfoy, Cassandra thought. Starched aloha shirt, pressed khakis, and designer slippahs looking absurdly out of place in the wild tropical setting. His cool, aristocratic tone and the way he sneered at them completed the picture.

Cassandra had been a Harry Potter fan since she was thirteen, but meeting a real-life version of the villain was downright unsettling.

For just a moment, a shadow flickered across Nathaniel's face, gone almost as quickly as it appeared. Cassandra caught it, though. Maybe guilt. Anger. Fear. Whatever it was, it didn't match the haughty bravado in his voice.

Lance tugged on Diego's shirt and nodded toward the house. He'd read Nathaniel's body language loud and clear. Finally, Diego caught on.

As Cassandra turned away, she heard Nathaniel mutter darkly, "Keep digging, and the ghosts will find you."

His words were laced with something heavier than annoyance. He wasn't talking about the stories Angela or Mahina had told them. He was talking about something real.

His gaze drifted past them, locking onto the banyan tree with an intensity that made the hair on the back of her neck stand up, like he was watching something move in the shadows.

They double-timed it back to the house.

By the time they slipped back inside through the sunroom, her gaze instinctively sought the framed family photo in the hallway. Her great-grandmother and great-great-aunt stood frozen in time among the Oliver estate workers.

Her pulse kicked up again. If Mr. Oliver was already suspicious, watching them closely, there was no telling whether they'd be allowed back in.

Move.

Thinking fast, Cassandra yanked out her phone and snapped rapid-fire shots of the framed images along the gallery wall. The plantation workers, Edward, Maggie, and Jean Oliver, the coffee plantation grounds, anything that might be useful later.

She didn't pause to study them. There wasn't time.

Shoving her phone back into her bag, she caught up with the students, forcing a steady breath.

Nope, nope, nope. She wasn't about to let some rich guy with a Malfoy complex spook her.

She exhaled slowly, calming herself. But she had a feeling Nathaniel Oliver III wasn't the only one keeping an eye on them.

Chapter Nine

CASSANDRA'S PHONE BUZZED IN her pocket as she and the students left the Oliver estate. Her mind still lingered on Nathaniel's veiled threats, the weight of his words hanging heavy. She glanced at the screen and felt her pulse hitch: Marcus Fischer.

She answered quickly, hoping his familiar voice would settle her nerves. But as soon as Marcus spoke, her hope evaporated. "We need to talk," he said, his tone clipped and tense. "Something's going on with the construction project. It's... bigger than routine renovations."

Cassandra slowed her pace, signaling the students to walk ahead. "Bigger? What are you talking about? I thought it was just maintenance work."

Marcus hesitated, the kind of pause that warned her the news wouldn't be good. "Bob Soukup is back on campus."

Cassandra stopped walking. "What? I thought he was laying low after the scholarship mess last spring."

"Apparently, Fran Morrison doesn't care about bad optics. She's been pushing this 'legacy project' hard behind the scenes, and Soukup's suddenly back in the fold. Every time I look for details, I hit a wall."

Cassandra's stomach tightened. "Fran and Bob working together? That's definitely a red flag. What do you mean by 'hitting a wall'?"

"It's like there's a script everyone's following," Marcus said bitterly. "I've been shut out of meetings. There's money moving around. Big money. And none of it adds up. Fran's making moves I can't get ahead of, and I don't like it."

Her thoughts raced. Fran Morrison had worked with Marcus in the past, but there were layers to their relationship that Marcus rarely spoke of. Now those layers seemed ready to break open.

"Do you think it's illegal?" she asked, keeping her voice low even though the students were out of earshot.

"Not illegal," he said after a pause. "But unethical? Absolutely. And it's giving me flashbacks to Iraq."

The mention of Iraq stopped her cold. Marcus never talked about his and Fran's time in the military, but the weariness in his voice told her this wasn't just about the college. Something serious had happened between them, and whatever it was, it was clearly bleeding into the present.

"What do you mean?" she asked carefully.

"Fran wasn't always... straightforward back then," Marcus admitted, his voice barely above a whisper. "There were times I covered for her. Times I probably shouldn't have. I didn't ask questions because we were in the middle of something bigger, and it didn't seem like the time to pick a fight."

"And now?" Cassandra pressed, her heart pounding.

"Now it's starting to feel the same," Marcus said grimly. "Except this time, I'm not sure I want to keep her secrets."

The unspoken tension hung between them like a live wire. Marcus had always been steady and calm. Hearing him sound uncertain was deeply unnerving.

"You need to be careful," Cassandra said finally. "Whatever happened back then—"

"I know," he cut her off, frustration showing. "But, Cass... whatever she's doing, it's not just about the college. It could ruin her. And... everyone she's tied to. That includes me, and maybe even you."

The implication hit her like a gut punch. Cassandra had thought she'd left Nebraska's problems behind, but they were catching up, fast. Her two worlds weren't colliding. They were entwined.

"We'll figure this out," she said softly, trying to sound more certain than she felt. "Just... don't get dragged down with her, okay?"

Marcus let out a bitter laugh. "I'm trying, Cass. But it's hard to see the endgame when you're not sure who's holding the cards."

When the call ended, Cassandra stared at her phone, her thoughts a tangled mess. Fran Morrison, the construction project, Soukup. None of it felt like coincidence.

And Marcus, steady and strong Marcus, was starting to show cracks. Funding and politics aside, this was about trust and betrayal. Marcus and Fran's shared history cast a long shadow over the present.

She wasn't done with him. But right now, another ghost needed her more.

Cassandra sat on the hotel lanai, nursing a guava iced tea as the remnants of the sunset cast a soft orange glow over the beach. Dripping wet tourists carrying rented surfboards hurried back to the shack before closing time, sunburned faces beaming with satisfaction. She watched them with a twinge of envy. Maybe she could squeeze in one surf session before their trip ended, a brief escape from Nebraska's landlocked monotony.

The students gathered around her, sipping on colorful drinks topped with fruit skewers and snacking on sushi and Korean BBQ.

Logan's leg bounced under the table. "Okay, listen to this," he said, barely containing himself.

He held up his phone like a trophy. "Remember that coffee plantation exhibit inside the house in Manoa? We found a hidden drawer in one of the old desks. Like, secret latch, pop-open compartment, the whole deal."

Cassandra groaned. "You did not go full Scooby-Doo in someone's historic home. Please tell me you didn't take actual artifacts."

Brandon shrugged. "Technically not stealing. More like... strategic wandering."

Jocelyn clutched her head. "Oh no, lōlō. We are absolutely getting arrested, and my brother is going to hold this over me for years."

Logan waved a dismissive hand. "Worth it. Because inside the desk we found old business papers. But weirdly the names don't match anything we've seen from the Marauder packet. It's like someone was trying to erase who the land really belonged to."

That got Cassandra's full attention. "What do you mean the names don't match?"

Logan flipped through his phone. "Look."

The photo showed a stack of yellowed documents on a carved wooden desk. The coffee farm logo was stamped in the corner, but none of the names were Olivers. Several had been crossed out, thick black ink slashing through them like a warning.

Cassandra's breath caught. Someone had tried to rewrite history. And she had a feeling she knew who.

Lexi leaned in. "So... these people owned pieces of the estate?"

"Or thought they did," Jocelyn said.

"Could've been tenants," Ethan offered. "Or investors."

Maria shook her head. "Those names were crossed out. Like... erased. That's not paperwork. That's a hit list."

Jocelyn muttered, "Yeah, that doesn't scream above board."

Logan grinned. "So, did we just crack the case wide open?"

Diego laughed. "Let's not arrest anyone yet, Sherlock."

Cassandra exhaled, thinking. "We're not jumping to conclusions. But someone hid these papers for a reason. If they're just property records, why lock them away?"

Maria ran her finger down the screen. "Some of these names look... familiar. Like ones I pulled from the 1909 plantation payroll census."

Ethan squinted. "You think they were workers? Not owners?"

"It happened a lot," Diego said. "Back then, families got promised land if they worked a certain number of years. But most of them never got anything except verbal deals that went nowhere."

"So what, this desk drawer is the receipt for a giant lie?" Lexi said.

Ethan reached for his phone. "I'm logging this under 'Historic Shady Deals: Confirmed.'

"If these names got erased back then... it might explain why the Olivers are still so desperate to cover things up now," Cassandra murmured.

And just like that, the group went quiet, absorbing the full weight of what they'd uncovered.

Before Cassandra could voice another theory, a loud squawk shattered the moment. Skipper launched from Andrew's shoulder, knocking over a plate of untouched sushi near Diego's hand.

"Bro!" Diego cried, as the parrot snatched a piece in his beak and flapped away. "That was mine!"

Skipper circled above them, triumphantly swallowing his prize as rice rained down like confetti.

Andrew sighed, though he couldn't hide his grin. "Sorry, braddah. He's food-motivated."

Laughter rippled through the group. Cassandra smiled. Even in the middle of unraveling a century-old mystery, there was something satisfying about watching a parrot outwit them all.

Lexi wiped a grain of rice off her arm. "Okay, back to the drawer. What else was inside?"

Brandon scratched the back of his neck. "Just a handkerchief with some dried flowers folded inside. It had initials embroidered in the corner—'J.O.' Maybe belonged to the wife or daughter?"

Cassandra frowned. "Jean Oliver?" Her pulse kicked up. If Jean had hidden the map, maybe the handkerchief was hers too. Like a breadcrumb, meant for someone who knew how to read the trail.

Maria leaned in. "Dried flowers. Maybe she was trying to hold onto a memory."

Ethan nodded. "If it was sentimental, why hide it in a drawer with business records?"

"No idea," Logan shrugged, "We ran out of time. The old lady checked on us, and we didn't want to get caught."

Ethan sighed. "So no bloody rope. No hidden knife under a ledger book. No confession signed by the Mānoa Marauder?"

The table chuckled, but Logan stayed quiet, staring at the photo on his screen like it meant more than he could explain.

Cassandra clocked the shift in his expression, less excitement now, more weight.

Brandon cleared his throat. "Still. Those property records felt... wrong."

He hesitated, then added, "In our research for our conference presentation, we found letters. Testimonies really, where immigrants were promised land or better jobs. Most never got either."

Diego nodded. "Yeah. Whole communities vanished from the records. No explanations, just... gone."

Brandon glanced down at Logan's screen again. "What if those crossed-out names are the ones who pushed back? The ones who tried to hold someone accountable?"

Cassandra turned to Andrew. "Any chance this is part of the exhibit? Some planted clue for the competition?"

Andrew shook his head. "If the stuff in that drawer was planted, nobody told me. I just read the lines they gave me and keep the headset batteries charged."

"Reverse escape room," Ethan muttered. "Instead of breaking out, we're trying to lock the killer in."

Diego leaned back. "Except the killer's a ghost. We're chasing shadows."

Cassandra's tone sharpened. "Maybe for you it's a game. For me, it's justice. These were real people, and we're close to something. I don't believe in coincidences."

The group quieted again. Even Andrew nodded solemnly.

Maria took a breath, then spoke, her voice low but steady. "I looked into Mary Pauahi. One of the victims. The police dismissed her because they labeled her a sex worker. Didn't even question it."

She exhaled hard. "But her family said she worked an office job. She was taking night classes. She was just starting out. But she was Hawaiian. Not rich enough. Not important enough."

The silence deepened. Cassandra reached out, squeezing her shoulder. They weren't chasing ghosts anymore. They were chasing stories of people who'd been silenced. It wasn't theoretical. It was personal.

Maria lifted her glass. "I don't care about the prize. I want justice. For her. For all of them."

The others followed, glasses raised. "To Mary Pauahi."

"To justice."

Cassandra stood, setting her glass down. "We're heading back to the estate tomorrow. Mr. Oliver chased us off before we found the well. We shouldn't submit our solution before checking everything."

Jocelyn crossed her arms. "And if we expose Oliver family skeletons, good. Let the ghosts haunt *them* for once."

Cassandra looked to Andrew. "You in? Now's your chance to back out."

Andrew nodded, serious for once. "Got it, Dr. Sato."

Cassandra breathed deep, letting the salty air steady her. "Goodnight, ya hooligans."

As they dispersed, she lingered on the lanai. Above her, stars began to appear.

Nathaniel Oliver's veiled threats echoed in her mind, tangling with Marcus and everything she'd left behind at Morton.

One puzzle was enough to keep her up at night. Two might pull her under.

But she had a team. A plan. And a resolve that wouldn't break, no matter what shadows waited ahead.

Chapter Ten

C ASSANDRA WAS SIPPING HER coffee the next morning when four of her students shuffled into the hotel continental breakfast area looking like they hiked up Koko Head. At sunrise. With no water.

Ethan, Diego, and Lexi all avoided eye contact, sliding into their seats like they'd made a silent pact to act normal.

Cassandra arched an eyebrow. "Let me guess. You all stayed up way too late watching Paranormal Investigators and now you're sleep-deprived conspiracy theorists?"

Lexi made a vague, noncommittal gesture. "Something like that."

Jocelyn smirked behind her coffee cup. Unlike the exhausted students, she was bright-eyed and polished, foundation flawless. Cassandra narrowed her eyes. Jocelyn never put this much effort into her appearance unless she was trying to impress someone.

Cassandra filed that mystery away for later.

Jocelyn teased, "Looks like some of our 'ohana didn't get much sleep last night. What were you *Menehunes* up to?"

Lexi shot a look at the others, a silent *should we tell them?* flashing between them.

Andrew dropped into a chair with a heavy sigh. "Okay, we have a confession to make."

Cassandra lowered her coffee. "Do I need to call a lawyer?"

"Nothing criminal," Ethan said, grinning. "But you're gonna want to hear it."

Diego nudged him. "Yeah, because she totally loves it when we go rogue."

Cassandra folded her arms. "Start talking."

"We Ubered back to the Oliver estate," Andrew said. "Last night."

That landed. Cassandra blinked once. Then again. "You're serious."

"We didn't break anything," Lexi said quickly. "Just cut through the shrubs behind the neighbor's place and wandered through a couple of conveniently unlocked gates. Maybe two."

Jocelyn shook her head, smiling. "Go on. You clearly rehearsed this."

"We thought the well might have some evidence," Ethan said. "Trying to stay ahead of Kualoa's team. But we didn't exactly strike gold."

Lexi leaned in, unable to hold it any longer. "We strapped a GoPro to Skipper and let him fly recon."

"You put a surveillance camera... on a parrot," Cassandra said flatly.

Diego held up his phone. "And it worked! Look."

They clustered around the screen as grainy night footage played back. In one frame, three figures crouched near the tree line, a flashlight glinting off paper.

"Pause," Jocelyn said. "Who is that?"

"That's Kualoa's team," Ivy murmured.

"They have the same map," Brandon said. "Or someone gave them a copy."

"Or they've got help from someone who doesn't want us solving this," Cassandra muttered.

Logan tapped the screen, then looked at Diego. "And the well?"

Diego reached into his hoodie pocket and plopped a bright blue stress ball onto the table.

Cassandra raised an eyebrow. "We're collecting desk toys now?"

Lexi flipped it over. "Look, it has a logo and QR code."

Andrew scanned it. "Vendor swag. HiloTech. One of the booths at the exhibit hall."

Jocelyn groaned. "Great. Now the nerds are spying too."

Diego tossed it from hand to hand. "Or Kualoa's team is leaving breadcrumbs like cartoon villains."

"Or they're taunting us," Ethan added. "Letting us know we're being watched."

"There were footprints," Andrew said, "Different sets. One had dress shoes."

Lexi shook her head. "Who wears heels to a haunted well?"

Maria folded her arms. "So Kalia's crew was at the creek. Someone else at the well."

"None of them were assigned to the estate," Cassandra said. Her mind was already connecting threads. "Maybe Mr. Oliver's security threat was a bluff."

Nakano had laid out rules. But Kalia wasn't following them and no one was stopping her. That was a problem.

Maria stirred her coffee, eyebrows knit. "You know, that tour guide Mahina said something about the creek yesterday. About workers avoiding it after dark."

Cassandra sat up straighter. "Right. She said they'd walk the long way around instead of going near it."

Diego tapped his fork against his plate. "Yeah, I get why. That place was creepy at night. It felt... off. Like we weren't alone."

Lexi smirked. "Skipper the stalker?"

Jocelyn leaned in. "It's more than that. You hear stories like this all over Hawaii. Places people refuse to go no matter how convenient. My tutu used to say the land remembers."

Logan looked thoughtful. "So you think something really happened near the creek?"

Jocelyn gave a small shrug. "If Mahina mentioned it, that means the memory stuck around. People might not know the details anymore, but something left a mark."

Brandon leaned forward, catching the thread. "Okay, but we're not just chasing ghost stories. If people avoided that spot, maybe someone used it because no one would go there. Like hiding something where it won't be found."

A beat passed.

Cassandra glanced around the table. Lexi and Diego exchanged a look. Ethan fidgeted with his fork. Clearly the students were doing some silent mind wrestling, but no one wanted to talk first.

Finally, Andrew leaned in. "So... about the well."

Ethan groaned. "Here we go."

Andrew dropped his voice. "Picture this: horror movie vibes. Wind howling, well hissing... and one weird stone with carved symbols."

Diego nodded. "Didn't budge. But totally out of place. We snapped photos."

Andrew nodded. "We thought it might be a lever or something. Secret tunnel entrance? Disappointingly, just a rock."

Maria held up a hand, mid-sip. "Hang on. I'm logging that. Where does 'howling wind' go? In the mystical vibes column?"

Ivy grinned. "New board. Paranormal... and Possibly True."

"Total letdown," Ethan said. "Until—" he dropped his voice dramatically, "we heard footsteps."

Lexi widened her eyes. "I thought we were dead. Like, Secret Service was about to rappel from the roof."

"Andrew ducked behind the well like he was in a spy movie," Diego said, grinning.

Andrew raised his hands. "It was dark! I panicked responsibly."

"So what was it?" Jocelyn asked.

"Chicken," Ethan said. "Just a stray chicken."

That set off another wave of laughter.

"Then Skipper," Lexi said, "decided to squawk like a pterodactyl and dive-bomb the well."

Andrew winced. "We thought he drowned."

"He didn't," Diego added. "But the splash was Olympic. And the footage? Pretty solid."

Ethan smirked. "Skipper's a total pro. Like a feathered ninja."

Cassandra finally cracked a smile. "So let me recap. You snuck onto the estate, startled a chicken, lost your parrot to a water feature, and poked at ancient rocks hoping for treasure."

"Pretty much," Ethan said brightly.

"But—" Andrew held up a finger, "while Skipper was flapping out, I saw something. A hollowed-out space inside the well wall. Like an alcove. It was empty, but it looked... intentional."

Someone had hidden something there. Deliberately. And whatever it was, it mattered enough to remove. Cassandra leaned forward. "And you saw that from where?"

Andrew gave a sheepish shrug. "I might've gone a few rungs down the ladder. Super careful."

Lexi looked betrayed. "He just started climbing! Like we were gonna form a rescue team!"

"I didn't go far," Andrew said quickly. "But I'm telling you, something used to be in that alcove."

"Do you have photos?" Cassandra asked.

"I handed my phone to Ethan before I went down," Andrew said. "Didn't want to drop it."

Ethan held up his hands. "Sorry! Was too busy making sure our bird didn't get sucked into an underground spring."

Cassandra closed her eyes briefly. "Next time you plan a covert expedition, maybe tell the faculty sponsor first."

"Where's the fun in that?" Jocelyn said.

Cassandra ignored her and turned to Diego. "Pictures of the symbols?"

"Right here." He pulled up a gallery of blurry night photos.

Ivy leaned over, scanning the screen. "Wait. Zoom in. I've seen this before."

Cassandra moved closer. "Where?"

"In the museum exhibit. On the employee's work shirts. That same brand mark."

Lance signed, *That mark was stamped on tools, burlap sacks, and crates. It means ownership.*

"Like a cattle brand," Brandon said. "Only this wasn't livestock. It was land. Workers. Their labor."

Cassandra studied the photo. The carving was rough, but deliberate. More like record keeping than decoration. Was someone marking a breadcrumb or claiming the space?

"What do we log on the timeline?" Diego asked, chewing the last bite of his granola bar. "No treasure. No ghosts. No villain monologue."

Maria pointed at the screen. "We log the symbol. The alcove. And the fact that someone went to the trouble to remove whatever used to be there."

"It's proof," Ivy said. "That someone tried to hide part of the story."

Ethan stood, stretching. "Okay, but if we're logging all that, I vote we also log naptime."

Diego nudged him. "Lightweight."

Lexi smirked. "Oh, we are absolutely talking more after lunch."

Cassandra stood too, the wheels already turning. "I'll check the VR exhibit again. Something's missing. It has to be hidden in the digital layers."

She looked at Ivy, Maria, and Diego. "Find those crate photos. The ones with the same symbol."

Everyone nodded. Cassandra lingered behind, tapping the rim of her coffee cup. Around her, the others buzzed with energy or peeled off for naps.

The timeline was tightening.

She opened her phone and added to their project tracking app: *Well symbol.* Then she started logging everything they could prove. No ghosts. Just evidence.

Chapter Eleven

C ASSANDRA WAITED FOR THE traffic light to change colors, her watch vibrating with yet another missed call. Her mom had left two voicemails in the last hour, and her sister had sent curious texts fishing for news. Clearly, people were talking about her and Jocelyn's investigation, and not everyone was thrilled.

This wasn't the time or place to answer, unless she wanted to risk getting flattened by a city bus or sideswiped by a tourist on a motorized scooter zipping through the intersection like an ant on a mango.

Several minutes later, she reached the hotel lanai and dropped into the chair that Jocelyn had saved for her. A row of plumeria trees obscured their view of the beach, their fragrance thick in the humid air. Cassandra sighed, setting her phone on the table.

Jocelyn looked up from her iced coffee and arched an eyebrow. "You've had that look all morning. You know, like you've been stuck at the DMV for an hour, and the clerk just taped a 'Back in 15' sign to the window."

"That's about right."

"Still dodging phone calls?"

"It's like everyone got the same 'worry about Cassandra' memo this morning."

Jocelyn snorted. "What gave it away? The potential trespassing charges or the part where you're now persona non grata with one of the oldest families on the island?"

Cassandra attempted a smile, but Jocelyn saw right through it.

"So, what's worse? Your family panic-texting you, or the part where your students broke into private property with a drone and a parrot?"

Cassandra groaned, rubbing her temples. "Too soon."

"What else?"

"Oh, just another headache to add to the pile." She pulled up an email on her phone and turned the screen toward Jocelyn.

FROM: OLIVER ESTATE LEGAL COUNSEL

SUBJECT: REVOCATION OF ACCESS

DR. SATO, DUE TO A RECENT BREACH OF CONDUCT, THE ESTATE'S LEGAL TEAM HAS DETERMINED THAT YOUR RESEARCH GROUP'S ACCESS TO THE OLIVER PROPERTY IS NO LONGER PERMISSIBLE. THIS DECISION IS FINAL AND NON-NE-GOTIABLE.

PLEASE REFRAIN FROM ANY FURTHER ATTEMPTS TO VISIT OR INVESTIGATE THE ESTATE GROUNDS. FUTURE TRESPASSING WILL BE MET WITH LEGAL CON-SEQUENCES.

Jocelyn scanned the email, then let out a low whistle. "Guess they are tired of playing hunt for the Mānoa Marauder. Someone doesn't like you asking questions."

"Gee, you think?" Cassandra muttered.

Jocelyn leaned back, crossing her arms. "Please. Like a cease-and-desist ever stopped you.

Cassandra hesitated. "Maybe we're getting closer to a plausible theory about who killed Jean Oliver."

"And they don't want the answer," Jocelyn said, a spark of excite-ment in her eyes.

"We have to be careful. Because if this gets back to Morton..."

"Then we better find the truth fast."

Her phone buzzed again. Her mom's name flashed on the screen.

Speaking of the worry memo.

"Guess I better take this," she muttered, putting the call on speaker. "Aloha, Mom."

Jocelyn grinned, lifting her drink. "Aloha, Auntie."

Her mother's voice was warm but edged with concern. "Aloha you two. You okay o' what?"

"I'm fine, Mom," Cassandra said, keeping her tone breezy. "Just... ya know, working."

Her mom let out a small *hmph*, the kind that said *No foolin' me.* "Working, eh? That's not what Mrs. Kobayashi said."

Cassandra paused. "Mrs. Kobayashi?"

"You know how she stay. Zippy's morning crew know everything before it even hit the news. And today? You da headline. 'Cassandra Sato digging into old *haole* business.' You like explain dat?"

Jocelyn raised an eyebrow, but wisely stayed quiet.

Cassandra took a sip of water, buying time. "Mom, it's just research. Nothing dangerous. We're mostly in the library."

Another *hmph*. "I neva say danger. I just saying... somethings, betta left where they stay."

"What do you mean?"

Her mom sighed, like she was choosing her next words carefully. "I dunno exactly where you been snooping, but I remember your Gran. She used to say, 'Keep da peace.' And she no just mean *our* side the family."

Cassandra's pulse ticked up. "Gran knew something?"

"She heard things. Back in the day. But she never talk. That's why she lived long and happy. No make waves."

Cassandra frowned. "So... what? You think I should just drop out of the competition?"

"No, no. I just saying watch where you dig. Some people, they no like when you pull up old dirt."

Something in her mother's tone sent a chill down Cassandra's spine. A warning without details. A door only halfway open.

"Mom, I gotta eat. We'll talk later, yeah?"

Her mother hesitated. "You take care now. Maybe take da students up to the pineapple plantation, go walk around, get one Dole Whip. Make everybody feel betta."

Cassandra swallowed, that old mix of love and warning tightening in her chest. "Thanks, Mom. Love you."

"Love you too, baby. Be smart."

Not just concern. Not just superstition. It felt like history warning her off. She needed to get a grip.

Jocelyn, sensing the shift in mood, nudged Cassandra's foot under the table. "Hey. Don't go full existential crisis on me right now. We've got enough to deal with."

"Right. No spiraling. Not today."

Jocelyn smirked. "Good girl. Now, if we're done with ominous parental warnings."

A flicker of movement caught Cassandra's attention at the far end of the lanai. A tall, ridiculously good-looking haole guy in an aloha shirt and khakis navigated the tables with practiced ease, his gaze locked onto them.

Jocelyn's entire demeanor shifted in an instant. With a grin, she sprang up, kissed him on the cheek, and pulled out the chair beside hers. "Cassandra, meet Jeff."

Ah. *So that explained the fancy hair and makeup.*

Seconds later, Meg and Connor arrived, carrying a bag of plate lunches, the smell of BBQ and curry filling the air. They parked a stroller beside the table, Olivia still knocked out from the car ride.

"Tony went fishing with your dad. Looks like we brought lunch just in time," Meg said with a grin, catching Cassandra's expression. "Everything okay?"

"Just got off the phone with Mama Sato."

Jocelyn slid a styrofoam container of food in front of her. "Here, have some spareribs. You'll feel better."

Connor dropped into a chair, shooting Cassandra a knowing look. "We didn't tell her anything, I swear."

Meg added, "But somehow your mom knows every step you take."

"Hasn't changed since I was in middle school," Cassandra replied. "What's more powerful than radar?"

"Probably LiDAR," Connor supplied.

Cassandra pointed at him with her chopsticks. "Yep, my mom definitely has LiDAR when it comes to her family." She took a bite of sparerib and groaned. "*Ono* isn't even good enough to describe this taste. I miss this food. Why can't Nebraska have ribs like these?"

"Too busy eating kolaches and Runzas," Meg chuckled, raising a sparerib to tap against the one Cassandra was holding. "Cheers!"

They ate in contented silence, the chopsticks clicking against takeout containers, waves crashing softly in the distance.

Meg dabbed at her mouth with a napkin. "So? Any breakthroughs today?"

Cassandra leaned back. "I spent the morning rechecking the Mānoa Marauder exhibit. The press at the time was obsessed. Full-on tabloid energy. Anything suspicious was blamed on the Marauder, even years later."

Meg frowned. "But only three murders were officially attributed to him?"

"Right. Even though Jean Oliver died during the same time period, they ruled it an accident."

Jeff set his drink down. "Speaking of the Olivers... I did a little homework. Okay, so the Oliver family's land deals? On paper, they looked normal. But once I dug a little deeper, there's a definite pattern."

Jocelyn gave him a smug grin. "Told you he was useful."

Jeff brushed a napkin across his lap like he was easing into a boardroom pitch. "Often the land gets 'sold' to someone—usually a cousin, or a name that doesn't show up again—then magically ends up back in the Olivers' hands. Sometimes they use inheritance claims. Sometimes the deed just... changes."

Quiet theft didn't make it any less repulsive. Contracts in name only, trust used as camouflage. How could she not root for the underdog when this kind of erasure played out decade after decade? A sour aftertaste rose in her throat, nearly overpowering her plate lunch.

Meg frowned. "So... no actual transaction?"

"Not in any meaningful way. The land barely left the family's control. Especially if the original buyer wasn't someone with power. Like a worker who thought they were earning ownership over time," Jeff said. "That happened a lot. Verbal deals, handshake agreements. Zero paper trail. And then poof, those families get cut out."

Cassandra leaned forward, her chopsticks forgotten. "We found a list of names hidden in a drawer at the estate. They were crossed out, like someone was keeping track. Could've been tenants, or workers... or something else. At first we didn't know what it meant."

"But now it fits," Meg said softly.

Jeff nodded. "Exactly. I couldn't find hard proof, but the timing lines up with labor surges on the estate like they were promising land in exchange for work, then pulling the rug later."

"Maybe," Cassandra said. "If those people thought they had a stake in the land and then got pushed out, it changes the whole story."

Jocelyn tapped the table. "It gives them a motive. Or makes them victims."

Jeff looked thoughtful. "And if anyone tried to push back, raise a complaint..."

Meg's voice lowered. "That could get dangerous fast."

Cassandra didn't reply right away. She sat with it, chewing her thoughts as the pieces began to click. "We'll recheck the names. See if any match the plantation rosters or labor rolls. If even one of them was promised land—"

"Then the motive wasn't just money," Jeff said. "It was control. And silence."

"And a bigger story than just one family's dirty history,"Meg added quietly.

Cassandra's eyes narrowed. "I'd bet Nathaniel's still doing it. He's pulling the same land grab, just using trusts and shell companies now."

Jeff shrugged. "It's the same game. Just modern tools. He'd use corporate trusts now. Much harder to trace."

Meg wiped her hands on a napkin. "You always seem to fall into the legal gray areas."

Cassandra let out a short laugh. "Funny you should say that. Got an official 'cease and desist' from the Oliver estate this morning. Apparently, we've been 'intrusive and unauthorized.'"

Jeff raised an eyebrow. "You don't say."

Jocelyn grinned, gesturing toward Cassandra with her chopsticks. "Told you. Stirring things up is her specialty."

Cassandra leaned back and flicked an invisible crumb off her shirt. "They wrapped it in lawyer-speak, but it was basically a passive-aggressive PDF."

Meg groaned. "Hasn't changed."

"It's my job," Cassandra protested.

They spent the next hour tossing around theories, the conversation drifting from crime-solving to conference panels.

Cassandra's watch buzzed with a text from Andy Summers and she tapped to read the full message.

Andy

Howdy. Hope your trip is good. Murphy is settling in great. He and Buckley are getting along like bros.

"It's from Andy," she murmured as she tapped a thumbs up reply. It warmed her to hear that. Murphy, her rescue Westie of six months, still didn't like to be cuddled and occasionally peed indoors, but he was learning. Andy added,

Andy

Sensing some tension on campus with new Prez. If I hear anything specific will let u know.

Tension on campus seemed like code for political nonsense she didn't have time for. She sent an eye roll emoji and left it at that.

Meg eyed her. "More weirdness from Morton?"

Cassandra sighed. "I hope Fischer knows what he's doing."

"You might want to prepare yourself." Connor set down his drink. "Fischer's a good guy, but he's got shadows."

"Anything specific?"

Connor hesitated. "Nothing I can say for sure. Just... be ready. Sometimes the truth is more complicated than we want it to be."

Cassandra absorbed that, the weight of too many questions settling in.

"Thanks for the break," Cassandra said. "We need to head back to the conference center for today's last session. It's a Q&A about the historical context of the Mānoa Marauder."

Thirty minutes later, Cassandra tucked her tote bag under a ballroom chair, as participants settled in for the panel.

Jocelyn slid into the chair beside her, dropping a PastForward branded phone battery pack into her tote like she'd won the lottery. "These tech companies have righteous swag," she whispered. "I waited ten minutes for a smartphone printer. The dude handed me this flashlight pen instead." She held it up with an mock solemnity. "Not the same level. Not at all."

She goofed around with the penlight, clicking it on and off until the LED ray stabbed into Cassandra's eye like a car's high beams.

Cassandra winced and looked away, muttering, "You're going to get us kicked out."

Jocelyn grinned. "Relax. I'm being educational."

Cassandra exhaled. Being around Jocelyn always felt like riding a tandem bike with a Labrador. Chaotic. Distracting. Unpredictably loyal.

But also, sometimes exactly what she needed.

"Look who's here," Jocelyn added, nodding toward the front.

Cassandra followed her gaze. There sat Kalia Chun, flanked by her matching army of hyper-competent students in pressed aloha prints and conference lanyards.

Of course.

"Guess we're not the only ones taking this seriously," Jocelyn muttered.

Cassandra scowled. "We caught them snooping around the estate. She's probably here to sniff out what we've found."

"She's bold," Jocelyn said. "But the question is how much does she know?"

The panel launched into a discussion of archival reporting and how the press shaped the Marauder mythos. Her mind chewed on the many ways descendants had been harmed. By the murders, and by the quiet theft of land cloaked in legitimacy.

Cassandra half-listened, until Kalia's familiar voice cut through the polite Q&A.

"Can you speak to how families were compensated—or not—after suspicious deaths on large estates? Particularly when land ownership or inheritance was in dispute?"

Cassandra's head snapped up.

Not royal artifacts. Not serial killers. Land. The same path they were following but repackaged for the public. Clean. Academic. Plausible.

Jocelyn leaned over. "That sound familiar?"

"Too familiar," Cassandra whispered. "Only difference is, we found the smoking drawer."

Cassandra's eyes narrowed. They'd started with a treasure map. Kalia had skipped to the end credits.

And yet. Kalia's question hit hard because it was carefully crafted. She hadn't said "murder." But the subtext was clear: if someone was erased from the books, who benefited?

Cassandra glanced toward the Kualoa team. One of Kalia's students whispered something behind a hand. Another smirked. Kalia didn't turn, but Cassandra could feel the shift in posture, the tilt of her chin. Deliberate.

That familiar smirky McSmirkface. The same one Cassandra had seen a dozen times in faculty meetings at O'ahu State right before Kalia hijacked a project or slid her name onto a grant proposal she barely touched.

Classic.

Cassandra pulled out her phone, kept it low, and started typing in the group chat.

Cassandra

> Kalia asked about land disputes tied to suspicious deaths. She's circling the same clues. Trello timeline update: Flag worker deaths near estate land transfers. Look at Reyes, Ybarra, Naehu, and the others. What if the pattern goes beyond the Olivers?

Lexi

> Wait, are they stealing our theory??

Cassandra

> She's guessing. We're closer.

Logan

> So… time to drop a red herring?

Cassandra

> Tempting.

Three dots hovered in the chat for several seconds.

Lexi

> Breaking news: Diego's about to crash and burn. Don't miss it.

Cassandra sighed.

This could not possibly end well.

Chapter Twelve

AFTER THE PANEL AND a healthy, yet deeply unsatisfying salad from a nearby takeout place, Morton's team decamped to a quieter hotel lounge, away from snooping eyes. She set down her notebook as the students clustered around the table, the energy immediately shifting. This was less of a post-mortem analysis and more of a casual recap.

Meg had already gone back to Waipahu, meaning they were sans interpreter, but Lance was proactive about making gestures anyone could understand and using his voice-to-text phone apps to follow along.

"Alright," Cassandra said, eyeing them. "Who wants to explain why I was receiving live updates on Diego's social downfall?"

Lexi smirked. "Tragic and unexpected."

Maria shook her head. "Honestly, we thought it was a sure thing."

Brandon gestured vaguely. "I mean, he's Diego. Even he thought it was a sure thing."

Ivy sighed dramatically into her phone mic. "Listeners, what you're about to hear is a classic tale of hubris, miscalculation, and one very poorly timed attempt at charisma."

Cassandra shot her a look. "Are you seriously recording this?"

Ivy grinned. "Relax, Dr. S. It's for posterity."

Lexi leaned forward, grinning. "We had a real *Only Murders in the Building* moment. Saw Angela between sessions, figured we'd take a shot at some casual sleuthing."

Cassandra did an eye roll. "By sleuthing you mean stalking a tour guide for secret clues?"

Maria grinned. "We thought we could be podcasters. Nothing to it, right?"

Ivy waved a hand. "Correction. I already am a podcaster. You guys were just playing guest hosts."

Brandon gestured vaguely. "We figured she'd be more open if someone charming approached her."

Logan raised an eyebrow. "So, I was attending the panel discussion *as assigned*—" he smiled like a child comically sucking up, "—and you chose Diego because he was the next best thing?"

Lexi sputtered. "No offense, Logan, but Diego was the logical choice."

Brandon nodded. "I mean, yeah. He's obnoxiously symmetrical."

Maria shrugged. "It was a calculated risk, but statistically sound. We grossly underestimated Angela's immunity to charm."

Lance typed into his phone, and the AI voice read it aloud. "So... it was an overconfidence problem."

Lexi pointed at him. "Exactly."

Cassandra pinched the bridge of her nose. "Please tell me he didn't open with a pickup line."

Lexi grinned. "We all thought he had the best chance of keeping her talking."

"And did he?"

Ivy narrated like she was doing a crime documentary voiceover. "Listeners, when last we left our unsuspecting protagonist, he was about to make his move. A seasoned charmer. A man of mystery. Or so he thought..."

Maria shook her head. "He tried to be smooth. Hit her with the 'ah shucks' smile, the classic eye contact."

Brandon scowled. "And it worked... for about two minutes."

Lexi leaned forward. "At first, Angela was super casual. Said the tour job pays well, the hours fit her class schedule. She likes history, but she's not making it a career. All normal."

Maria nodded. "Then Diego mentioned the police search in the 1950s. Angela didn't flinch, but something in her posture changed."

Ivy shuddered. "And suddenly we're in *Frozen*. Full-on Elsa mode. If she had raised her hands, the whole convention floor would've turned to ice."

"The ice queen? Just like that?" Cassandra snapped her fingers.

Lexi narrowed her eyes. "She didn't even ask what we meant about police re-opening the case. She already knew."

Cassandra raised an eyebrow. "What exactly did Diego say?"

Brandon squinted, thinking. "All he said was that the cops didn't search the whole estate. Just the main house. He wondered if someone hid stuff somewhere else."

Cassandra drummed her fingers on the table. Angela's reaction hadn't been surprise, it had been calculation. She wasn't worried about the old investigation being remembered. She was worried about it being finished.

Maria sighed. "We all legit expected Diego to walk away with a date and an inside scoop. Instead, he got nothing but emotional damage."

Brandon crossed his arms. "She hit us with stink eye. Just like yours, Dr. Sato. You know, the one that says 'I am five minutes from quitting academia and moving to a goat farm.'"

Was her stink eye that aggressive? Cassandra bit her lip. She made a mental note to maybe tone it down. But still... these kids were so exasperating. How did parents raise actual children without losing their minds?

Logan exhaled. "Yeah, that sounds like someone who doesn't want questions."

Lance tapped his phone for a few seconds before the voice read. "Or someone who knows there are answers and doesn't want anyone finding them."

For a moment, Cassandra flashed back to Angela as a nervous freshman. The same girl who had once been terrified of breaking rules now stood firm, casually brushing off questions about a century-old crime like she was part of the Oliver family's inner circle.

"Did she say anything useful before she shut down?"

Maria brightened. "Actually, yes. She gave us a fun little behind-the-scenes tidbit."

Ivy leaned forward. "So, apparently, Mrs. Oliver, Nathaniel's great-grandmother, hated living in that house."

Brandon raised an eyebrow. "Wouldn't even sleep in the master bedroom."

Cassandra frowned. "Why?"

Lexi wiggled her fingers dramatically. "Ooooh, because of the whispers in the night."

Maria rolled her eyes. "Allegedly."

Ivy grinned. "Angela said there was a rumor that Mrs. Oliver swore she heard voices in the master bedroom. Nobody ever proved anything, but she refused to sleep in there."

Logan crossed his arms. "That's weird. And also exactly the kind of thing rich people don't like to talk about."

Cassandra nodded slowly. "Alright, so she gives you this random but interesting estate gossip... then shuts down the moment you press her about real history?"

Lexi smirked. "Pretty much."

Lance made a *keep going* twirl of his finger.

Brandon tapped the table. "One more thing. Then she threw shade at Hawai'i Unforgotten. She said something like, 'Nakano's people have been circling this estate for years. They want a scandal. Doesn't mean they'll find one.'"

Cassandra exhaled. "Did she mention Kualoa or the other teams? If Angela's protecting someone, we need to figure out who."

Ivy shook her head. "She didn't name names. But she did complain that three different conference teams had been hounding her for estate secrets. Said everyone has an angle when it comes to history."

Cassandra mused over that. Apparently they had more competition than just the Kualoa students.

Lance signed something quick, and Logan translated. "She was too smooth. Like she practiced saying it."

Cassandra nodded. "It's possible. Did she say anything about Mr. Oliver?"

Lexi hesitated. "Not directly. But she did say, 'It's funny how people love to tear down the families who built this town.'"

Maria made a face. "Right. Casually, like an offhanded comment, but it felt rehearsed."

Ivy exhaled. "And then she mentioned a black-tie event she went to at the estate last week. Something with big donors, high-profile guests. Said it was incredible to be in a room with people who actually make things happen."

Cassandra felt a weight settle in her stomach. Angela was starting to believe the hype about protecting the Oliver family's reputation.

Lexi mimicked Angela's clipped tone. "She said, and I quote, 'This little amateur detective routine won't end well for any of you. Some things are better left alone.'"

"And then, like a true villain, she smiled and walked away." Ivy leaned back in her chair, all smug satisfaction. "Season finale energy, right?"

Cassandra narrowed her eyes. "Well, that sounds familiar."

Maria frowned. "Wait. What do you mean familiar?"

Cassandra pulled out her phone and scrolled to her emails. She turned the screen toward them.

"I got a very similar warning from someone else this morning."

She waited while they read the email from the Oliver estate lawyer.

Ivy's podcast voice dropped to a whisper. "Coincidence? Or is Dr. Sato being targeted by a shadowy academic conspiracy?"

Cassandra arched a brow. "Ivy."

Ivy grinned. "Too much?"

"Dial it back one notch," Cassandra said, but she wasn't entirely joking. "If Angela said the other teams are also peppering her for an advantage, we need to go over everything again. We can't afford to fall behind."

Heads lowered while they worked their phones, checking the lists on their project app.

Ivy scrolled through estate photos from earlier in the week. "Wait, wait, wait."

Cassandra frowned. "What?"

Ivy spun her phone around. "I took this earlier when I was snapping B-roll for my podcast's Behind the Scenes segment." She swiped to a close-up of a quilt spread neatly over a four-poster bed. "The quilts in the bedrooms are beautiful, but something about this one is different."

Lance leaned over, his eyes narrowing. *Those flowers...* he signed, pointing to an embroidered quilt block.

Logan caught the message. "Wait, those flowers look familiar. Are they on the estate somewhere?"

Ivy flipped between images. "It's not just flowers. See that wavy line? Could that be the stream?"

"And this," Cassandra pointed to another appliqué. "looks like an old-fashioned key."

Remembering how Hana had protected Jean's map, Cassandra wondered if she'd stitched more than one message into the fabric. A backup plan, hiding symbols in plain sight?

Maria grinned. "If we get our own Netflix series, Selena Gomez plays me. You see the resemblance, right?"

Logan gestured, *connection. Let's compare this to the map.*

Cassandra nodded. "If these symbols match up, we'll know exactly where to look next."

Unless Kalia's team already found it first.

Then her phone buzzed. She glanced down, expecting another message from her mom. It wasn't. It was a call.

From Ethan.

She frowned. *Students never called. They texted. Always.*

She held her breath and swiped.

The phone barely had time to connect before Ethan's panicked whisper broke through. "Dr. Sato?" His breath was shallow. "We need help."

Cassandra sat up straighter, scrambling to catch up. "Why? Aren't you at dinner?"

"We—we're at the vacant property next to the Oliver house. Diego's gone."

Cassandra's pulse slammed. "What do you mean, *Diego's gone*? He walked off?"

Ethan's voice wavered. "I hear voices. I can't see anyone. But they're talking. And Diego—he was just here. I think they're looking for something. What if he followed them? Or—" He broke off. "I don't know. I just—I can't find him."

The wide-eyed, slack-jawed stares from the other students told her none of them knew about this side adventure.

Cassandra shot to her feet. "Ethan, drop me a pin. Right now. Stay out of sight. We're coming."

As she ended the call, she pointed a stern finger at the group, channeling the strict administrator she tried not to be 95% of the time.

"Do not say a word about this to anyone. And none of you'd better get any bright ideas about going off on your own."

Logan and Lance were already at the door. "We're coming with you."

Extra muscle might come in handy. Cassandra gritted her teeth. She turned to Jocelyn. "Where's your car?"

Jocelyn's face went pale, but she grabbed her bag without hesitation. "In the garage across the street. Let's go."

Cassandra power-walked, muttering under her breath.

"I knew those boys would pull something stupid."

Chapter Thirteen

CASSANDRA GRIPPED THE PASSENGER door handle, her knuckles white as Jocelyn navigated the winding streets leading toward the jungle-covered edge of the valley. Her grim face clearly showed her mind running through the worst-case scenarios, while Lance and Logan huddled in the back seat, both signing nervously to each other.

"Diego and Ethan can't resist a challenge," Cassandra said. "But they're in over their heads this time."

When they reached the turnoff for the vacant property next to the Oliver's, Jocelyn parked the car a few houses down. The night air was thick with humidity, and the moonlight barely cut through the dense trees surrounding the area.

They slipped through the overgrown shrubbery, their footsteps muffled by the soft underbrush. The sound of rustling palm leaves and distant voices reached their ears, sending a shiver down Cassandra's spine. Somewhere ahead, Ethan was hiding and Diego was missing.

As they moved deeper into the property, Cassandra whispered and signed, "Stay close. We don't know who else is out here."

Jocelyn nodded, "This feels like the start of every bad decision in a *Magnum P.I.* episode, but okay."

A sudden crack of a branch to their left made Logan freeze. Lance, walking close behind, bumped into him hard, eyes wide. Cassandra's arm shot out, pointing toward the sound.

They stood frozen, breath held, the night pressing in around them. Nothing.

They took a few more steps. The moonlight hit the edge of a rusted lawn chair, then the corner of a crumbling brick patio. Shadows shifted between trees, and a gust of wind rustled the ferns near an old chicken coop.

"Maybe this was a mistake," Logan whispered. "What if we're not the only ones out here?"

Then, movement. A dark shape slipped from behind the small building. Cassandra's pulse surged. She nearly shouted—

Ethan.

A squeak escaped before Cassandra clamped her hands over her mouth.

His face was pale, his eyes wide with fear. He pointed toward the back of the property.

"I don't know where Diego went," he whispered, his voice shaky. "I thought he was right behind me, but then... he just disappeared."

It took several seconds before her heart rate slowed enough that she could focus on him in the dark. "Did you see anyone else?"

Ethan swallowed hard. "I heard voices, but didn't see people. They were close though."

Before they could respond, the sound of rustling came from the brush behind them. Jocelyn's hand shot up, signaling them to freeze, while the air around them suddenly felt stifling. Footsteps drew closer. Cassandra's pulse quickened as she turned, prepared for security guys with machine guns.

Three figures emerged from the darkness, illuminated by the faint glow of the moon. It took a moment for Cassandra to recognize Kalia and two of her students from Kualoa University. They'd traded school polos for black t-shirts, but their smirks were unmistakable.

Kalia folded her arms, raising an expertly groomed brow. "You're following us," she hissed. "Ran out of your own clues, huh? Just like grad school when you couldn't do anything without a group."

"That was called collegiality, Kalia," Cassandra snapped. "You ought to try it sometime if you want to ever finish that dissertation, Ms. ABD."

A gentle touch to her back from Jocelyn reminded her not to stoop to Kalia's level of cattiness. After a quick cleansing breath, Cassandra said, "We're not here for clues. One of my students is missing. Diego has been gone for..." Her voice trailed off and she gave Ethan a questioning expression. "...at least an hour."

The seriousness of her statement seemed to pierce Kalia's facade. Her expression shifted slightly, a hint of concern crossing her face. She exchanged glances with her students.

"We haven't seen him," she said, her voice a bit softer now. "But between the wild pigs and the homeless people living in the jungle, you might want to widen your search."

Out of the corner of her eye, Cassandra saw Logan signing to Lance to keep him up on what they were whispering.

Jocelyn said, "We'll search here. Can you check next door? If you find anything, let us know."

Kalia hesitated, but her competitive nature took a back seat. She nodded. "We'll head that way."

With a final glance, Kalia and her team disappeared into the darkness, heading toward the Oliver mansion.

Cassandra breathed a sigh of relief and turned to Ethan. "Show us where you last saw Diego."

Ethan led them toward the back of the property where the trees grew denser, their tangled branches blotting out what little moonlight remained. The air was thick with damp earth, and the darkness pressed in, swallowing their flashlight beams like hungry shadows.

"I was near a big banyan tree," Ethan whispered.

After nearly half an hour of searching, Logan took a step forward... then vanished.

One second, he was there. The next, he was gone.

A startled shout ripped from his throat as his foot caught on a hidden dip in the ground. His arms pinwheeled backward, barely catching himself before sliding down a ravine tangled with vines and roots.

Cassandra froze. "Logan?"

Then, from the darkness below, a groan.

"Took you long enough," Diego's voice croaked up at them.

Cassandra exhaled sharply, tension easing.

She aimed her phone's flashlight down. At the bottom of the ravine, Diego lay slumped, clutching his ankle. His face was twisted in pain, but the way his shoulders sagged when he spotted them said everything.

Cassandra chest unclenched. "Stay still. We're coming down."

Logan groaned, sitting up and rubbing his hip. "For the record, I meant to do that."

"Sure," Jocelyn snorted. "Because gravity was an essential part of the search strategy."

Logan grunted as he got to his feet. "Hey, it worked, didn't it?"

Jocelyn rolled her eyes and dug through her bag. "Well, since someone dropped their flashlight in the process, it's a good thing I've got this."

She pulled out the tiny penlight from the conference swag booth, clicking it on with a smug flourish.

Cassandra blinked. "Are you seriously bragging about a giveaway flashlight right now?"

Jocelyn aimed the beam dramatically at Diego. "Look at that. Direct hit. High-tech precision."

Diego sighed. "Great. I'll be sure to write a glowing review. Right after I get the papaya-sized lump off my ankle."

Jocelyn scooted halfway down the ravine, while Cassandra and Lance stayed above, securing a rope Jocelyn had found stored in her trunk. Working together, they carefully lifted Diego out of the ravine, making sure not to worsen his injury.

Diego winced but managed to stand with help, leaning heavily on the others. His ankle was swollen, clearly sprained or broken. As they slowly made their way back to the car, the breeze shifted, bringing a sharp chill that raised goosebumps along Cassandra's arms.

Chicken skin.

She ignored the temptation to run. They were close to a clearing now, shaped like an old campsite, with large logs circling piles of rocks. At its center, a fire pit lay overgrown with grass, its charred wood long since cold.

Something or someone sat motionless on one of the logs.

Cassandra's breath hitched.

At first, Cassandra thought it was a statue, like one of those eerie wooden carvings left to watch over sacred places.

But then, the shadows shifted, and she realized... it was breathing.

A frail figure, hunched and still, wrapped in a threadbare muumuu and a moth-eaten shawl.

An old woman.

Her wrinkled face remained expressionless, her dark eyes fixed on a distant point.

Jocelyn gasped, stepping closer. "Is she... alive?"

Cassandra's stomach tightened.

The whispers in the night. The master bedroom Mrs. Oliver refused to sleep in. Angela had laughed when she told the students the ghost stories... but she'd also gone ice cold the moment they asked real questions.

Cassandra swallowed.

Before anyone could speak, the woman blinked. Slowly. Like an owl. And then... her gaze shifted.

She saw them.

Her thin, weathered hands rose, fingers curling, and she began to move them.

Lance stiffened. Then, as if on instinct, he stepped forward. His hands moved too, signing in a way Cassandra had never seen before. Not casual, not modern. More precise and deliberate.

The woman responded, her movements measured, poetic.

Even Logan who had taken several years of sign language classes seemed lost.

Seeing as they weren't walking anymore, Ethan and Logan helped Diego sink onto a tree stump. Cassandra felt torn between getting him immediate medical attention and this eerily compelling woman.

Cassandra concentrated intently, ignoring individual signs, while trying to understand their facial expressions and gestures. She caught a few things and whispered them to the others. "Something about a grandfather... and digging... and gone." She glanced at Jocelyn and shrugged. "That's all I got."

"If this were a television show, now something even worse would happen because we're all distracted by this creature," Jocelyn whispered, evaluating the area again. "Look at those rock stacks. I bet this area is an old heiau. Is she even alive, or is she an old Hawaiian ghost?"

"Lance sees her," Cassandra said quietly. "And by the way they're talking, he seems to think she's real."

The words hung in the air, heavy with possibility.

Cassandra locked eyes with Jocelyn, who stage whispered, "Promise me no one with a white mask and chainsaw is creeping up behind me?"

Jocelyn was good at cutting tension, but this time her jokes were freaking Cassandra out. She rolled her eyes and hissed, "We are *the adults*, Jocelyn. Knock it off."

The old woman's hands stilled. Her expression didn't change, but there was a finality in the way she sat back, her gaze drifting away as if she had already dismissed them.

Cassandra swallowed. "That's it?" She spoke and signed, "She's done?"

Lance hesitated, then nodded. *Yeah. She said what she wanted to say.*

By the time they reached the car, the sticky night air had cooled, leaving behind a damp chill. The adrenaline had faded, replaced by the bone-deep exhaustion that only comes after a near-disaster.

Cassandra quickly texted Meg to let her know they were heading to the clinic with Diego.

The moment the SUV doors shut, the interior filled with the scent of sweat and jungle grime.

Ethan wedged himself next to Diego in the middle row, while Logan and Lance crammed into the way back, their hands signing rapidly, concern etched into their expressions.

Jocelyn drove in tense silence, and before long, she pulled up to a small urgent care clinic. Logan and Ethan helped Diego inside, his weight leaning heavily on them. The waiting room was nearly empty, aside from a tired-looking nurse at the desk, who took one glance at Diego's swollen ankle and pushed a wheelchair over without asking.

After checking in, Diego sank into the chair, adjusting his foot with a wince.

Despite the pain, he smirked. "Well. That was an adventure."

Cassandra thunked her tote bag onto her lap, her patience hanging by a thread. "This is why we don't sneak around abandoned properties in the middle of the night."

Diego sighed, rubbing his ankle. "Lesson learned. Probably. Maybe."

Jocelyn snorted. "Yeah, that sounds about right."

Cassandra's glare made it very clear it was not funny.

Jocelyn glanced at the check-in counter, then back at Cassandra. "Why would a piece of land that close to the Oliver estate still be sitting vacant?"

Cassandra blinked, the question hitting her square in the adrenaline crash. "That's what I was just thinking. Mānoa real estate doesn't sit empty unless someone wants it that way. I know there's a piece we've been missing."

As the nurse wheeled Diego back to be seen by the doctor, Cassandra turned to Lance, who had been unusually quiet. She nudged him gently. *So... what was that woman telling you back there? I caught bits and pieces.*

Lance's hands moved fast, his face serious. Logan, watching intently, tried to keep up but finally threw up his hands.

Hold up, bro. Just type it, he signed. *I'm missing half of this.*

Lance grabbed his phone, typing with quick, deliberate taps before turning the screen toward Cassandra.

Cassandra's stomach tightened as she read aloud: "The woman's name is Linda. Her grandfather, Daniel Ybarra, was the Oliver estate's groundskeeper. He found Jean's body in 1910. But he always said he saw something before that. Something awful."

Cassandra looked up. "What did he see?"

Lance typed: "HE TOLD LINDA THAT JEAN DIDN'T FALL. MAGGIE PUSHED HER. SHE HATED JEAN. THOUGHT HER ACTIONS EMBARRASSED THE FAMILY."

Maggie? That didn't fit. She was the golden wife, the polished one. But it explained so much.

Logan frowned. "So Daniel kept quiet?"

Lance nodded: "HE SAID EDWARD MADE IT WORSE. COVERED IT UP. OR MAYBE HE KNEW WHAT MAGGIE DID. LINDA DIDN'T KNOW. BUT DANIEL BURIED SOMETHING. TO KEEP IT SAFE. SAID IT COULD RUIN THEM ALL."

The group went quiet.

Joslyn frowned. "Wait, Maggie Oliver?"

"Jean's sister-in-law," Cassandra clarified slowly.

Ethan looked disturbed. "Are we saying she pushed her? Like... actually pushed her?"

"LINDA SAID DANIEL BELIEVED IT," Lance typed. "THOUGHT JEAN'S DEATH WASN'T AN ACCIDENT."

"Then Edward covered it up to protect his reputation," Logan added grimly.

Lance typed more, and Logan read it aloud: "She said others came looking. Asking questions. But none of them saw her."

"They weren't paying attention," Cassandra said. "Or they didn't believe she mattered."

Jocelyn's eyes narrowed. "Was there evidence... something Maggie changed about Jean's stuff, and Edward covered it up..."

"Something worth killing for?" Cassandra said it too easily, her own voice giving her pause.

Lance nodded: "She kept saying, 'my grandfather saw the truth.' And that what he hid would bring the family shame."

Nobody spoke for a long moment.

Then Cassandra exhaled. "If Jean's death was tied to Maggie, then it makes sense someone would do anything to keep it hidden."

Logan whispered, "We're not just dealing with an old mystery anymore. If Linda's right... that whole family's been lying for a century."

Just as Cassandra opened her mouth to reply, her phone buzzed.

She glanced down, expecting a text from Meg—

Unknown Number.

Her breath caught. Her gut screamed don't answer. But she did. "Hello?"

Silence.

Then, breathing. Low. Rough. Measured.

"You should've stayed out of this, Dr. Sato." The voice was gravelly, each syllable deliberate. "This is your last warning. Drop the investigation... or you won't like what happens next."

Click.

Cassandra's fingers were ice around the phone.

"Cass?"

Cassandra barely heard Jocelyn. The voice echoed in her head. *You won't like what happens next.*

"Cassandra." Jocelyn grabbed her wrist. "Who. Was. That?"

She exhaled sharply, forcing herself to meet her friend's gaze. "Someone's watching us. Could've been Nathaniel?" Her voice felt distant, like it belonged to someone else. "Or someone who wants us to think it was him."

Logan nodded. "They don't know about Linda, though."

The air in the clinic suddenly felt too tight, too small.

They had come looking for Diego, but it seemed they had unearthed something far more dangerous.

Chapter Fourteen

S OON THE ADRENALINE DRAINED from Cassandra's system. Exhaust- ed, she wandered down a hallway of the urgent care clinic until she found a bathroom, which was thankfully empty this late at night.

Cassandra caught sight of herself in the mirror and nearly jumped. Somehow, her tight hair bun had survived the chaos, but the rest of her? Not so much. Leaning in, she plucked a leaf and a smudge of dirt from above her ear, scowling at her own reflection. The makeup she'd so painstakingly applied first thing in the morning had rubbed off, replaced by layers of sweat and dust.

She needed sleep. Desperately. A normal person would be in bed right now, curled up in an oversized t-shirt, dreaming about malasadas.

Instead, she was stuck playing crisis management for a group of students who had all, at some point, decided they were immune to consequences.

No one needed to see her raw, unfiltered, sleep-deprived face. Even her own mother had probably forgotten what she looked like without at least a layer of concealer.

She dabbed at her cheeks with a damp paper towel, careful not to smear what little makeup remained. It was a losing battle, but at least she wouldn't look like she'd just crawled out of a crypt.

She was this close to ripping off her now-muddy platform sandals and walking barefoot like a true island girl.

Then she glanced at the floor.

Nope. She did not need a new kind of bacterial infection on top of everything else.

Staring herself down in the mirror, she whispered, "Suck it up, wāhine. You've survived worse."

Tossing the paper towels into the trash, she straightened her top and marched back out to the waiting room.

In the far corner, the students slouched in pairs, sprawled across sturdy armchairs, scrolling through their phones with vacant expressions. Probably wishing they were in bed, too.

But maybe the team could put this time to better use. Hadn't they passed a coffee shop on the same block as the health clinic?

Shortly after, Cassandra returned, a hero bearing gifts. A tray of Americanos.

Ethan nearly dove over a row of chairs to grab one. "Dr. Sato, I would take a bullet for you."

"Let's hope it doesn't come to that," Cassandra said dryly, passing the rest around.

The group perked up immediately, groaning in collective caffeine worship as they took their first sips.

Cassandra sat next to Lance and Logan. She spoke and slowly signed at the same time. "Lance, can you tell us more about Linda. She was... strange, yah?"

Logan said, "At first I thought she was a ghost."

"She claimed her grandfather was the estate's groundskeeper?"

Lance slowly explained with signs and gestures. *Linda's signing was old-school. I've seen videos of old Hawaiian sign language. The Deaf community on the islands used HSL long before American Sign Language spread from the mainland.*

Cassandra leaned in, keeping her expression calm but skeptical. "Lance, are you sure? If she was using old Hawaiian signs, how do you know you understood?"

Lance gave her a patient look. Like he'd been waiting for this question.

It's like talking to someone with an accent, he signed. *You might miss a word or two, but you understand the meaning.* He paused before adding, *Deaf people are better at filling language gaps than hearing people. You'll just have to trust me.*

Cassandra sighed. Fair enough.

Lance typed more on his phone and turned it toward her. "She said others came before us. Asking questions. Looking for something. But they didn't know where to look. Her grandfather did. He said he buried the truth."

Jocelyn leaned forward. "What kind of truth?"

Lance typed: "She repeated this over and over. 'My grandfather saw the truth. He buried it. And what he hid would bring the family shame.'"

"So... what, a confession? A letter?"

"I keep thinking about that photo," Cassandra murmured. "The one of Edward Oliver in his study where he's holding something. Looks like a small carved box."

Logan frowned. "No fancy boxes like that on display."

Jocelyn's brow furrowed. ""Exactly. Which means it either disappeared a long time ago... or it was never meant for display."

Lance nodded, then typed again. "Linda said her grandfather buried something valuable. Maybe it does tie to Jean's death."

Silence stretched long moments until Cassandra leaned back, crossing her arms. "Okay. We have to go back."

"And you," Jocelyn pointed at Ethan, narrowing her eyes. "We betta not catch you and Diego sneaking off again. You two have a talent for causing trouble."

Ethan put a hand to his chest, feigning innocence. "Hey! It's not like we planned for Diego to fall down a ravine. That was just... an unexpected detour."

Jocelyn crossed her arms. "Unexpected detours are how people end up in ERs, braddah."

Ethan huffed. "I wasn't the klutz who fell into a hole."

Jocelyn arched an eyebrow. "No, but you were there, which means you had the opportunity to prevent it."

Ethan sighed dramatically. "Great. So now I'm Diego's babysitter?"

Jocelyn smirked. "Apparently, someone has to be."

Cassandra held up her hands to stop their bickering. "Enough. No more sneaky sneaking. We are this close to solving the murders. Find the evidence before the other teams figure it out."

Suddenly, the clinic doors swooshed open. Kalia and a student stormed in pushing a wheelchair, looking flustered. Slumped in the chair was Andrew, pale and dazed.

What now? Cassandra jumped to her feet.

"Andrew?" She rushed forward, but Kalia waved her back.

"He's okay, just a little concussed," Kalia said, breathless. Her usual composure was gone, strands of hair escaped her sleek ponytail, a sheen of sweat on her forehead.

"We found him at the Oliver estate, half-conscious. Figured we'd bring him here before anything worse happened."

For several heartbeats, Cassandra locked eyes with Kalia, instincts on high alert. Was this just another way for Kalia to one-up her? Or was this the rare occasion where rivalry took a backseat to actual human decency?

Kalia folded her arms, "Has a gnarly bump on the back of his head."

Jocelyn let out a low whistle. "Lucky t'ing he got one hard, stubborn head."

Andrew, looking foggy but awake, managed a pained smile. "Guess I took one for the team."

Cassandra crouched beside him, concern outweighing irritation. "What were *you* doing there? Nobody sent you."

"I just wanted to be useful," Andrew muttered, blinking against the harsh clinic lights. "I thought maybe I'd find something before Kalia did. I didn't think anyone else would be out there."

Ethan stared. "So you just wandered over solo? At night?"

Andrew winced. "I had my flashlight. And Skipper. Who, by the way, is an excellent early warning system."

Jocelyn muttered, "Tell that to your skull."

Kalia motioned to her student, who stepped forward, holding up a plastic evidence bag. "We think this was used to clock him."

Jocelyn leaned in. "A rusty garden tool proves someone got hit, not who did it. Or why."

Lance, watching from behind, signed, *The tool's old. Could've been left years ago.*

Kalia answered, "He was half-buried in mulch, lying next to one of the old flowerbeds. Looked like he'd been trying to dig something up."

Andrew said, "I was poking around the edge of the flowerbeds... Thought I saw something, then boom. Next thing I know, I'm in a wheelchair."

Before she could process the implications, the clinic doors slid open again. Two Kualoa students entered, one with a very disgruntled parrot perched on his arm.

The sleepy night nurse at the front desk barely looked up. Then she spotted the parrot. "Sir, that is not a service animal—"

Kalia threw up her hands, exasperated. "Take this bird already. My ears need hazard pay. Detective Bird's been shrieking 'clues' for an hour straight. I was this close to calling animal control."

Skipper flapped his wings indignantly. "Find the clues!"

Cassandra suppressed a laugh. "Guess Skipper saved the day."

Ethan leaned over to let Skipper hop onto his shoulder.

Andrew, still woozy, fished a peanut from his pocket and held it up. "He's got my back."

Kalia glared at the bird, her patience clearly frayed. "Next time I hear 'clues,' I'm tossing him in the koi pond. Don't say I didn't warn you."

Skipper fluffed up proudly. "Detective bird!"

Ethan stepped outside with Skipper, just as a nurse wheeled Andrew back for further treatment.

Kalia moved closer to Cassandra, voice low, "Looks like we're ahead now, Sato. You sure you're ready to lose?"

Cassandra squared her shoulders. "For real, Kalia? You found a rusty old tool. So what."

Kalia's eyes gleamed. "Maybe. But we're closer to solving this than you think."

And with that, she spun on her heel and walked out.

Cassandra's coffee soured in her stomach. Kalia was ahead. Not just in artifacts. In nerve. And tonight, Cassandra conceded she was losing her edge.

Long past midnight, Andrew returned, his concussion confirmed to be mild.

"Aww guys. I'm touched that you waited for me," he crooned, grinning despite his injuries.

Around the room, students roused from various stages of dozing.

Diego, booted foot propped up, looked annoyingly chipper. "Sooo... we breaking and entering again, or are we taking the boring, legal route this time?"

They still didn't grasp how close they'd come. Or maybe they did. And they were choosing laughter anyway.

Cassandra's gaze hardened. "We don't have a choice. Someone's willing to hurt us to keep their secrets hidden. Finding what Daniel Ybarra hid might be the key to everything."

The threat was real now. And personal.

Chapter Fifteen

A s Cassandra stepped outside the clinic, a familiar, tense figure strode up the walkway. Pono's face was hard, his jaw clenched as he took in Diego's booted ankle and Andrew's bandaged head.

Confused as to how he knew where to find them, Cassandra shot Jocelyn a questioning glare. Jocelyn shrugged.

Pono closed the space between them with a quiet, deliberate intensity, his presence pressing down on Cassandra like the weight of a wave just before it crashes. He didn't stop until Cassandra could feel the heat rolling off him, his breath thick with coffee and anger.

He leaned in, voice low and rough as gravel. "Four days, Sato. Four damn days, and you got guys broken and bleeding. You try set a record?"

Pono's glower locked onto hers, unblinking, like he was daring her to argue.

Cassandra fought the urge to take a step back but her feet had other plans. She shifted half a step away, enough to get some breathing room without making it obvious. No need to poke the bear.

Jocelyn, sensing the crackling tension, casually interjected, "Hey, at least they're still alive, yah?"

It did not have the calming effect she was probably going for.

Cassandra's pulse thumped as she took another slow step back, keeping her expression neutral. "I mean, technically, only one's bleeding."

She did a mental forehead slap. Why did Pono always arouse her inner child?

An image of Pono at twenty-years-old flashed in Cassandra's memory. He'd used that bossy tone with her several times during the now infamous summer she'd gone off the rails.

Pono had never lectured her back then. He'd let her brother Keoni do all the smothering, while he'd quietly steered her away from worse choices. A steady hand, nudging without shoving. She hadn't realized it at the time, but now, standing here with his scowl drilling into her, she wondered: Had she ever thanked him?

She plastered a fake smile on her face, "Hey, braddah! Perfect timing. We were just wondering how we were gonna Uber all these banged-up bodies home. You got space for some poor life choices in that truck of yours?" At the same time, she threw an arm behind Pono's back and nudged him away from the group of students.

Quietly, she said, "Look, I don't know how you found us. Neither of these guys got hurt because of me. I didn't tell them to go sneaking around late at night."

Pono didn't raise his voice. "I saw my sister's phone ping at the medical clinic instead of tucked up in bed at the hotel. And I knew she had to be with you. Because of you, these kids are in over their heads with this cold case thing. You think the Oliver family's ghosts only haunt old newspaper clippings?"

The weight of his stare alone pinned her in place. "You're poking through paperwork people spent a long time making disappear. Keep shaking this tree, and I guarantee something worse than coconuts is gonna drop on your head."

Cassandra folded her arms. "I promise to be careful. But the students are adults. Making decisions as adults. I'm not their babysitter."

Pono snorted. "You tell yourself that all night if it makes you feel better. But we both know you'll be the one explaining it to your Cornhusker bosses if something worse than a sprained ankle happens."

Oof. Pono really knew how to cut straight to her heart. She'd always feel responsible even if the courts or her board didn't hold her accountable.

Pono was still squared off with her, their stances mirroring a childhood argument ready to boil over, when a shift in the shadows caught Cassandra's eye. A figure, small, unmoving just beyond the halo of the streetlight. White hair draped over a faded mu'umu'u, her gaze steady, waiting.

When Lance walked over to join her and started signing, Cassandra knew the woman was Linda.

Cassandra hadn't told Pono about meeting her or their communication ace-in-the-hole, Lance. So she faced Pono away from Linda and Lance who were signing in quick, urgent conversation.

"It's late," she said. "Can we quit the lectures and just get these folks back to the hotel, please? Is that your truck?"

She pointed to his personal extended cab pickup, hoping he'd continue gazing away from Lance.

Pono rubbed his face, and for the first time, Cassandra noticed the faint lines framing his eyes. He was also up past his bedtime and probably had to show up early tomorrow for his next shift. "I got you," he said resignedly. "I can take three of 'dem. You get the parrot, though, eh?"

Diego, Lance, and Logan followed Pono while the rest piled into Jocelyn's car. Even Skipper showed a modicum of discretion and kept his beak shut. Fifteen minutes later, they shuffled into the hotel lobby, rumpled and bleary-eyed. But before they could collapse into bed, Cassandra had to ask one question.

Cassandra signed as she spoke, her fatigue battling her curiosity. "Lance, what did Linda say? And how the heck did she know where we'd be?"

Maybe she followed Kalia? He shrugged. *She said to meet her at the back gate of the Oliver estate at dawn.*

"At dawn?" Ethan repeated. "You mean like the one four hours from now?"

Grimly Lance nodded.

Cassandra's brows knit together. Something about the message felt too convenient, like a nudge in a direction she wasn't fully choosing. But she'd already gone this far. There was no turning back now.

"Alrighty then," Cassandra closed her eyes briefly as she made a decision. "I'll be in the lobby at 5:00 a.m. sharp. No questions, no delays. This isn't on the official itinerary, and if you come, you need to understand the risk. We've already had injuries, and whoever attacked

Andrew is still watching. No one will judge you for sleeping in and hitting the beach your last couple of days."

Jocelyn's hotel door was across the hall from Cassandra's. Before they went inside their rooms, Jocelyn leaned on the frame and waved good night. "I will absolutely judge if you're a no-show."

Even at their lowest energy level, Jocelyn still knew how to make Cassandra smile. Sometimes that's exactly what you need from a true friend.

Despite her exhaustion, Cassandra barely slept. By the time her watch alarm buzzed at 4:45, she was already awake, staring at the ceiling in the dim light of her hotel room, Pono's warning playing on repeat: "I guarantee something worse than coconuts is gonna drop on your head."

At 5:00 a.m., she met her team in the hotel lobby, exchanging groggy nods before leading them to the rental van. No one spoke. The energy was different this morning: charged, expectant, as if they all sensed that whatever they found today would change the course of their investigation.

The van's headlights cut through the pre-dawn mist as they wound toward the Oliver estate, windows down, cool breeze. The streets were silent, wrapped in that eerie hush just before sunrise, where shadows stretched long and secrets felt closer than usual.

They parked near the back gate, the lush valley wall above them barely visible in the silver light of dawn.

Then, a rustle.

Linda emerged from the shadows, her presence sending a ripple of unease through the group. Her long white hair seemed to glow in the dim light, and for a brief second, Cassandra had the wild thought that she was more ghost than woman.

She gestured for Lance, signing quickly, her movements sharp and urgent.

Lance nodded, his expression serious. *She says to follow her.*

Linda led them across the overgrown grounds, where mist curled along the pathways, and the faint scent of damp earth filled the air. Unlike before, she moved with absolute certainty as if every footstep had been carefully placed a hundred times before.

She stopped at a secluded landscaped berm near the tree line. She pointed. No explanation. Just an instruction: *Dig.*

The students exchanged glances before dropping to their knees. Ethan pulled out a few metal spoons and whispered, "I might've borrowed these from room service for just this contingency."

Logan and Ethan took turns clearing away the soil, while Lexi and Lance helped brush away the loose dirt, clawing it deeper with their fingertips.

Then, a rough edge. Something solid.

They dug faster, and within minutes, a fabric-wrapped object came into view.

It was old, a coarse work-shirt, stained with time and dirt.

Lexi reached forward, gently unfolding the fabric, revealing the faded imprint of a coffee company logo.

Wasn't that the same logo they'd seen on the coffee plantation photos? Cassandra's pulse kicked up a notch.

This felt like a time capsule, for real. Not like the grainy film at the conference VR game.

Beneath the fabric, a small, intricately carved wooden box rested in the dirt.

It was beautiful in its simplicity. The surface smoothed by time, delicate engravings still visible beneath the grime. Hawaiian symbols traced its lid, ones Cassandra recognized from the map, the quilt, and even the markings on the stone near the well.

Cassandra's throat tightened. The box was a message from the past. Wrapped in dirt and silence, waiting for someone to finally listen. And somehow, they'd been the ones to find it. But why them? Why her?

Hands trembling slightly, she tried lifting the lid.

Locked.

Gently she held the box near her ear and shook it. Nothing rattled. Like it was empty. Cassandra's stomach twisted. Had they come all this way for an empty box? Or was this something meant to be earned, not stumbled onto? Maybe Linda had only led them here to see if they were worthy of what came next. And if that was true, what did it mean that the box hadn't opened for her?

Ethan exhaled. "Seriously?"

Lance looked to Linda, who stood motionless, her eyes not surprised.

Cassandra ran a hand over the outside of the box, feeling for hidden latches. Another puzzle piece. A final clue. But what was missing?

"She already took whatever was inside," Cassandra whispered. "Or maybe she never let it be found... until now."

Cassandra tapped Lance and signed, *Ask her what happened to her grandfather?*

Lance turned to Linda. They conversed back and forth for a long moment, the rest of the group watching helplessly.

Finally, Lance interpreted: *Her grandfather worked here until he died. Not a groundskeeper. Only as a gardener. He was scared for his family, so he never complained. But he always believed maybe one day, he could get the land back. For him and the other workers.*

Logan, staring at the shirt still in Lexi's hands, was the first to put it together.

"Oh... wow." He turned to Cassandra. "The workers in the estate photo. The ones standing beside Jean Oliver. The house staff and estate workers wore these shirts."

Daniel Ybarra. Linda's grandfather.

Her pulse pounded in her ears, she was so dialed in.

"Linda's the reason we're here," Jocelyn whispered, brushing soil from her hands. "She wanted us to walk in her grandfather's footsteps. She pointed at the lie. The one her grandfather saw... the one Maggie buried."

Before Cassandra could process the weight of the discovery, heavy footsteps crunched against the gravel path.

Nathaniel Oliver stepped into view, his jaw tight, his gaze flicking from their faces to the freshly dug-up soil. He exhaled sharply, the kind of sigh that carried more than just irritation. Like he'd already known how all this would end.

Something flashed in his eyes. Relief? Disappointment? Frustration?

Just as quickly his expression hardened, masking whatever had slipped through.

"I warned you," he said, his voice low, raw with something unspoken. "Stay off my property. You don't belong here, digging up things you don't understand."

Lance, standing nearest to Cassandra, instinctively grabbed the small box and shoved it behind his back in one rapid movement.

No one spoke. No one moved.

Cassandra kept her face neutral, not daring to glance at Lance or the box.

Nathaniel didn't notice. His gaze was locked on the hole.

Slowly, like a man carrying a weight too heavy for his frame, he stepped forward and crouched at the edge of the disturbed soil.

A long silence stretched between them.

When he spoke again, his voice had lost some of the anger, replaced with exhaustion. "You think I haven't already looked?"

Cassandra froze.

Nathaniel's fingers pressed into the loose dirt, as if testing it, as if willing something to appear. He let out a bitter chuckle, one that didn't reach his eyes.

"I've dug up every inch of this place," he admitted, barely above a whisper. "Most everywhere, but not here. I thought the answer couldn't be this obvious. And you know what I found?"

He looked up, meeting Cassandra's gaze head-on.

"Nothing."

A chill swept over her skin. Was Nathaniel guarding family secrets or had he been searching for them too? And he'd found nothing.

Cassandra kept her voice steady. "Maybe you were never meant to find it."

Nathaniel's lips pressed into a thin line.

She saw the momentary flicker of understanding, the realization that maybe, just maybe, the answers he'd been chasing had been kept from him on purpose. Kept from him...

By Linda. By Daniel Ybarra. By the people who had been trampled by his family's power.

His fists clenched. "Whatever story you're trying to rewrite, Dr. Sato, it won't work. You can't change what happened."

Cassandra took a step closer. "No. But together we can finally tell the truth."

The weight of her words hung between them. An offer. A way out.

Nathaniel's jaw tightened, his fingers curling into the dirt one last time before he let it fall away. Then, just like that, the mask of the untouchable Oliver heir slid back into place.

He exhaled sharply and stood, brushing his hands against his pants. "Keep playing your childish history game," he said, his voice cutting but less certain than before. "You're out of your depth. And if you keep digging, you might find yourself buried along with your so-called 'truth.'"

With that, he turned and walked away, disappearing into the morning mist.

Her gaze followed his retreat, and she caught a glimpse of the second-floor windows through the tangled branches. The master bedroom, if she remembered the floor plan right.

Maggie Oliver hated that room. Refused to sleep there. Maybe she knew what kind of secrets the ground outside her window was hiding.

Only when she heard the faint sound of the back door clapping shut did Cassandra let out the breath she'd been holding.

She should've felt victorious. But instead, heaviness settled in her chest. The truth had cost them something they hadn't fully named yet. Nathaniel was angry. Moreover, he was hurt. And part of her knew: this wasn't the end of the story. It was the beginning of the fallout.

Lance, still clutching the small, carved box, finally exhaled.

Cassandra turned to Linda.

She was watching Nathaniel disappear, her face unreadable. Finally, she looked back at Cassandra. And for the first time, she smiled. Not a smug smile. Not a triumphant one.

A knowing one. As if to say, *You see now. You see why it had to be you.*

Cassandra swallowed hard. She wanted to believe she was the right person for this. But impostor thoughts scraped at her composure.

What if they failed to finish what Linda started? What if choosing her had been a mistake?

This was a test. A challenge. And Cassandra's team had been the ones to pass. Not Kalia's.

The weight of it pressed down on her as they made their way back to the van. Now they had to figure out what to do next.

Lance pointed at the box. *If it's not what's inside that matters... maybe it's where it was hidden.*

If Linda trusted her to keep digging, she needed to learn to trust herself too. Cassandra nodded. "We need to check the land records. See who owns that vacant parcel now."

Jocelyn blinked. "You think Nathaniel bought it?"

"Or tried to. If Daniel Ybarra's family ever owned it, there'd be a paper trail. Somewhere."

Cassandra rubbed her temples. "Whoever hit Andrew, whoever called me, they're not reenacting the past. They're hiding something real. Now."

Logan raised a brow. "Not a cold case anymore?"

Jocelyn, buckling her seatbelt, cut the tension the only way she knew how. "Coffees for everyone, right? You owe us after this."

Cassandra put the van in Drive. "Oh yeah. Double shots. On me."

Jocelyn smirked, staring at the estate as it faded behind them. "Good. Because I think we just woke up a whole lot of ghosts."

Chapter Sixteen

A FTER FINAL POSTER SESSIONS and lunch, they reconvened outside the conference ballroom for their final team event.

Ivy practically bounced on her toes. "I love escape rooms! My family does one together every winter break, and we always solve it with time to spare!"

Brandon yawned dramatically. "Y'all look like you need a nap. I still can't believe you didn't text me last night."

"I'm just glad I wasn't with you," Maria folded her arms. "How would a misdemeanor look on my grad school applications?"

Cassandra closed her eyes and muttered, "No one is getting arrested. If I don't see another police officer before this trip ends, I will be perfectly content."

She met Jocelyn's gaze and held it.

A silent understanding passed between them that by *officer*, she meant Pono. No more scolding, no more lectures, no more students acting like they were starring in some true crime reenactment. Even if it meant not solving the cold case of the Mānoa Marauder or winning the grand prize.

Yeah, right. Like she could let it go now.

"C'mon, Maria. It's just puzzles!" Logan's eyes gleamed with excitement. "Nobody's gonna call the cops on us for being too smart."

Lance rolled his eyes and mimed drinking before fingerspelling, *3 E-S-P-R-E-S-S-O.*

Diego groaned, adjusting the boot on his sprained ankle as he nursed another coffee. "Y'all are gonna have to carry the team on this one. I'm just here for moral support and caffeine."

A booming voice cut through the chatter. "Welcome to the Honolulu PastForward Expo's 'Unlock History' Escape Room Experience!"

Andrew, his aloha shirt aggressively loud, small steri-strips covering the gash on his forehead, grinned like a game show host and raised both arms dramatically. Theatrics, as usual.

"You're about to time travel through some of Hawaii's most pivotal historical moments. Your mission: crack the codes, solve the puzzles, and maybe, just maybe, escape before the timer says pau."

A ripple of chuckles ran through the crowd as Andrew leaned into the mic. "For those of you who know me from the Mānoa Marauder exhibit earlier this week... surprise! They made me the escape room guy, too. I'm your guide for all things 'pretend you're smarter than history.'"

Without turning her head, Cassandra glanced sideways at Kalia's team.

Of course, they looked annoyingly well-rested, practically glowing. None of them had met a ghostly hippie Deaf lady in Manoa, narrowly avoided an arrest, or been threatened by a rich landowner at dawn.

Kalia caught Cassandra's glance and winked like she'd already won.

Cassandra exhaled through her nose. Kalia had pulled that look in so many faculty meetings...

Andrew waved toward the signs around the room. "K' folks, each escape room is themed on a key event in Hawaii's past. Let me tell you, it's gonna take teamwork. So, if you the one who's planning to play hero and do it all yourself, good luck."

He read from a laminated card and dropped his voice into dramatic narrator mode: "First up, in the 'Victory on the USS Missouri' room, you'll relive the dramatic final moments of World War II. Make sure the surrender signing goes smoothly. Crack codes, stop saboteurs, and finish the treaty before it's too late."

His grin widened. "But hey, no pressure. It's just world peace, yeah?"

The crowd chuckled as he continued.

Meg stood slightly to his side, her hands moving quickly as she interpreted Andrew's heavily accented Pidgin for Lance and a few other Deaf participants. She shook her head slightly at one of Andrew's more exaggerated phrases, her lips twitching like she was trying very hard to control her facial expressions.

Lance leaned over and signed, *Yeah, he's a comedian now*, earning a smirk from Meg.

Cassandra shook her head. Andrew hadn't changed much since undergrad, except now he was professionally annoying.

"In the 'Statehood Struggles' room, you'll navigate the heated debates surrounding Hawaiian statehood in 1959. You'll face legal webs, discover hidden documents, and try to sway key figures to your side. Or if you're feeling rebellious, maybe keep Hawai'i out of the Union altogether. Your choice!"

Someone in the back groaned. "Great, more debates. Just like Thanksgiving dinner with my family."

Andrew laughed. "Eh, at least no Auntie screaming about the turkey being dry, yeah?"

"And there's 'Real Estate Boom and Bust,' where you'll play detective with shady contracts, missing property records, and corrupt developers. Can you keep the land in the right hands? Or you gonna sell the beach for cheap?"

His smirk widened. "Pro tip: crooks always leave clues in the fine print. You just gotta find 'em before they find you."

Cassandra's ears perked up.

Missing property records? Corrupt developers? That was... uncomfortably close to the real-life mystery they were investigating.

She cast a sideways glance at Jocelyn, who raised an eyebrow as if thinking the same thing.

Andrew, oblivious, kept going. "For those of you who love drama, our 'Kingdom of Hawaii' room takes you back to the monarchy days. Protect the crown jewels, play politics with the royal court, an' see if you can stop a coup. Or, who knows? Maybe *you* the one pulling the strings, huh?"

Andrew scanned the crowd, clearly loving the attention. "So, which one will you get stuck in, yeah? Hope you lucky."

Cassandra glanced at Kalia again. The other woman smiled knowingly, like she was already ten steps ahead.

Andrew raised a hand. "Now, I know you folks love working with your crew, but we gotta keep things interesting. Here's the twist you've all been waiting for... You're getting shuffled."

Groans rippled through the crowd.

"Eh, no shame. You folks like to complain, but it's more fun this way. Yes, this means you may end up with strangers. Think of it like Survivor. Alliances optional, but no backstabbing, yeah?"

Her students exchanged glances, clearly disappointed they wouldn't be working together. Cassandra's stomach sank.

Andrew held up a lanyard, "Check the back of your name tag for a colored dot. That's your team. Find your matching sign and try not to act like it's speed dating for nerds. Once everyone's in place, a volunteer will bring you your first clue."

His grin turned mischievous. "Gonna be fun, promise. And remember if you get stuck, blame the guy who thinks he's the smartest in the room. Every group's got one. Gotta work with the team. If you no can, good luck, cuz the timer don't care."

Slowly, the crowd funneled through the ballroom doors like fish swimming down a rocky stream. Inside, neatly arranged moveable walls had chopped the huge ballroom into smaller spaces, each marked by a door and a large, color-coded sign.

Kalia stood near the green-marked door, arms crossed. Cassandra stopped in her tracks. *Of course she's in my group.*

Kalia sighed like she was equally cursed by fate. "Don't even tell me you're green."

As Meg passed by with her team, she caught Cassandra's eye, pausing just long enough to sign: *Good luck with that.*

Cassandra stifled a groan.

The Real Estate Boom and Bust scenario was loaded with political and cultural landmines. It was a direct mirror of Hawaii's tangled real estate history including the shady land grabs that played into the Oliver family's past.

If Cassandra and Kalia could be civil, this challenge might actually help their cold case investigation. But who was she kidding? Kalia was never civil when Cassandra was in the room.

Cassandra rubbed her temples. "You can have green. I'm not in the mood."

"Chicken," Kalia taunted.

Cassandra shot her a glare. "What are we, eight? That's not gonna work."

Kalia leaned in slightly, her voice dropping into a knowing murmur. "You want me busy in here while you spoon-feed your students the answers to the Mānoa Marauder challenge? I know how you operate. You don't trust them to win on their own."

Cassandra stayed quiet, even as irritation prickled at her spine.

Kalia tilted her head, smirking. "And honestly, why would you? A bunch of corn-fed hicks from Nebraska trying to untangle the intricacies of Hawaiian territorial law? Please. They've been out of their depth since baggage claim."

Cassandra could handle insults about herself. But her students? Her good students, who had uncovered more in four days than Kalia's matching-polo clone army had in an entire semester?

That was a line too far.

"Those so-called corn-fed hicks are already so far ahead of your creepy little cult of overachievers," Cassandra shot back. "By tomorrow's luau, they'll have this case tied up in a bow. And trust me, it won't be Kualoa green."

No, she didn't actually stick out her tongue. But she wanted to.

Just then, Andrew handed their group the first clue: a weathered deed and a stack of cryptic historical documents. "You're good to go. Timer starts as soon as you open the door."

As he passed Cassandra, he murmured quietly: "Sorry, Dr. Sato. The randomizer was cruel today. But, uh... good luck with her."

Cassandra barely had time to glare at him before he scurried away.

Inside, the room was set up like a bureaucratic nightmare.

The first challenge was a real estate map matching game: A large, color-coded map of O'ahu covered one wall, with parcels labeled *Leasehold*, *Fee Simple*, and *Government Reserved*. Below it was a list of early developers and landowners. The task? Match each name to the correct parcel, then identify which ones were later converted and why.

A lanky student in glasses squinted. "Why is most of this map yellow?"

A petite woman with a clipboard, already trying to take charge, tapped the laminated instructions. "Yellow's leasehold land. Blue is fee simple. Green is government. We're supposed to assign the names, figure out which lands got converted, and basically solve for motive."

Cassandra leaned in, scanning the grid. "Most of this area was managed by royal descendants. See here? Bishop Estate owned most of Waikīkī at one point."

Kalia barely glanced up. "Yeah, yeah, everyone knows about Bishop Estate. What about these?"

She pointed to a cluster marked *Converted to Fee Simple.*

Cassandra traced the names. Native Hawaiian families. "Some of their land was lost through predatory lease agreements. A few bought it back, but..." She paused. Several names were crossed out.

Kalia began assigning names to parcels without consulting anyone. "Let's just move forward," she said briskly.

Cassandra's jaw tightened. "Maybe try matching them correctly first."

The lanky student frowned. "Wait—what's fee simple again?"

"Fee simple means full ownership," Kalia said, distracted. "Leasehold is more like long-term rent from a trust or estate. Most people in Hawai'i don't actually own the land under their homes. Just the right to use it."

Cassandra cut in, her voice sharper. "Which worked out just fine for the ones holding the deeds. Not so much for the families who'd lived there for generations."

She jabbed a finger at a section labeled *Lost Land.* "Like this Kekoa family. When their lease ran out, the estate sold the parcel to a developer. No renewal, no buy-back. Just gone. And the rules were never made to protect them."

A flannel-clad student raised a hand. "Uh, so do we match the original lessee or the developer who took it over?"

"Both," Cassandra and Kalia said in unison. They locked eyes. Neither smiled.

The tension hung in the air as students glanced at each other.

Flannel shirt guy spoke up, clearly trying to smooth things over. "Uh, okay, maybe we can just agree to disagree and keep moving? The timer's ticking."

Then came Part Two: the board.

In the middle of the escape room, a game table was set up with a wooden map divided into land parcels. The group had to protect as many parcels as possible by placing shaped markers before time ran out. But the shapes didn't fit neatly, and every move was a trade-off.

"This is like... Tetris meets colonization," someone muttered.

Cassandra scanned the map, recognizing several of the names printed on the wooden parcels. "Wait—Some of these are the same names as the land conversions we just mapped. If we protect the wrong names, we're siding with the developers who took over. We need to prioritize the original families who lost everything."

Kalia scoffed. "Not everything's some epic land justice crusade, Sato. It's just a game. Solve the puzzle, win the points. Move on."

Cassandra's stomach twisted. "This isn't just a game. The way land gets sliced and reshaped on that board is exactly how families like the Kekoas lost everything. And families like the Olivers made sure the rules stayed that way."

A student in a Waikīkī ball cap chuckled nervously. "You two have... history, huh?"

"Just a little," Cassandra muttered.

They managed to piece together a few shapes before time ran out, but Kalia's rush left others vulnerable, and the board told its own story.

The last challenge was a locked safe, its heavy steel door covered in dust like it had waited decades to be cracked.

Kalia grabbed the dial before Cassandra could stop her. "I've got this."

She twisted too hard. The mechanism jammed.

Cassandra muttered. "Maybe if you stopped trying to prove you're the smartest person in the room, we'd actually finish this,"

Kalia scoffed, not letting go of the dial. "Just 'cause you no can do solo don't mean I need help."

A student near the back cleared their throat awkwardly. "Uh... we're, like, right here? This is getting uncomfortable."

The safe finally popped open, revealing a faded, typewritten note folded neatly on top of a single, rusted key.

Cassandra unfolded the paper, reading the words aloud: "What was taken remains locked behind the veil of bureaucracy. Look beyond the fine print."

On impulse, Cassandra slipped the rusted key into her pocket. No idea why. Just... felt like something to keep. No one noticed. They were too busy thinking.

It wasn't part of the challenge. It wasn't even hers. But the idea of leaving it behind or letting someone else find it first made her chest tighten. Was this about the game, or the real puzzle still waiting outside this room? She wasn't sure. But the key felt heavier than it should have.

Kalia frowned. "Locked behind... what does that mean?"

As the group groaned in frustration, Cassandra caught a subtle movement in the corner of her vision.

A beige curtain fluttered slightly against the far wall.

Kalia saw it too.

A storage space. Big enough to hold whatever had been hidden away.

Without thinking, they both sprinted toward it.

Cassandra reached first, yanking back the curtain. A plain, non-descript door labeled 'Supply' stood before them. She grabbed the handle. It turned easily.

Kalia huffed. "This better not be a dead end."

The moment they stepped inside, the door clicked softly behind them. The softest, sneakiest door lock in history.

Cassandra froze. Turned. Jiggled the handle. Shoved it harder.

Nothing.

She exhaled slowly, pressing her forehead against the door. "Great. Just what I needed. A team-building exercise."

Chapter Seventeen

CASSANDRA GROANED, "OH, COME on," before stepping back, glaring at the stubborn door as if it might suddenly develop a conscience.

Kalia leaned against the nearest shelf, arms crossed, smirking. "Great. What's your big plan now, Nebraska?"

Cassandra shot her a withering look. "I'm thinking. Maybe you could try it for once instead of just standing there like you're above it all."

Kalia sauntered over, giving the handle a slow, deliberate twist. When it didn't budge, her smirk faltered. "Locked, huh?"

"Brilliant deduction," Cassandra muttered, slumping against a wall. "We're officially in a sitcom."

The muffled sounds of other teams drifted in from the escape room. Phones had gone into a basket before the game started to prevent cheating. Now, they couldn't call for help either.

Kalia knocked. "Hello? Anyone out there!"

Silence.

"Someone will notice we're missing."

"Ugh. This is exactly why I hate group activities."

A pause settled between them. Long enough to feel the walls pressing in.

Then Kalia broke the silence. "Alright, while we're here, let's clear the air. What's your deal with the Olivers? You've been gunning for them like it's a family grudge."

Cassandra blinked at her. "What do you mean?"

Kalia shrugged. "Even back at O'ahu State, you had a thing about the old families. Now you're out here trying to burn the Olivers to the ground."

Cassandra rolled her eyes. "Cute. Read a history book. They profited off stolen land and artifacts, and they've been covering it up for over a century. If you actually cared about people instead of your resume, you might get it."

"Oh, spare me the lecture. We both know this is personal."

She wasn't wrong. Cassandra could feel her own silence pulsing. Kalia was watching her, waiting for the crack.

She dodged. "Fine. Let's talk about motives. What do you think Nakano's real angle is?"

Kalia hesitated. "I don't know. But whatever it is, he's not telling either of us."

That, at least, they could agree on.

"You're the one keeping secrets," Cassandra said. "We know you snuck onto the Oliver property. What did you find?"

Kalia smirked. "Always sure you're the smartest in the room. Classic Sato."

Cassandra laughed. "You're projecting again."

"Hardly. We found something before you. Records linking Nathaniel Oliver's lawyer, Joseph Aukai, to a secret auction in the 1950s. Held at the estate. Royal artifacts. Hawaiian quilts. Plantation equipment. And a lockbox."

Cassandra's breath hitched. *No way.*

Kalia noticed. Her eyes narrowed. "A carved wooden box. Ornate. Native symbols."

Cassandra froze her face. No way was she giving that reaction air.

Kalia pressed. "The records list it for auction. No receipt. No buyer."

Cassandra's thoughts swirled. Was it never sold? Was it buried instead?

Then Kalia tilted her head, voice dropping. "You sure Nakano's not using you?"

Cassandra's stomach tightened. "Excuse me?"

"You think Nakano gave Morton College the plantation field assignment because of your brilliance? No. He's working angles. Just like he's working me."

"Glad we agree on something."

Kalia's smile disappeared. "My team—actual Hawaiians, by the way—got shoved into a dusty archive while Stanford rolls in with AI cheat codes and UCLA interviews kūpuna. Tell me that's not rigged."

Cassandra frowned. "Wait. UCLA interviewed locals?"

Kalia nodded. "Families whose ancestors worked the estate."

Cassandra laughed, sharp and bitter. "And you saw those East Coast historians on the panel explaining Hawai'i to Hawaiians."

Kalia groaned. "Don't remind me."

They let it settle. Just two women who knew how the game worked, and hated it.

Cassandra exhaled. Then, slowly, pulled a folded photo from her bag. She hesitated. Sharing this meant something. Meant trust.

She smoothed it over her knee and handed it across.

Kalia studied the photo and frowned. "Wait... is this the box?"

The same ornate box now sitting in her hotel room after they'd dug it up.

"Maybe." Cassandra said. "Or maybe it's just a snapshot. My great-grandmother and her sister worked at that coffee plantation. One of them died there. Mānoa Marauder."

Kalia gasped, then went quiet. "So Nakano... he's feeding you clues?"

Cassandra exhaled slowly. "I found that photo during the tour. Buried in plain sight among the Oliver family's private gallery. Too convenient."

Kalia traced a finger over it. "And it just happens to match the competition."

"I don't like being used."

Kalia refolded the photo and passed it back. Her voice softened. "You've always been caught between doing what's right and what's practical."

Cassandra blinked, surprised.

"You don't seem to struggle with that," she said.

"Wrong," Kalia said, leaning against the opposite wall. "I'm stuck. Kualoa's a dead end. No one takes me seriously. I work twice as hard for half the credit."

Cassandra noticed the shift: stiff jaw, lowered gaze.

She softened. "First time I ever hear you talk real kine."

Then Kalia blindsided her. "I'm sorry."

Cassandra blinked. "For what?"

"For... Paul. When he died. I didn't know what to say, so I didn't say anything. I respected him."

The name hit hard. Paul. Her fiancé.

Cassandra swallowed. "Thanks. He was a good guy."

"He believed in you. A lot of us didn't have that."

"Is this an apology or a setup?" Cassandra asked, wary. "You're impossible."

Kalia smirked. "So I've been told."

Cassandra shook her head. Still didn't trust her. But she couldn't deny the moment.

"If the box leads somewhere," she said, "you'll get credit. At the luau."

Kalia tilted her head. "Maybe we work together. Just for the luau. Not as friends. Just for the truth."

A flicker of something passed between them. Not friendship. Not trust.

But maybe something more useful.

Then the door handle rattled and swung open.

"Ho, you two stuck in here all this time? What you doing, planning one slumber party?" Pono leaned against the doorframe, grinning. "Little sister, I swear. Only you could turn an escape room into a closet conference."

Cassandra groaned. "Outta all the cops on this island, had to be you, huh?"

"Eh, you keep finding trouble, they keep calling me." He stepped aside. "Come on. Before the hotel charge you rent."

Kalia stepped out first, brushing herself off. "Thank goodness. She insisted we check that room for the final clue. I told her it was a bad idea, but..."

Cassandra's jaw dropped. "That is not what happened—"

Pono waved them off. "Don't care. Just don't get locked in any more broom closets, yeah? I get enough paperwork already."

The crowd had gathered. Snickers. Side-eyes.

Cassandra caught Kalia's glance. That smug little smirk. The sting of betrayal was familiar, but this one landed deeper than it should've.

Was any of that real? Was the auction story true, or bait?

Cassandra shoved the doubt down. She'd play the game. But not Kalia's game.

Pono gave her a final, pointed look. *Little sister strikes again.*

She set her jaw. Walked past them both.

Didn't flinch. Didn't blink.

She didn't need validation. Didn't need anyone.

As the ballroom doors shut behind her, she told herself what she always did: *Figure it out alone.*

Cassandra trudged back to her hotel room, every step heavier than the last until the weight of the evening crashed down. The humiliation. The frustration. The creeping doubt.

She flopped onto the bed, staring at the ceiling. Pono's words still rang in her head. *Little sister strikes again.*

She was past being underestimated. Past second-guessing herself. But tonight had unraveled everything.

The case. The threats. The truth twisting in too many directions. And now Kalia, feeding her just enough information to make her doubt what was real. Was Dr. Nakano using her team? Was Linda? Had they been played from the start?

Her phone buzzed on the nightstand. A text from Andy Summers lit up the screen:

Andy

Need to vent? Late-night call's no problem.

She stared at the message, her thumb hovering over the reply button. Finally, she typed:

The faint glow of the bedside lamp cast long shadows across the room. She could switch it off. But she didn't.

It wasn't the darkness around her that unsettled her.

It was the darkness inside. The whispering doubt that she wasn't enough.

She set the phone down, her fingers brushing against the edge of her tote bag. Inside, nestled beneath her notebook, was the box.

She pulled it out and stared at it for a long moment. Hidden for decades. Still locked.

Then she remembered the escape room. The rusted key. She fished it out of her pocket, squinting at its worn shape under the lamplight.

"Worth a shot," she muttered.

She slid it into the box's keyhole. Didn't turn. Didn't even catch.

Cassandra sat back, half-expecting that. Still, it stung. "Guess some of this competition really *was* just a game."

She turned the escape room prompt over in her mind again: *What was taken remains locked behind the veil of bureaucracy. Look beyond the fine print.*

Not a puzzle. A warning. The key wasn't for the box.

It was for her brain.

"Bureaucracy," she said aloud. "Property. Paperwork."

That was the lock. Not a box or a filing cabinet. The land deeds. The trusts. The paper trail built to keep the truth buried just deep enough.

And who designed that escape room challenge?

Dr. Nakano, of course. The man wore aloha shirts and sandals like a decoy. But underneath he was the Willy Wonka of Hawaiian academia. Cryptic. Crafty. And annoyingly pleased with himself.

She shook her head. "You couldn't just send a text, old man?"

Nope. He had to create a week-long scavenger hunt to drop a hint.

The box sat waiting on the bed beside her. She let it rest, her fingers slipping away. The lamplight burned steady. Stubborn. Refusing to flicker.

It didn't waver in the face of doubt. She wished she could say the same.

Tomorrow, she'd go after the paper trail.
Tonight, she let the light keep watch.

Chapter Eighteen

C ASSANDRA PUSHED OPEN THE double doors of the conference center, chilled AC sweeping away the humid air. Students clustered at tables, scrolling footage, scribbling notes, murmuring over laptops. Finally! A room full of people treating this mystery like actual homework.

Jeff spotted her and waved her over, already spreading out a controlled jumble of printouts, zoning maps, and marked-up legal forms.

Cassandra approached with cautious curiosity. "Please tell me you found something sketchy."

He gave her a smug look. "Oh, it's sketchy with a capital S."

He held up two maps—identical in layout but not in content. One was clean, professionally printed, labeled with the Oliver estate and surrounding parcels. The other was worn, photocopied, and marked with a spiderweb of notes in yellow sticky flags and red ink.

"This first one," he said, tapping the clean version, "came from Dr. Nakano's Hawai'i Unforgotten archive. What the team got in the private papers."

Cassandra nodded. "I remember. It had the estate boundaries but no internal divisions."

Jeff laid the annotated copy on top. "But this one? This came from the city zoning office. Look here—" He pointed to two parcels outlined in red. "Same land. But suddenly, it's two separate holdings."

She leaned closer. One section was marked *Trust Transfer, 1953*. The other had a note reading *Aukai Legal Filing—No Sale Price*.

Her eyes narrowed. "Joseph Aukai?"

Jeff nodded. "The Oliver family's lawyer. Same guy. I traced the legal filing back to a zoning complaint: someone objected to new fencing. The pushback uncovered a quiet land transfer. No sale. No announcement. Just—poof—under a new trust name."

Cassandra's mind raced. "1953. That's when the Marauder case was reopened."

"Exactly. And now look—" Jeff flipped to a second sheet. "Same pattern in 1957. Different parcel. Same lawyer. Same evasive paper trail."

Cassandra set down her coffee. Her voice was low but firm. "Once is coincidence. Twice is a pattern."

"That's what I thought. The Marauder case wasn't just about murder. It was about erasing land lines."

Jocelyn appeared at her elbow, holding two waters and a bag of kettle chips. "I leave you alone for ten minutes and you're conspiring like a crime podcast."

Jeff grinned. "She's a good influence."

Cassandra gave him a mock solemn nod. "Your boyfriend just cracked open a cold case. I'm gonna need more chips."

Jocelyn gave Cassandra a long look then returned her focus to the maps.

"We found a list in the estate house," Cassandra explained. "Names, then lines drawn straight through them. Like someone was wiping them off the record."

"Tenants?" Jeff asked.

"Maybe. Or workers. Or families who were promised land and got pushed out. This might explain why."

Jeff flipped back to the original map. "If this pattern holds, it wasn't just erasure. It was consolidation. Strategic, quiet, and legal enough to avoid suspicion."

Cassandra's fingers drummed on the table. "We need to start logging land transfers that coincide with deaths. Not just at the Oliver estate. Anywhere their trust reached."

Jocelyn blinked. "You think it's bigger than one family?"

Cassandra nodded slowly. "If this went beyond the Olivers, we're not looking at a scandal. We're looking at a blueprint." The pattern had been there all along.

Jeff whistled softly. "And we thought this was just a cold case."

Jocelyn popped a chip into her mouth. "I was promised academic tourism, not corporate espionage. I wore the wrong shoes."

Cassandra turned from the table, spotting Lexi and Ethan hunched over a laptop two rows away. Lance and Logan were nearby, reviewing video footage frame by frame.

"Hey," she called and waved to get their attention. "Quick huddle."

The students gathered, pulling their chairs into a loose semicircle. Lexi balanced her boba tea precariously on her knee. Diego showed up with a half full box of malasadas, offering the remaining pastries to the others.

"We've got something new," Cassandra said, lowering her voice slightly as she nodded toward the papers Jeff had spread out. "Multiple land transfers tied to the Olivers. Quiet. Unlisted. Same lawyer involved named Joseph Aukai. Same pattern every time. One of them was in 1953, right when the Marauder case was suddenly reopened."

Lexi frowned. "So they were hiding something?"

"Or trying to bury it before anyone else looked too closely," Jeff said. "A transfer like that? No price listed, and the new owner's name links right back to the family. It was a shell game."

"Remember," Cassandra said, tapping the margin of the 1953 transfer, "no charges were ever filed in 1910. But then, forty years later, something spooked them."

"What happened in 1953?" Diego asked.

"Possibly nothing," Jocelyn said. "Or someone, maybe a descendant of one of the original workers, stepped forward with a land claim. And suddenly the Olivers had to bury the evidence. Literally and legally."

Cassandra added, "And if the police reopened the murders around that same time, it's no coincidence. They were probably sniffing too close to the truth."

Lance signed, eyes narrowed. *So the Marauder was both a killer and a distraction.*

Meg translated, and the group went quiet.

Maria was the first to speak. "And those crossed-out names? They weren't bad tenants or unpaid debts. They were threats. People who knew too much."

"Or people who were owed something," Ivy said. "If you want to disappear someone's land rights, first you erase the person."

"They'd shut it down the same way," Logan finished. "Lawyers. Quiet deals. Or worse."

Lexi was mid-reply when Cassandra noticed a flicker of movement behind them. Two students from NYU, seated not far away, had stopped typing and were clearly watching their table.

"Show's over, folks." Cassandra cut her eyes toward them, then leaned in. "Whatever. They still have to write their own report. They can't plagiarize our genius."

Lance signed, *Next meeting in a treehouse. Passwords required.*

"Noted," Cassandra dropped her voice. "We might not know who the Marauder was. But we're starting to understand what he was protecting."

"Control," Logan said. "Land, reputation, all of it."

"And Nathaniel?" Lexi asked.

"He's clinging to that same legacy," Cassandra said. "Trying to preserve something he doesn't realize is rotten underneath."

Diego snapped his fingers. "Yikes. Hope he's got a crisis therapist on speed dial."

Cassandra picked up a pen and scribbled on the map's margin:. *Timeline Update: 1953 land cover-up tied to Marauder case reopening. Cross-check Aukai trusts with Reyes/Ybarra land parcels.*

She looked around the table. "We've got to tighten the theory by tomorrow. If we can prove the pattern, we might not need to solve the murders first. The motive's right here, we just have to show our work."

"Alrighty then," Ethan muttered, dragging his hand down his face. "Homework and stale malasadas. Living the dream."

By late-morning, the conference buzz gave way to the lure of the ocean, and the Morton team eagerly headed to the beach for a much-needed break.

Cassandra went into full chaperone mode. "Remember folks, this is peak sunburn time. Maybe wear a swim shirt. Nothing like trying to sleep upright on a plane with sunburned shoulders. Reapply sunscreen now, thank me later."

Lexi groaned and pulled the collar of her shirt aside, revealing a pink, flaky streak on her shoulder. "Mine is starting to peel and it's so gross!"

"And Ethan is banned from helping anyone with the sunscreen!" Maria added, shooting him a pointed look.

Ethan groaned. "It was an accident! I really thought I got everything!"

"If her back was the size of your hand, then yes," Logan deadpanned.

Laughter rolled through the group as they scattered, some hitting the water, others staking out a spot under the palm trees.

Cassandra's ohana was already gathered near a shaded picnic table. Meg and Connor with Olivia, and Sarah wrangling her toddler, Diana, while their nephews, Kai and Makoto, darted barefoot across the sand with Tony.

Cassandra spotted her sister Kathy and plopped down beside her. "No Leilani or Keoni today?"

Kathy shook her head, watching the waves. "Leilani's halau is dancing at the luau tomorrow, so she's been busy rehearsing. And Keoni..." She sighed. "You know how he is. Work, baseball, repeat."

Cassandra followed her gaze. The boys were up to their armpits in the waves, laughing as they taught the college guys how to boogie board. The nephews were skinny as sticks, their olive-brown skin darkened from endless hours outside, their ribs visible every time they dashed back to shore. Bottomless energy. Black hair slicked back with saltwater. Grins wide with gap-toothed mischief.

Makoto bolted out of the water first, shaking his head like a wet dog, spraying her with saltwater. "Auntie Cass! Did you see my moves? Papa Sato says I could go pro!"

Cassandra wiped droplets off her arm, grinning. "If by 'pro,' he means you'll never leave the beach, then yeah. Olympic level."

Kai trotted over next, cradling something in his sandy hands. "This one's for you, Auntie." He held up a small striped shell, light brown with delicate ridges.

Cassandra's chest tightened as she took it, feeling the pull of home in something so small.

Moments like these. These were the reasons she missed Hawaii. The sound of the waves, the smell of the salt air, the bare feet buried in warm sand. The effortless way family just existed together. No grand plans, no calendar invites. Just showing up with a cooler, food, and love.

And yet, she'd chosen to leave.

She turned back to Kathy, swallowing the lump in her throat. "I wish I had more time with you guys."

Kathy shrugged, easygoing as ever. "Eh, we get it. Work trip. But next time, don't take so long to come home."

"Yeah." Her voice came out thin. "They're growing up without me."

Diana, who'd been busy gnawing on a baby carrot from a zippered snack bag, toddled over, her round cheeks still chubby with baby softness. She plopped onto Cassandra's lap without hesitation, tiny fingers sticky from half-eaten fruit.

Cassandra wrapped an arm around her, resting her cheek against Diana's curls, damp from the humid air. Maybe paradise was a state of mind.

"I'll come home next for winter break," she murmured. "I don't mind skipping the Nebraska snow for a few weeks."

Kathy nodded. "Yeah, yeah. I'll believe it when I see it."

Cassandra laughed, the sound light and easy. For the first time in days, her heart felt full. Family, sunshine, and a moment of peace she didn't have to analyze. A rare break from the puzzle. But breaks never lasted.

The scent of saltwater clung to Cassandra's skin as she stepped into the cool, polished lobby of the hotel. She could still hear the distant crash of waves, feel the warmth of Kai's small hand in hers as he pressed the shell into her palm. Everything had felt so simple: her family, the island, the sense of belonging she hadn't realized she missed so much.

Then she saw him.

Nathaniel Oliver stood near the front desk. Tall, old money Tommy Bahama vibes, his pale hair like a ghost among the living. Even in the busy crowd, he commanded attention. Not by presence, but by the space people unconsciously gave him.

Angela stood beside him, sharp lines in a synthetic blazer that looked expensive but didn't breathe.

Not confidence. Not even ambition. Hunger.

Angela had learned how power walked, how it smiled without meaning it. And now she was copying every step. She wasn't one of them, yet. But she was trying.

Nathaniel's gaze landed on Cassandra, and his lips curved into a smile that didn't reach his eyes. "Dr. Sato," he called out smoothly, his gaze dragging over her flushed face and beach coverup in a way that made her arms tighten reflexively around herself. "Making progress?"

Cassandra's good mood vanished like footprints in the sand at high tide.

She straightened her spine. "We're doing fine, thanks."

Angela stepped forward, her expression neutral, but her tone sharper than Cassandra had ever heard it. "Fine, is it? You're delving into matters that are, frankly, none of your business."

Cassandra raised an eyebrow. "Funny. The Angela I remember would've believed that truth and justice matter."

Angela's jaw twitched. For a breath, the mask slipped. Then she smoothed it over with a polite, chillingly corporate smile.

Nathaniel chuckled. "Justice? Is that what you're after? Or is this about scoring points at your little college in Nebraska?"

Cassandra's teeth clenched. "We're here to uncover the truth, Mr. Oliver. If that makes you uncomfortable, maybe you've got something to hide."

Nathaniel's smile faded, his cool arrogance replaced by a cold stare. "Careful, Dr. Sato. Digging too deep can have consequences. Not just for you, but for the people you care about. Your students, for example. Promising futures can be derailed by the smallest misstep."

Angela folded her arms. "We'd hate to see Morton College's reputation suffer over something as trivial as a misunderstanding."

Cassandra didn't look away this time. She studied Angela's face, searching for a crack, a hesitation, a flicker of the girl she used to know. Somewhere in the back of her mind, she'd hoped Angela could still be reasoned with. That maybe she hadn't sold out.

But there was nothing. Just the practiced, polished stillness of someone who'd already picked a side.

Cassandra's brain kicked back in, parsing what the mask meant. Had Nathaniel bought her? Was she a pawn in his power plays? Or had Angela convinced herself this was her best shot at something bigger?

Cassandra took a slow breath, centering herself. "Is that a threat?"

"Not at all," Nathaniel said smoothly. His smile returned, but this time, it was sharper. Hungrier. "It's advice. Some doors are better left closed."

Cassandra wasn't backing down. "Are those consequences legal, or are we talking about some vintage Oliver family intimidation tactics?"

Nathaniel's laugh was soft, almost amused. "Why not both?"

Angela's gaze didn't flinch at authority like it had a year ago. Now she carried herself like someone who thought you could buy confidence, sure that no one would notice hers came from a thrift shop.

"You've got good students," she said. "Don't let them ruin their futures chasing the wrong version of history."

She hadn't thought it was possible to dislike anyone more than Kalia, but Nathaniel and Angela were climbing the ranks. Nathaniel gave her one last unreadable glance before turning on his heel. Angela followed without hesitation.

Cassandra watched them walk away, their footsteps swallowed by the hum of hotel conversation and clinking glassware. She forced herself to unclench her fists, but the cold weight in her stomach remained.

She glanced around the lobby. No one else had noticed. The air smelled like orchids and sea salt same as it always did.

But something had shifted.

Angela wasn't bluffing. And Nathaniel wasn't done.

Chapter Nineteen

After her shower, Cassandra picked up her phone and saw Andy's unread text. She grimaced. Between the Oliver confrontation and the weight of everything else, she hadn't responded.

She was about to hit dial when another unread email notification caught her eye.

Her stomach dropped when she saw the sender.

From: Fran Morrison

Subject: Your Conduct at the Conference

Dr. Sato,

I have been made aware of concerning reports regarding your research activities during the PastForward Conference. While I trust your professional judgment, I must remind you that your actions reflect upon Morton College as an institution.

Please be advised that any additional incidents that compromise our reputation will trigger an immediate administrative review.

I look forward to discussing this upon your return.

Regards,

Fran Morrison

Cassandra stared at the screen, pulse ticking up. Polite HR language couldn't mask the real threat. She closed her eyes and let out a slow breath, a thousand thoughts colliding at once.

Concerning reports. Which ones? About the estate trespassing? Her students snooping on Angela? Was this just Fran flexing her power or was someone actively feeding her ammunition?

With the administrative shakeup back home, Cassandra's job was already in the crosshairs. This would be a convenient excuse to take her out quietly. She rubbed a hand over her forehead. Was it really just a year ago that she'd survived a tsunami, left everything behind, and moved across an ocean to take the first step toward her dream job?

Now her trip was cursed, and her job was imploding.

She tapped Andy's name.

He answered on the second ring, voice warm and easy. "Cassandra. To what do I owe the honor?"

Cassandra flopped back onto the hotel bed. "I let the students split up at our field research site, and now they all think they're auditioning for a true crime podcast. Also I may have accidentally confronted a corrupt millionaire in the hotel lobby wearing a swimsuit cover-up."

A beat of silence.

"That's... a lot," Andy said

"Tell me something great is happening back in Nebraska, because this trip is turning into a train wreck."

Andy whistled. "That bad, huh?"

"Just got an email from Fran Morrison." Her voice flattened. "You know the kind. All polite and passive-aggressive, but basically says, 'Sneeze wrong and you're fired.'"

Andy's tone shifted. "Hold up. You're not even in our time zone. How did you already make the enemies list?"

"You tell me," she muttered. "All my official updates have been squeaky clean. Students are engaged. Competing. Learning about history. The full brochure experience."

Andy didn't sound convinced. "Including the urgent care receipt I found on the shared travel expense drive?"

Cassandra groaned. "So I'm getting taken down by a teenager's foot. Fantastic."

"If I remember right it was a twisted ankle." Andy said. "At night. On private property."

"Allegedly. I was trying to keep Morton out of the paperwork."

"Fran's collecting red flags like Pokémon. That visit probably hit the daily briefing. And if your millionaire complains—"

"I doubt it. Nathaniel Oliver seems like the type who prefers threats that don't leave a paper trail."

Andy paused. "Be careful, Cass. You're playing chess with people who don't follow rules."

"I'm not playing," she said. "I'm trying to keep my students safe, solve a century old murder, and not get fired in the process."

"You've been texting me pictures of garlic shrimp, and shave ice like from a vacation," Andy said. "Meanwhile, you're running a covert op with a team of rogue undergrads and dodging HR like it's laser tag. Just hope they don't check the group chat."

"I sent you at least three 'mayhem in progress' texts last night. And that one of the hidden drawer!"

"Oh, right. And Angela Bachman's audition for 'Intern Who Would Sell Her Soul for a name badge.'"

Cassandra laughed, but it was thin. "It's not exactly covert. We knew about the team competition when we registered for the conference. More like semi-rogue. Extremely supervised rogue."

"I'm sure Fran will appreciate the nuance."

There was a beat of silence on the line. Cassandra could almost hear Andy putting the pieces together. Her vague updates, the expense report, the escalating mayhem.

"Yeah. That tracks," he said finally, with the resigned tone of someone realizing the circus had been in town all along.

Cassandra sat up. "Wait. What do you mean, that tracks?"

Andy hesitated. "I wasn't going to say anything yet, but... there's an emergency board meeting coming up. Fischer halted the construction project. Morrison's not happy."

Cassandra's heart kicked. "Fischer stopped it? He didn't tell me that."

"Probably wants to keep it quiet until he talks to Chairman Hershey and a few others. I only know because security's prepping for extra press."

She closed her eyes. A full-blown scandal was the last thing Morton College needed.

If Fischer was already on thin ice, and now Fran was lining up shots against her... this could spiral fast.

There was a time not even that long ago when her students joked about "The Queen of Doom Effect." Cassandra Sato: harbinger of chaos, destroyer of schedules, carrier of vibes so cursed she could derail entire events.

She'd laughed it off. Mostly.

But now she was thousands of miles from campus, juggling a cold case and a career implosion. Yeah. Maybe they had a point.

Andy's voice pulled her out of the spiral. "Don't panic. We've survived worse. You're Cassandra Sato. You eat bigger fires than this for breakfast."

She sighed. "It's not just Fran. It's the contest. The kids. The pressure. I feel like I'm constantly two steps behind."

"You're letting them get in your head. I've seen you shut down a student protest with a single raised eyebrow."

"That was different. You were there to run interference."

"I was also there when the Chinese consulate thought we'd stolen agricultural secrets, your dog treated the faculty lounge like his personal bathroom, and your roof caved in."

Cassandra groaned. "I thought we retired the Queen of Doom jokes."

"Never. That legacy is forever. You don't just cause chaos, Cassandra. You wreck time zones, Cassandra. *Time zones.*"

She smiled in spite of herself. "And yet, here you are. Still speaking to me."

"And Murphy's doing great, by the way. "

Her heart tugged. Not bad for a half-feral Westie who'd once refused to let her touch him. Andy had rescued Buckley a few weeks before she'd adopted Murphy, and the two dogs had bonded like littermates, making Andy the perfect sitter.

"Still sleeping on your sweatshirt like a neglected prince," Andy added. "I'm tempted to frame the look of betrayal he gives me when I don't let him on the couch."

Cassandra laughed, the tension in her shoulders loosening just a little. "He's manipulating you for peanut butter and attention."

"It's working."

She could picture it perfectly. Murphy, milking his tragic backstory for maximum effect. "I should probably just let you keep him."

"Nah," Andy said. "You're his person, like it or not."

Cassandra swallowed against the lump in her throat. She could deal with murder investigations and crumbling job security. But somehow the idea of Murphy waiting at the door, furry white tail wagging, expecting her to come home. That nearly undid her.

"Yeah," she whispered. "I guess I am."

Andy let the silence settle before shifting gears. "Alright. Enough heavy stuff. You solving this case or what?"

"I'm trying," she admitted. "But if this all blows up, I'm taking you up on that assistant security officer job."

"Murphy already claimed the good chair." Andy chuckled. "And I only pay in sarcasm and late-night donuts."

Cassandra smiled. "Tempting. But I think I'll stick to ruining my life on a slightly bigger stage."

Dinner was an informal visit to the food court, where the kids could order everything from plate lunches to noodle bowls and seafood without breaking the budget. It was loud, busy, and filled with Cassandra's favorite smells in one place: garlic, soy sauce, and grilled meats.

Afterward, the O'Briens drove back to Waipahu to spend their last night with Cassandra's parents. Jocelyn had a date with Jeff. Cassandra was peopled out, and the nearly dark horizon promised serenity.

She kicked off her sandals. The sand clung cool and fine to her toes, a welcome change from the heat of the day. Moonlight lit her way as she walked, soft and silver against the pull of dark water. At the edge of the tide, the waves swept in and out with steady rhythm, more breath than voice. She let the water brush her feet, then stepped back, just far enough to stay dry, and lowered herself onto the sand.

She hugged her knees, staring at the horizon's dark seam. It reminded her of Paul, and the nights they used to sit like this, dreaming up futures that now seemed impossibly far away.

"Paul," she murmured, thinking of how water carries spirits between this world and the next, how it touches land and leaves, again and again. She hadn't said his name out loud in months.

Scooping a handful of sand, she let the fine grains slip through her fingers, a quiet offering to the past. The wind caught the last specks, carrying them away, as if the ocean itself was listening.

"I don't know if I'm even meant to be here."

The words hung in the air, unanswered. She sighed and looked up at the stars, the weight of her doubts pressing down. "Am I even helping anyone? Or is this all just... noise?"

"Talking to yourself now?"

She looked up to see her brother standing nearby, his wiry silhouette unmistakable. He carried a small cooler and an easy smile that faded as he got closer.

"Eh, brah," she said softly. "You've been MIA."

He dropped the cooler onto the sand and sat beside her. "Jocelyn called. Said you looked like you could use some big brother time."

For a moment, neither spoke. The ocean stretched out before them, dark and endless.

Cassandra tried to smile but didn't quite manage it. "I thought you were too busy to stop by."

Keoni shrugged, pulling out two cans of sparkling water and handing her one. "Family's complicated. But you already knew that."

She accepted the can, tapping the top lightly before cracking it open. "I'm starting to think I don't understand family at all."

"That's the thing. You don't have to understand it to be in it."

Cassandra fiddled with the tab. "Some days I miss you all so desperately I can't breathe. But others, I'm clicking along at work and moving closer to making my dreams a reality."

He chuckled softly, shaking his head. "Queen of the college. Always so dramatic."

"You must be confusing me with Sarah." Cassandra glared at him, but it lacked heat. "I'm serious. Every time I think I'm getting somewhere, something or someone knocks me over."

He leaned back on his hands, the breeze ruffling his hair. "Let me guess. Paul?"

She stiffened, caught off guard. "What about him?"

"You tell me," he said gently. "You ever wonder if all this chasing justice is about proving something to him? Or to yourself?"

"I don't know. Sometimes, I can almost hear him laughing at me for taking on so much at once. He used to say I needed to take a breath and choose a battle." She smiled faintly. "And then he'd remind me to make sure I won."

"Sounds about right. Paul always thought you could do anything. So why don't you?"

"Because it's not just him." Her voice broke a little. "I keep thinking about Auntie Hana. We didn't even know her story. And no one told us a thing. Not Mom. Not anyone. I found out from a quilt, Keoni. A quilt." She swallowed. "She was ohana. And somehow... she got lost."

Keoni's jaw tightened. "She didn't just vanish, Cass. She fought back. She hid that map for a reason. You're the one who found it. You're the one who's gonna make sure people remember her."

She sighed, pressing her fingers into the cool sand. "So, you already know about the map and Hana?"

"You think I don't have my own sources?"

She narrowed her eyes. "Jocelyn?"

He cracked open his drink, taking his time before answering. "And Mom. And Dad. Pono too. You really thought we weren't keeping tabs?"

Cassandra exhaled, shaking her head. "Great. Mom's turned it into her own family gossip hour."

"Oh, for sure. She's narrating this whole investigation like a crime podcast. Except instead of analyzing the evidence, she mostly says you should eat more and get some sleep."

Cassandra gave a short laugh, but her shoulders stayed tense. "The map was just a start. Hana died, and nobody cared. They called it a tragedy, but they never looked too hard. She didn't matter to them. No one told her story. Now... I'm trying. I really am."

He bumped her shoulder lightly. "So don't let them bury it. Finish what she started."

She stared at him, her eyes glistening. "What if I can't?"

Keoni sighed, running a hand through his hair. "You think you're the only one with doubts? Every day, I wonder if I'm doing enough for my boys, for Leilani, for myself. It's not like I've got it all figured out either, Sis. But you keep showing up."

She let out a bitter laugh. "Between Nathaniel Oliver threatening me, Kalia undermining me, and the ghosts of this case... I'm wondering if I should just go back to Nebraska and let them win."

He grinned faintly. "You're Cassandra Sato. You don't quit. No matter how hard the waves hit, you hang on."

She blinked, the weight of his words settling into place.

"Besides," he added with a smirk, "I'm pretty sure Miss Perfect Hair would lose her mind if you actually solved this thing."

"What's that supposed to mean? Are you saying *my* hair isn't perfect?" She snorted.

He tilted his head, pretending to assess. "Nothing wrong... if you're going for 'windswept professor who forgot to pack her hairbrush.'"

She swatted at him, grinning as he ducked away. "Rude." she huffed, but the tension in her chest loosened just a little.

"Hey, you asked." He nudged her knee with his. "But seriously... when did you stop trusting that you're the right person for this?"

Cassandra laughed softly, wiping her eyes. "You really know how to ruin a perfectly good pity party."

"That's my job. Yours is standing up for people who don't have a voice."

Cassandra blinked, the realization hitting like a wave crashing against the shore. "That's it, isn't it?" She whispered. "That's the connection."

She pulled out the Oliver family photo again, her fingers tracing the worn edges. "The ties that bind," she murmured. The phrase looped through her mind, connecting Nathaniel's threats, the missing property, and the wooden box they'd unearthed. "They were never just hiding stolen land. They were hiding the truth."

He dropped his empty can into the cooler. "So what's next? You just gonna sit here all night?"

Cassandra stood, brushing sand off her legs. "Let's see what he's hiding."

Keoni rose beside her, his smile warm. "That's my sister."

They paused in silence, the moonlight dancing across the waves.

Cassandra studied the water, waiting for the right moment.

She was ready to ride. Or wipe out trying.

Chapter Twenty

CASSANDRA AND MEG STROLLED across the lush green expanse of Kapi'olani Park, the morning sun already warming the air. The salty breeze drifted from nearby Waikīkī Beach, mixing with the smell of fresh-cut grass and someone grilling nearby. Towering banyan trees cast shifting shadows across the picnic tables where her students had gathered.

Despite the peaceful setting, her team was buzzing.

Andrew sat cross-legged in the shade, Skipper perched comfortably on his shoulder. Next to him, Ethan wore a smug grin like he'd just solved the Wordle of the day in one guess.

Logan and Brandon hunched over a laptop, their laughter punctuated by exaggerated gasps of horror.

Diego sprawled on the picnic table, tossing a hacky sack in the air while Maria scribbled notes in a journal.

It would have looked like any other group of college kids cramming for finals. If not for the intensity in their faces.

"Do I even want to know?" Cassandra asked, setting her coffee on the weathered wooden table.

"Oh, you absolutely do," Logan replied, tilting the laptop screen toward her. "We were reviewing Skipper's GoPro footage of the epic fails from the past few days for laughs, but... this isn't funny."

"Hey!" Andrew feigned indignation. "I'll have you know Skipper doesn't fail. He improvises. And besides, this—" He pointed at the laptop triumphantly. "—is the real deal."

"Just keep him away from my sandwich," Diego muttered.

She stepped over the bench and sat down. "Show me."

Cassandra leaned in while the video played in grainy, slightly nause-ating footage as the camera bounced in sync with Skipper's flight path. The hotel lobby came into focus, and Cassandra's stomach dropped. She recognized this moment.

Nathaniel Oliver and Angela appeared on screen near the front desk. Her arms were crossed, and her whole body tensed .

Cassandra said, "There. Pause it. Go back. She says something. Look at her body language."

Jocelyn squinted. "She's annoyed at Nathaniel, but not surprised."

Diego sighed. "Should've let me handle it. I was one Elsa icicle away from breaking her."

"Yeah," Ethan scoffed. "You can't build a snowman in Hawaii."

Diego grinned, "No, bro. I was gonna make her Let Go of her secrets!"

The Frozen thing was funny, but enough already. She knew they were just excited and trying to make the game fun, but she was having a hard time acting like it wasn't personal. She shot him a stink eye.

Logan resumed the recording, picking up with Nathaniel and Angela squared off in the lobby, unaware of the silent witness above them.

Nathaniel's voice was sharp, edged with frustration. "They know something. I saw it on their faces. Somebody gave them a trail to follow."

Angela crossed her arms. "They're students, not FBI agents."

"They were digging," he growled. "In my landscaping. With *her*. That old woman has lived rent-free in the groundskeeper's shack for decades. Now she's giving tours?"

Angela looked wary. "Linda? She barely speaks. She signs."

"Exactly. And I was fool enough to think that meant she didn't have an agenda." His voice dripped with disdain. "They were standing over a fresh hole like they'd struck oil. I don't know what they pulled up, but I know who helped them."

Angela lowered her voice. "You really think Linda gave them some-thing?"

"She's been sentimental for years. Always planting flowers by the memorial trees. Skulking around at night like a ghost. Watching. Judg-ing."

Angela's face tightened. "They'd still have to prove it."

Nathaniel's tone smoothed, but his eyes were flinty. "If they try, we'll shut it down. That cottage is still on my land. Her grandfather earned that cottage. She didn't."

Angela's voice dropped. "You'd really evict her?"

Nathaniel's tone turned smooth, almost casual. "If they're getting close, she's not just a liability. You know what that means."

Angela didn't answer at first. Her jaw worked slightly, like she was chewing on something bitter. She asked quietly, "You'd really go that far?"

He didn't respond. Just adjusted his cufflinks and turned toward the elevators.

Angela stayed frozen for a beat, her eyes fixed on the floor. When she finally moved, it was slower, like her heels had suddenly grown heavier.

For a full ten seconds, no one spoke. Cassandra's pulse roared in her ears. If the Olivers discovered they had this footage... what could they do?

Then Diego let out a low whistle. "That's not great."

"Not great?" Maria gaped. "That's straight-up movie villain dialogue!"

Cassandra didn't speak. Her thoughts spun too fast, colliding. Linda's warning, Nathaniel's threats, the box, the photo. As much as she wanted to win, this was about telling the story. And consequences.

Lexi was already typing furiously on her phone. "Like a true crime podcast. 'The Chilling Last Words of the Oliver Dynasty—'"

They were so close to solving at least part of the puzzle. But deciding the approach required subtlety. Not exactly her team's strength. Cassandra held up a hand, forcing herself to think past the adrenaline. "This... is evidence. Real evidence."

Andrew pumped his fist. "Boom! Case closed. We won. Game over."

The luau was the obvious setting to reveal the GoPro video, but the stakes were dangerously high.

"Let's not get ahead of ourselves," Cassandra said. "We need to figure out how to present this without implicating ourselves. Divide and conquer."

"Logan and Brandon, start with the video. Transcribe the audio clean, clip what we need, and check earlier footage for more red flags."

"On it," Logan said, already pulling up files.

"Diego, Ethan, you map our timeline. From the VR exhibit to the estate dig. Every clue, every contradiction."

"Or," Maria countered, arms crossed, "suppose they figure out we have this? I don't think Nathaniel's idea of 'handling it' involves hugs and apologies."

Lance signed, *You're assuming we'll even get the chance to use it. The conference leaders might shut us down if they think we stepped outside the competition rules.*

"The Olivers have connections," Brandon added. "What if they get us expelled? Or arrested?"

"Oh, please," Ethan said with a dramatic wave of his hand. "Are we seriously worried about that guy? He's just a spoiled old dude with Malfoy hair."

"And access to a lot of lawyers," Ivy pointed out. "Ethan, this isn't a joke."

"I'm not joking," Lexi said. "We have real evidence. It's about justice for Dr. Sato's Auntie Hana and the other victims."

Their evidence for identifying the Manoa Marauder was sketchy, but if they could just push Nathaniel into doing something reckless, maybe he'd reveal what he knew.

"Lexi, Maria, Ivy—you're on framing. Tie the property records to Linda's family story. Sure, we'd like to catch a killer. But more importantly, we're restoring stolen voices."

Lexi grinned. "Got it. We'll make it unforgettable."

"Linda kept her secret all these years because she didn't trust anyone," Meg said quietly. "Or maybe she was scared the truth would die with her. Either way, she bet on our team. And somehow, it worked."

As the team bickered about whether this was a win or a get-out-of-town moment, Cassandra's eyes swept over the scattered notebooks, laptops, and zipper bags filled with old photos, receipts, and hastily scribbled notes. They were pulling everything together.

"Okay, let's focus," Cassandra cut in. "Did everyone bring their physical clues this time?"

Diego dropped his blue stress ball in the pile with a dramatic flourish.

"RIP to the creepy well theory," he said. "That dead end nearly cost me my free flashlight swag."

Lexi snorted. "It felt haunted, but there was nothing there."

Cassandra nodded. "No bodies. No secret hatch. Just a metaphor, apparently."

The group chuckled, the tension easing a notch. Declaring the well a bust allowed them to let go of a shared ghost.

Meg said, "Same with the creepy phone call you got. Could have been anyone trying to get us to back off. Even one of the other teams."

"I'd say it was NYU or the Stanford bros," Andrew guessed, "but you're right. Hard to prove."

Cassandra caught Brandon glaring meaningfully at Logan. Soon everyone was quietly waiting for him.

Logan froze mid-chew on a piece of mango. "I didn't steal anything valuable," Logan protested. "I picked up paperwork, and the hankie with the pressed flowers. Better than letting them rot in a drawer."

Lexi perked up. "Wait. What kind of flowers?"

Logan rummaged through his backpack, pulling out a delicate, timeworn handkerchief with faded pressed flowers inside. "I dunno. I just thought it looked kinda sentimental, you know?"

Maria's expression changed. "Logan, where exactly did you find this? It has J.O. on it. For Jean Oliver, right?"

He frowned, thinking. "The hidden drawer in the estate's exhibit room. Same place as the business papers."

Cassandra's mind raced. If Jean or Hana had hidden it together intentionally, then it was evidence.

Andrew raised his hand. "And me? What's my role, boss?"

"You," Cassandra said, pointing to the parrot on his shoulder, "keep Skipper's footage under wraps. No accidental leaks, no showing it off. We can't risk the Olivers catching wind of this."

Andrew placed a palm over his heart solemnly. "Oh, Captain, my Captain."

Meg shot her a look, remembering another Dead Poet's Society moment in Nebraska. Cassandra coughed into her hand to cover a laugh.

As Ethan took another look at the handkerchief and flowers, then passed it to Diego, Cassandra exhaled and pulled out her phone. She needed more visuals to jog her memory.

Her fingers scrolled quickly through her photo gallery, past grainy screenshots of documents, newspaper clippings, and—there. The shots she'd taken in the Oliver estate's gallery.

She hadn't had time to study them properly. Her fingers hovered over the phone screen. She swiped again. One image, then another, before pausing on a different photo.

Jean Oliver, seated near a window, with two young seamstresses. Cassandra had seen the photo before, but something felt different this time.

Her gaze moved lower, taking in the sewing projects on their laps. One of the young women held a piece of folded fabric in her hands, but the other...

A doll.

A small fabric doll, faded with age, its stitches neat but well-loved.

Her mother's words echoed in her mind. Something about a doll from her great-grandmother's things, stored in Waipahu.

Cassandra's pulse jumped and chicken skin crawled down her shoulders and arms. The photo was history, family, and justice rolled into one.

The pieces of this investigation were chaotic and frustrating, but this was real. Something she could touch, something that had been held by the woman whose memory she was trying so hard to honor.

Jocelyn frowned. "What is it?"

Her throat tightened. "The doll. Mom said she still has one from that time. I just—I need to hold it."

Jocelyn studied her for a moment, then nodded.

Cassandra grabbed her bag and announced to the students. "I'm going to Waipahu."

Jocelyn didn't even argue. She just grabbed her bag and followed.

As they hurried toward the parking lot, she barely registered the students shifting into action behind her. Lexi and Maria huddled over the maps. Logan booted up the laptop, and Andrew whispered something to Skipper, who let out an indignant squawk.

Cassandra's instincts screamed that they were on the edge of something big.

She just hoped she wasn't too late.

Chapter Twenty-One

C ASSANDRA PULLED INTO HER parents' driveway in Waipahu, killing the engine and gripping the steering wheel for an extra second. The house was quiet, no sign of her parents' cars under the carport, just a couple of bikes leaning against the house where her nephews had probably left them.

Jocelyn unbuckled. "Okay, game plan?"

Cassandra drummed her fingers on the steering wheel. "We go in, find the plastic tub, and get out before Mom decides we've lost our minds."

Jocelyn smirked. "So, a heist."

"A well-intentioned heist," Cassandra amended.

They slipped inside with the key Cassandra had never returned after college, not that Mom ever noticed. The house was still and cool, the scent of rice and Spam lingering from breakfast, mingling with the ever-present lemon-scented cleaner.

The closet in her parents' bedroom was exactly as she remembered: a few dresses, two suits, and the rest stacked with precariously balanced plastic totes.

Cassandra pointed. "She said it's in here somewhere."

Jocelyn reached for the sliding wooden closet door and gave it a tug. It groaned but didn't budge.

Cassandra scowled. "Figures. The track's old. Probably rusted."

Jocelyn wiped her hands on her jeans. "Okay, so, do we need a crowbar?"

Cassandra huffed, marching off to the bathroom closet. She returned with a can of WD-40, shaking it dramatically. "Nah, just good old-fashioned problem-solving."

She sprayed along the metal track, then gave the door another shove. Still stuck.

Jocelyn raised an eyebrow. "So... are we still calling this a heist or just admitting we've broken into your mom's house and immediately failed?"

Cassandra growled in frustration, grabbed the top edge of the door, and gave it one last determined yank.

The entire thing popped out of its track and crashed to the floor with a WHAM.

Jocelyn winced. "Okay. Not exactly subtle."

Cassandra placed her hands on her hips. "Look, Mom, we broke into your house, but we fixed the closet door."

Jocelyn doubled over laughing. "Yeah. Real smooth."

They spent ten minutes wrestling it back into place, grumbling the entire time.

Jocelyn wiped her forehead. "Look at us. Just two responsible adults. Breaking and fixing the same thing in under ten minutes."

Cassandra checked her watch. They didn't have time to waste. If this key or clue was real, they needed to be moving.

Just as Cassandra successfully slid the door open, a sharp knock at the front door made them both freeze.

Jocelyn's eyes widened. "If that's a ghost, I'm out."

Cassandra peeked through the blinds and groaned. "Worse."

Mrs. Kobayashi.

Cassandra cracked the door open, immediately met with the sharp-eyed scrutiny of her parents' longtime neighbor.

"Ohhh, your mom not home?" Mrs. Kobayashi peered inside, clearly assessing the situation. "You two looking real suspicious."

Jocelyn, with forced brightness: "Aloha, Auntie! No worries, just—uh, just grabbing something for Cassandra's mom."

Mrs. Kobayashi folded her arms. "That car outside. Who staying over? One boy?"

Jocelyn's eyes widened. "No! No boys. Just us. Just the two of us."

Mrs. Kobayashi squinted. "Hmm. You sure?"

She was grilling them like they were still twelve. Cassandra sighed, trying to keep her patience. "Auntie, we're just here to pick up something. No scandal, yah."

The woman remained unconvinced but finally shuffled off, muttering something about 'haole friends' and 'too much drama lately.'

Cassandra shut the door, locking it for good measure. "I swear, if I ever decide to commit an actual crime, I'm doing it in another neighborhood."

Jocelyn snorted. "Nah. She'd still know."

They returned to the closet, pulling down bins and sorting through old photo albums, school yearbooks, and Christmas decorations.

Jocelyn groaned. "Respect to your mom for the organization, but *where* is the doll?"

Cassandra sighed, shifting another box aside. "She said it was in storage. Maybe she forgot which bin?"

Finally, buried under an old suitcase, they found a dusty bin so old the lid was cracked.

Jocelyn heaved it out. "Jackpot."

Cassandra tucked a stray hair behind her ear. "C'mon, let's at least make this worth it."

They lifted the lid, both leaning over expectantly.

Inside were neatly folded quilts, a few small trinkets, a silver brooch, and—

The doll.

Cassandra's breath hitched.

It was exactly like the one in the old photo—hand-stitched, worn soft with age, the fabric slightly discolored from time.

She picked it up gently, fingers running over the tiny, embroidered face. For a moment, she just... held it.

Jocelyn nudged her. "You okay?"

Cassandra nodded, swallowing against the unexpected lump in her throat. "Yeah... I just—"

She'd seen this doll in the photo before. But holding it now felt real and fragile, touched by Hana's hands. The nostalgia hit harder than expected. Mom had known it was here. But had she ever looked at it, really looked? Or had it become another relic of a painful story no one wanted to tell?

The front door opened.

Both of them froze.

Then—

"Why is there a strange car in my driveway?" Her voice carried from the front hall, sharp, but laced with something else. Worry.

Cassandra and Jocelyn whipped their heads toward each other. Mom.

Footsteps stormed into the house, followed by the unmistakable flick of the kitchen light.

"Cassandra. Kéhau. Sato."

Jocelyn muttered, "Ohhhh, you're in trouble."

Cassandra shoved the bin lid shut and sat on her hands like that would somehow make her look less guilty.

Mom appeared in the doorway, arms crossed. Not quite nuclear, but she was definitely teetering on the edge. "Why does it look like a raccoon broke into my closet?"

Before she could answer, another voice chimed in from behind her mother.

"You do realize breaking and entering is a crime, yeah?"

Pono.

Cassandra groaned. "Mom, we did not break in. I used my key."

"Oh," Mom said. "So you just thought you could waltz in here like it's Costco samples? Help yourself?"

But instead of yelling, she just sighed and shook her head. "You could've called, you know."

Pono stepped into view, arms folded, grinning like he'd just caught her red-handed. Which he had. "I told you it was only a matter of time before you got arrested."

Jocelyn sighed. "Well, if I'm getting arrested, at least it's with Cassandra."

Pono chuckled, shaking his head. "Oh, this is good."

Cassandra shot him a stink eye. "What are *you* doing here?"

"Your mom called when she saw the rental parked in her drive-way," he replied bluntly. "You've stirred up a hornet's nest, Cass. I heard your name in the station before I even clocked in."

Cassandra's stomach clenched. "Wait. HPD guys are talking? I didn't realize how far this went."

"I don't know. I'm just a lowly Sergeant. I heard some guys at the station talking about the Mānoa Marauder. Not a coincidence, eh? You're walking into a storm, and I'm not sure you're ready for it."

Cassandra crossed her arms. "Thanks for the vote of confidence. I know it's just a bunch of college kids playing detectives, but they are smart college kids."

Mom let out a slow, exasperated breath and gestured at the closet, frowning at the tools still on the floor. "And what happened here?"

Jocelyn said, "...Structural failure."

Cassandra, added deadpan, "We fixed it."

Mom squinted. "Fixed it or broke it first?"

Cassandra hesitated. "...Both."

Jocelyn demonstrated the smooth sliding of the door. It worked perfectly, twice. Then stuck again.

Mom pinched the bridge of her nose. "Kitchen. Now."

Cassandra and Jocelyn trudged into the kitchen like two teenagers awaiting sentencing.

Mom poured herself tea, settling into her seat across from them with the unimpressed stare of a judge deciding whether to hand out life in prison or just hard labor.

Pono leaned against the counter, arms crossed, smirking.

Mom folded her hands. "So. Explain."

Cassandra exhaled and set the doll on the table.

Mom frowned. "That old thing? You tore apart my closet for *that?*"

Cassandra's voice stayed steady. "Mom, this isn't just a doll. It's Hana's. It might be the only thing she left behind."

A flicker of something passed through Mom's expression. Worry, or memory, or both.

Jocelyn lifted the bin lid and pulled out a quilt, smoothing the soft, floral fabric across the table.

Pono crossed his arms. "You folks got me thinking. I drove past the Mānoa estate earlier today. Saw security patrolling. A lot of security for a so-called *historical site*. Made me wonder what's in there that's worth protecting?"

Cassandra's stomach twisted. "That's what I've been trying to tell you. They're hiding something."

Pono nodded. "With the security I saw, I think you got them spooked."

Mom exhaled, rubbing her forehead. "I know you're chasing answers, but Cassandra, this... this is bigger than you think. Does Dr. Nakano even know you're doing all this?"

Cassandra stiffened. "Why would you ask that?"

Mom gave her a knowing look. "Because everyone's talking. Mrs. Kobayashi's daughter works at the conference. She said there's tension."

Cassandra hesitated. Nakano had *steered* them in the right direction hadn't he? But there were too many coincidences. Too many missing pieces.

Pono leaned against the counter. "You might not like the answer if you start digging there."

Cassandra swallowed hard. Before she could respond, Jocelyn suddenly stiffened.

"There's something else," she murmured.

She ran her fingers over the quilt's seams and found a stitched pocket.

Mom leaned in. "What are you—"

Jocelyn slid her hand inside.

Empty.

Mom frowned. "It's empty?"

Jocelyn checked another quilt. Same thing.

Pono frowned. "You're saying someone hid stuff in there before?"

Auntie Hana's hands had stitched these quilts. She had hidden something before. Cassandra's pulse quickened. Her gaze dropped to the doll. She pressed her thumbs into its stiff fabric. Something felt... wrong.

Jocelyn caught her hesitation. "What?"

Cassandra turned the doll over, running her fingers over the seams. A few stitches were loose. Carefully, she pulled at them.

A small, metallic *clink* hit the table.

Silence.

Mom's eyes widened. Not just at the key, but at the look on her daughter's face.

She didn't say anything, but her hand moved instinctively toward Cassandra's arm. Just for a second.

Pono leaned forward, staring at the aged key now lying on the table between them.

Jocelyn let out a breathless laugh. "No way."

Cassandra swallowed hard, picking it up.

Auntie Hana had left behind memories.

And a message.

Pono finally broke the silence. "Okay," he said. "Who wants to tell me what that unlocks?"

Cassandra set the doll down on the kitchen table, her pulse still hammering from the discovery. The tarnished key sat beside it, catching the light. It had been buried inside the doll's seams for who knows how long, waiting.

Jocelyn rubbed her temples. "I can't believe we actually found a key inside a doll."

Pono crossed his arms. "I can't believe you two are surprised. At this point, I wouldn't blink if you pulled out statehood documents, though that might actually be less complicated than this case."

Cassandra barely heard them. Her mind was already racing ahead.

The box.

She spun toward the doorway. "Be right back."

Pono raised a brow. "Where are you going now?"

She slipped out the door, hurried to the rental car, and popped the trunk. There, wedged between her tote bag and Jocelyn's sweatshirt, sat the old wooden box. Cassandra grabbed it, tracing her fingers over the carved details as she carried it inside.

Back in the kitchen, she placed it gently on the table. The wood was worn smooth, the metal latch dulled but sturdy.

Jocelyn inhaled sharply. "Moment of truth."

Pono nudged her. "Any bets on what's inside? I say gold bars."

"Land deeds," Jocelyn countered. "Or a confession from a serial killer."

Mom eyed the box warily, arms crossed. "If a centipede crawls out of that thing, I'm burning it."

Cassandra ignored them, slotting the antique key into the lock. It fit perfectly.

She turned it.

Click.

The latch gave way.

Cassandra hesitated for just a beat, then lifted the lid.

Silence.

Jocelyn frowned. "Wait... what?"

Pono muttered a curse. "You gotta be kidding me."

Mom leaned in, eyes narrowing. "Well? What's in there?"

Cassandra swallowed hard, her fingers tracing the edges of the contents. The weight of the past sat heavy in her hands.

She exhaled.

"This..." Her voice was barely above a whisper. "This proves they were connected. And someone wanted them both silenced."

Inside, nestled on a faded velvet lining, was a black-and-white photograph. Two figures stood side-by-side in front of the Oliver estate. Manuel Reyes, unmistakable in his work shirt, and a woman in a city clerk's uniform. Her name was scrawled on the back in faded ink: Mary Pauahi.

Chapter Twenty-Two

T HE RHYTHMIC POUNDING OF pahu drums reverberated through the luau grounds, a heartbeat of tradition that made Cassandra's own pulse quicken. The scent of roasted kalua pig mingled with the floral sweetness of plumeria lei, and despite the stress of impending doom, she inhaled deeply, as if she could store the moment in her pores.

The air buzzed with laughter and clinking glasses, but Cassandra knew better. This was a battlefield masquerading as a party.

She adjusted her tote bag, where the wooden box, the map, and the photograph of Mary Pauahi and Manuel Reyes were securely hidden. Nearby, her students were stationed like chess pieces, blending in but alert. Maria and Ivy hovered near the stage, phones poised like tourists, but ready to document everything. Andrew stood a few feet away, Skipper perched on his shoulder, the parrot's bright gaze scanning the crowd.

Cassandra eyed the guests. No sign of Kalia. Her stomach sank. Kalia had promised to help, hadn't she? Was she planning to let Cassandra's team crash and burn, only to swoop in at the last second for the credit?

At the bar, Nathaniel Oliver stood laughing with a group of local businessmen, wearing his pressed aloha shirt and leather sandals. To any outsider, he looked at ease, fooling anyone who hadn't heard him threaten her the day before. But Cassandra noted the way his fingers tapped against his glass, restless. And how his eyes darted across the crowd. Not just watching but searching.

Angela hovered nearby, her sharp gaze flickering through the guests like a predator. Cassandra had no doubt she was scanning for threats.

Near the buffet, Lance and Logan chatted animatedly in ASL pretending to argue over the merits of poi. Ethan pointed at a mountain of pork, gesturing wildly while Lexi yanked on his arm. Cassandra could just make out their voices.

"You think I could eat this whole pig by myself?" Ethan boomed.

Lexi swatted him. "I think you could embarrass us all by trying. Focus, genius."

Just then, Leilani appeared from the performers' tent, her elegant floral muʻumuʻu swishing as she approached. Cassandra's sister-in-law looked stunning, but her face was drawn, and her usual brightness seemed dimmed.

"Leilani," Cassandra said, stepping away from the group and giving her a gentle hug, careful not to mess up her fancy updo. "It's so good to finally see you!"

Leilani offered a small smile. "I'm sorry I haven't been around, Cass. Things have been... busy."

Cassandra hesitated, sensing more beneath the words. "Is everything okay?"

Leilani's smile wavered, but she nodded. "I promise, we'll catch up soon. Keoni said you've got your hands full with your students. And in his words, 'you're looking for trouble, again.'" She smiled kindly. "I just wanted to say ...whatever happens, you've got this. You've always had a way of willing your goals into being. It's inspiring."

Cassandra swallowed the lump in her throat. "Thank you. That means a lot."

Leilani squeezed her arm, her eyes briefly glancing toward the main stage. "I should get back. The hālau's up next. If you need anything just yell. Loud."

"Don't tempt me," Cassandra said with a wry smile. Leilani laughed softly and disappeared into the crowd.

Cassandra gazed after her but didn't have time to wonder what was really going on with Leilani and her brother, because the drums quieted for a heavyset man who sat on a stool and began strumming a slack-key guitar. The lilting melodies of his clear voice quieted the crowd and as one they shifted toward the stage.

The haunting music sent a spark directly to her heart, pulling her into the island's history and folklore. "Don't lose focus," she whispered to herself.

Cassandra moved closer to the tiki bar. She set her bag on a high stool, removing a sandal to clear a pebble that had been rubbing the edge of her foot.

Cassandra stage whispered to the students nearby, "You all know the plan. Keep it subtle. We don't want to tip them off too early."

Brandon muttered, "Define subtle."

Right on cue, Skipper swooped overhead like a tactical spy, his chest-mounted GoPro gleaming under the tiki torches.

"Because *he* didn't get the memo," Brandon added, pointing skyward.

Maria glanced at her phone, her eyes widening. "You need to see this," she whispered. "Now."

Cassandra took the phone. Onscreen a scanned newspaper clipping showed a legal notice from 1910, listing Mary Pauahi as the certifying clerk on a property transfer.

A ripple of realization passed through her. "Where did you find this?"

"After you showed us the photo of Mary Pauahi and Manuel Reyes, Lexi and I dug deep into Mary's background. Turns out, she worked for the city." Maria tapped the screen. "She handled land deeds. If she saw anything shady, like forged records, she'd have known."

Cassandra's mind raced. The Oliver estate. The missing land records. Mary had been a witness.

"If she and Reyes were involved," Maria continued, "maybe she was trying to help him fight to keep land for the workers or tenants?"

Cassandra exhaled sharply. "She wasn't in the wrong place at the wrong time. She was a threat. And someone made sure she never exposed the truth."

Moments later, Andrew sidled up next to her.

"Skipper's on the move," Andrew whispered, his phone raised to track the GoPro feed. The parrot squawked loud enough to turn a few heads.

"Can you tell him not to blow our cover?" Cassandra hissed, her hand tightening on her bag. Inside, the contents felt heavier than ever.

Andrew grinned. "He's a bird, not a secret agent."

"Then maybe we should've brought an actual spy," Logan quipped, signing his words to Lance as he spoke.

Lance rolled his eyes and signed back. *This bird is going to get us all kicked out.*

"Keep it together," Cassandra said, her voice low but firm. "The luau is crowded, but that doesn't mean we can't be seen."

"Or heard," Logan agreed.

A rustling movement caught her attention. Angela had turned sharply, her hawk-like eyes locking onto the stool where Cassandra's bag rested.

Angela's gaze snapped back to Cassandra. Her expression darkened. Angela's voice crackled into her comms, sharp and urgent. "They've got the original documents. We have a theft in progress. Intercept the girl with the messenger bag."

Moments later, several men in all-black outfits fanned out across the luau, moving with quiet, deliberate steps.

Cassandra hefted the bag onto her shoulder. "Heads up, folks," she said, voice low but urgent. "Scatter!"

The students dispersed like startled chickens into the crowd just as a vendor cart rumbled past. Cassandra seized the opportunity, darting toward the food stalls, hoping to lose herself among the brightly lit signs for shave ice and malasadas. She caught a glimpse of Nathaniel, watching from a distance, unreadable.

"Don't let her get away!" Angela barked, joining the chase.

Cassandra cursed quietly and wove through clusters of tourists, narrowly avoiding a vendor pushing a cart of coconuts.

"Watch it, lady!" the vendor shouted as one of the coconuts toppled off and rolled straight into Angela's path. She stumbled, nearly losing her balance.

"Nice assist," Cassandra muttered, darting toward a row of folding tables covered in cheap beaded jewelry and pareo fabric.

Angela surged after her again, grabbing at the strap of Cassandra's bag. She yanked her arm free. T-shirts exploded in a rainbow cascade. "Sorry!" she shouted, breathless, as the vendor cursed behind her.

Her resolve faltered. If Angela or security got the bag, it was over. The documents would vanish. The truth, buried again. She'd be detained for sure. Fired, probably. The Olivers would walk. And Nakano? He'd play neutral until the dust settled.

The only way to protect the evidence, the students, and the truth was to go public, *now*. They needed a spotlight. A crowd. A way to force Nathaniel's hand before security shut them down.

She bolted toward the stage, nearly colliding with a hula dancer holding a large prop spear.

Cassandra yelped, ducking under the weapon and vaulting onto the stage, panting and disheveled. The drums faltered, the dancers fading back.

And there, among them, was Kalia. Her pā'ū skirt swayed as she turned, her poised expression unreadable. Was she here to help or to sabotage?

Leilani stood near the edge of the stage, arms crossed. Watching like Manono, the ancient Hawaiian warrior princess.

For a moment, Cassandra's confusion spiked. Were Kalia and Leilani working together?

Angela stormed forward, flanked by security.

Cassandra's students raised their phones.

Nathaniel Oliver stepped into the center of it all, calm but coiled tight. "Dr. Sato," he said smoothly. "Care to explain what exactly you're doing?"

Cassandra lifted her chin. "I think you already know."

Angela hovered close, her stance rigid and ready. The all-black security detail loomed at the edges of the crowd, ready to pounce at a moment's notice.

Lexi's voice rang out, cutting through the crowd. "She's got the missing documents! The ones Oliver's been hiding!"

Murmurs swept through the audience. Rival teams started booing.

Cassandra saw the opportunity click on Dr. Nakano's face. The stakes, the opportunity, the drama.

"Let them finish," he said, his voice calm but calculated. "The steering committee will evaluate the evidence in its entirety before awarding the cold case cash prize."

Though his support steadied her, Cassandra's gut churned with unease. Nakano's calm control hinted at ulterior motives, but she pushed the thought aside, focusing on the moment.

Then, Kalia stepped forward.

She moved with the effortless grace of a dancer, the flickering tiki torches casting long shadows across her poised figure. "This is what you're looking for." Kalia pressed a folded paper into Cassandra's palm.

Cassandra frowned, unfolding a scanned newspaper clipping. A black-and-white funeral announcement filled the page.

MRS. LILLIAN NAKANO, 80, PASSED AWAY PEACEFULLY IN HONOLULU. SHE IS SURVIVED BY HER SONS, MASARU AND KENJI NAKANO, AND HER GRANDCHILDREN AND GREAT-GRANDCHILDREN. SHE WAS A DEDICATED ADVOCATE FOR HISTORIC PRESERVATION AND AN EARLY SUPPORTER OF THE HAWAI'I UNFORGOTTEN INITIATIVE, DEVOTED TO RETURNING STOLEN HAWAIIAN ARTIFACTS AND LAND. SHE WAS PRECEDED IN DEATH BY HER PARENTS, KEALOHA AND MALIA PAUAHI, AND HER BELOVED SISTER, MARY PAUAHI.

She looked up sharply. "Mary Pauahi was Dr. Nakano's great-aunt."

Gasps rippled through the crowd.

Cassandra studied Nakano's expression, her fingers tightening around the obituary. "You knew," she said, voice steady but cutting. "You knew Mary Pauahi was your *ohana*."

"Of course I knew," Nakano said. "But what I never knew—what I still don't—is *why*."

Cassandra didn't let up. "You orchestrated this entire investigation. You made sure we got access to the estate. You fed us just enough clues to lead us here."

Nakano's fingers curled into a fist. "Because no one else would."

Nathaniel Oliver scoffed. "This is ridiculous. He's just as manipulative as you are."

Several heartbeats of silence. At last, Nakano spoke. "Justice isn't always clean. But it was the only way to make people listen."

The crowd was watching Nakano now. She could feel the weight of his choices pressing against him. Cassandra's pulse pounded.

"She was just a name in my family's past," Nakano continued, his voice taut. "Another forgotten victim of history. I spent years digging through archives, but there was nothing. No records of why she was there that night. No reason she should have been a target."

Angela, who had been standing rigid beside Nathaniel, turned sharply. "What else aren't you telling us, Professor?"

A wave of whispers and gasps spread through the festival-goers.

Nakano said, "It doesn't change what needs to be done."

Nathaniel Oliver's family had covered up crimes. Dr. Nakano had hidden truths. And between them, Mary Pauahi had been caught in the middle.

Cassandra's fingers tightened around the wooden box in her tote. "This is bigger than any of us," she said. "But it's coming out now." She felt a surge of relief as she caught Kalia's eye. Whatever their past, she had chosen to stand with them.

And then, Skipper swooped down, landing dramatically on a large speaker. His chest puffed, his feathers gleaming under the torches. "The family secret!" he squawked, loud enough for the entire luau to hear.

Someone screamed. A drink spilled near the stage. The MIT coach got smacked in the face by a flying paper umbrella.

Nathaniel Oliver stood frozen. His mask of composure had cracked, leaving something raw and vulnerable underneath.

Phones lifted. Cameras flashed. The truth was finally loud enough for everyone to hear.

Taking a deep breath, she readied to call her students forward, when Nathaniel's voice cut through the night. "And what exactly do you think you've uncovered?"

The words snapped everyone's attention back to him. His voice was calm, too calm. A dangerous kind of quiet. "A funeral notice?" He tsked, shaking his head. "That's your big reveal?"

Angela, emboldened by his dismissal, took a step closer. "She's bluffing," she said, scanning the audience like she could convince them it was all a farce. "This means nothing."

Cassandra squared her shoulders. "Then why do you look nervous?"

Nathaniel's jaw tightened.

A beat of silence. Then Logan called out from the stage, casual as ever. "Guess it's time for some receipts."

Cassandra nodded toward her students.

Chapter Twenty-Three

C ASSANDRA STEADIED HERSELF ON the stage, adjusting her dress and smoothing her hair. The mess behind her told the story. Toppled chairs, scattered lei, and a sense of barely contained pandemonium.

Skipper flapped his wings, preening triumphantly, completely oblivious to the storm he had just helped unleash.

Angela stood at the stage's edge, glaring daggers, her fingers twitching at her side like she wasn't sure whether to fight or flee.

Nathaniel Oliver stood in the center of it all, his carefully composed mask slipping, piece by piece.

Kalia's poised figure remained near Cassandra, steady and unreadable, while Leilani stood at the stage's side exit, arms crossed, an immovable force of quiet strength.

The stage suddenly felt smaller, the bright spotlights harsh and blinding. Something could still go wrong. Cassandra glared helplessly at the crowd.

The murmurs grew louder. A baby cried in the back row; someone shushed them.

Sweat pricked along Cassandra's temple. Where was her anchor? Then, she saw her. Meg.

Standing near the front, her hands already raised, ready to interpret for Lance. Cassandra wasn't alone. She inhaled deeply.

And then, a sharp gesture from Logan set everything into motion. Diego and Logan bounded onto the stage, laptops and cables in hand. A few audience members gasped as Diego deftly connected wires to the AV system.

Lexi appeared next to Cassandra. She scanned the audience and grinned. "Oh look, the Stanford guys. Too bad they won't get to deliver their TED Talk on 'Why We Actually Won.'"

Diego scoffed. "More like 'Why We Should Have Won, But the Judges Were Biased.'"

Within moments, the screen behind them flickered to life. Diego adjusted the feed, his fingers flying across the laptop keyboard. "Ready when you are."

The screen lit up with a newspaper clipping of the first land deed.

Lexi stepped forward, holding the microphone like a gavel. "We know the Mānoa Marauder murders were never random."

Behind her, the screen flickered with historic land deeds, faded signatures, and maps marked with overlapping boundaries. A handwritten list, each name slashed through with careful precision.

"These documents show that, at the time of the murders, the Oliver estate encroached on land belonging to Manuel Reyes and others who later disappeared. These men weren't guilty. They were scapegoats."

A UCLA student heckled, "Still way less dramatic than a ritual sacrifice."

Nathaniel folded his arms, tight across his chest. "Old land squabbles don't prove anything."

A professor from the East Coast team nodded in agreement. "Land records alone won't hold up in court."

Lexi didn't blink. "Maybe not." She clicked forward.

"The Oliver family stole land. Parcel by parcel, deed by deed. We believe Jean Oliver created this map to track those acquisitions, and that Hana Nakamura later hid it inside a quilt for safekeeping."

The screen shifted: a sepia-toned scan of the quilt, then a photo of the wooden box, grainy, half-buried, caught in flashlight glare. "That's where we found it. In a shallow pit behind the estate."

Lexi tapped the next slide. "The map marks specific locations across the property. We don't know exactly what's buried at each site, but we believe some hold stolen cultural artifacts."

She paused. The air felt charged.

"Whatever it is... someone in Edward Oliver's family was willing to kill to keep it hidden."

Cassandra's breath caught. The hair on her arms lifted.

Nathaniel's smile faltered, a bead of sweat just visible at his temple.

A Stanford coach crossed his arms. "Still circumstantial. Show us proof."

Lexi's gaze didn't waver. "Gladly, bro. Some of these stolen artifacts were supposedly sold at a 1950s auction. But the records don't match. Either the Olivers faked the sales, or they covered up what really happened."

She turned to Cassandra. "Dr. Sato?"

Cassandra nodded. The next image filled the screen. Manuel Reyes. Mary Pauahi. Standing before the Oliver estate.

Silent recognition rippled through the crowd.

Even Kalia flinched, barely, her fists clenched at her sides.

Nathaniel stopped breathing.

Cassandra stepped into the mic. Her voice sliced like obsidian. "Mary Pauahi wasn't some unfortunate casualty. She was a city clerk who certified land transfers."

The slideshow cut to a legal document. In the corner: CERTIFIED BY CLERK – MARY PAUAHI.

Nakano jerked like he'd been slapped.

Lexi's voice dropped, dead calm. "She saw something. Maybe forged signatures. Land fraud. Maybe worse."

Cassandra narrowed her eyes at Nathaniel. "She was a threat."

Nathaniel's head whipped toward Nakano. His suspicion was a loaded gun.

Nakano's voice was gravel. "Your family knew she worked for the city. They knew she was involved with Reyes. And they silenced her."

Nathaniel took a step back. "I didn't know. I didn't—" His voice cracked. "I swear, I didn't know!"

The screen changed again: a land deed stamped with HAWAI'I UN-FORGOTTEN.

Nakano froze. The color drained from his face.

"You think men like the Olivers give back what they stole?" he rasped. "You think truth rises on its own?"

He threw a hand toward the document. "I've watched the truth rot in archives. I had to dig it out."

Cassandra's eyes burned into him. "You didn't just dig. You planted seeds."

Nakano's tone iced over. "I made them listen."

A groan from the audience.

A UCLA professor shouted, "This is why peer review exists."

Nathaniel's hands curled into fists. His breath came shallow. With a sudden roar, he tore off his lei and flung it. "This is a setup! You used this contest to smear my name. My family has protected this land for generations!"

Gasps.

Angela inhaled sharply, but said nothing.

Cassandra stepped forward, her voice like a judge delivering the sentence. "Protected the land?" she said. "Or hoarded it?"

A kupuna near the front row muttered, "Shameful."

Nathaniel's eyes darted toward the stage exit.

Lexi didn't move. "And then there's this."

The projector flicked again showing grainy GoPro footage. Night vision. Students creeping through overgrown brush. Then, a shadow. Andrew's yelp and the sickening thud of a body hitting the ground. A figure retreating.

Andrew leaned forward. His own voice echoed from the recording: "Hey! Ouch!"

Lexi spoke over the noise. "And considering Oliver's minions chased Cassandra through the luau not even an hour ago, we all know exactly who was behind that assault. They aren't afraid to get physical."

The audience watched in stunned silence as the footage flipped to Angela and Nathaniel's exchange in the hotel lobby. Nathaniel's final order: "You know what that means."

The noise of pursuit. Angela's voice from the recording: "Grab her bag. Find the papers."

Angela flinched. She stepped back from Nathaniel like he'd caught fire. "You're on your own."

That did it.

Nathaniel's face twisted. His voice cracked. "You rigged everything. You wanted to destroy me!"

Dr. Nakano met his eyes, unwavering. "No, Nathaniel. You did that all by yourself."

Nathaniel turned to Angela. "Did you know?"

She met his gaze without emotion. "You asked me to protect the legacy," she said. "You never asked for the truth."

"It was my legacy!" His composure fractured. "I had a right to know!"

Nathaniel exploded, charging the stage exit—

But Leilani was faster.

With the grace of a warrior, she pivoted, swept his leg, and let gravity do the rest.

Nathaniel hit the floor hard.

Before he could rise, Pono Yakamura and HPD officers closed in.

The crowd erupted, some gasping, others cheering.

As Nathaniel sagged in the cuffs, his shoulders finally collapsed.

Cassandra spotted Nakano slipping into the shadows.

She followed. "You shaped the story," she said. "That's not the same as truth."

Nakano's face was unreadable. "Justice isn't always clean," he said. "But at least now... they listened."

Cassandra wasn't entirely satisfied, but not entirely angry either.

He didn't wait for her forgiveness. He simply stepped further into the dark, his presence already fading into the background of the luau.

Behind her, Kalia extended her hand. Cassandra took it, steadying herself.

"Bringing truth into the light of the Hawaiian moon honors those who came before us," Kalia said softly.

Cassandra let the words settle deep. Relief and pride washed over her as she turned back to the celebration. Her students stood near the stage, hugging, high-fiving, and snapping photos. Their laughter blended with the drumbeats, the steady pulse reverberating in her ribs.

The reckoning had come. Now she had a decision to make.

The luau resumed, a whirlwind of sound and color. Cassandra lingered at the edge of the stage, her feet caught between two worlds.

Leilani turned to her, offering a borrowed pāʻū skirt. An invitation.

The vibrant fabric was heavy in her hands. Cassandra hesitated. She wrapped it around her waist, adjusting the ties with the ease of someone who had done this a hundred times before. And then she stepped forward.

The drumbeats quickened.

The dancers' movements were effortless, a story woven in motion, each step echoing generations of tradition. Cassandra's body remembered the rhythm before her mind could catch up. She stepped into the line of dancers, the hālau welcoming her with silent nods, shifting to include her.

The pā'ū skirt brushed against her legs, its weight settling her movements, while the scent of plumeria wrapped around her like an embrace. Her hips swayed, her arms cut through the air in fluid motions, telling a story of the ocean's embrace, the strength of the 'āina, and the endurance of the people.

Her students watched in awe. Lexi clapping enthusiastically, Lance signing *Beautiful!* to Meg. Logan holding his phone high to record the scene.

To them, she had always been Dr. Sato, their hyper-organized, always-prepared mentor. Now, they saw her as Cassandra Kēhau Sato, precious child born of the morning dew.

A woman who carried two worlds: Japan and Hawaii.

A woman who would always find her way home.

And, finally, a woman who knew where she was going.

As the dance ended, Cassandra held the final pose, her hands raised in an offering to the heavens. The crowd erupted into cheers, their applause rolling like waves over the stage.

Cassandra's chest tightened with emotion. The *mana* of her homeland surged within her. By blood, she was Japanese. By birth, American. But in this moment, she felt undeniably Hawaiian.

As she bowed alongside the hālau, Cassandra felt something click into place. The rhythm, the story, the legacy. It had always been there, waiting.

Chapter Twenty-Four

THE MOON WAS HIGH and the tiki torches long snuffed out, but the adrenaline hadn't quite faded. Cassandra sat cross-legged on the sand, a takeout box of malasadas balanced on her lap.

Around her, the Morton and Kualoa teams were scattered across beach towels and driftwood logs, eating their way through a mix of plate lunches and leftover conference stress.

The luau stage was a memory now, packed up and rolled away. Only the stars remained, along with a cooler full of soda and the hum of kids who'd just upended a century-old cover-up.

The rivalry wasn't buried, exactly, but it had softened, settling into grudging mutual respect.

"This is the best loco moco I've ever had," Logan said through a mouthful of rice and gravy.

Lexi, unimpressed, rolled her eyes. "It's the *only* loco moco you've ever had."

"That's what makes it the best!" Logan grinned, completely undeterred.

"Eh, eat now, argue later," Cassandra said, waving her fork like a weapon. "You don't want to waste good grinds. And slow down before you choke. We're not making a pit stop at Queen's ER before the airport."

"That's fair," Jocelyn muttered, eyeing Ethan, who had somehow managed to inhale half a plate of kalua pork without coming up for air.

Nearby, Pono sat back on his hands, his tanned legs stretched out in the sand. "You Midwesterners eat like you just got out of prison."

Ethan leaned back, licking gravy off his thumb. "Food tastes better when you've just solved a hundred-year-old murder."

The laughter rippled through the group, easy and unguarded.

Finally, it was over.

Diego, still bouncing with energy, tapped his chopsticks on an invisible drum. "Stanford just posted a 'well actually' thread about how they were onto something 'way bigger' and the judges just didn't get it."

Lexi groaned. "Of course they did. I bet they mention their AI chatbot at least three times."

The laughter faded as Lance paused, gaze distant. He signed something slowly. Meg translated, her voice low: "Linda kept that box buried for decades waiting for someone who'd care enough to finish what she started. How do you think she believed justice would ever come?"

The group fell quiet, the question hanging between them like mist over the sand.

Pono rubbed the back of his neck. "You don't protect something that hard unless you believe someone will find it."

Cassandra stared out at the waves. "Maybe she knew it had to happen this way."

Meg glanced over. "What do you mean?"

"She had enough to ruin them. But back then, the Olivers were untouchable. If anyone from Linda's family came forward, evidence would've been buried just like their murder cases." Cassandra thought some more. "Her grandfather kept the estate standing. Linda preserved the truth. She made sure it wouldn't end with her."

Ivy pointed with her fork. "We followed a quilt map, dug up a box, and found land records that traced straight to Linda's family. Even the old drawer with the 'J.O.' handkerchief; she left it all for us to find. A woman we barely knew... trusted us to finish what her grandfather couldn't?"

Logan nodded. "And the wooden box was wrapped in one of those old estate work shirts. The same ones from that gallery photo. All history, just waiting."

"Nathaniel and Angela tried to cover it up," Ethan said. "But Linda already had the pieces in motion."

Meg murmured, "She waited years for someone to listen."

"And she chose us," Cassandra said softly. "Not to accuse, but to remember. We may never get full proof. But we know who benefitted. And we know who paid the price."

Connor exhaled. "She played the long game."

Lexi nudged Logan. "See? Not everything is about charging in."

Logan rolled his eyes. "Okay, fine. Sometimes waiting is a strategy."

Maria grinned. "Someone write that down. Logan admitted he has self-control."

"Don't get used to it," he shot back.

Brandon, mouth half-full, raised a finger. "So we're just supposed to believe Linda had a master plan? Like, fate sent a bunch of college nerds to solve it?"

Pono shrugged. "Sometimes the right people show up."

Jocelyn chimed in. "Well, Hawai'i Unforgotten's doing a full audit now: land titles, donation records, estate holdings. Everything."

Kalia smirked. "Looks like the state wants to know how much shady history's been hiding behind those museum walls."

Maria let out a low whistle. "So... we kicked off a legit investigation."

"Looks that way," Kalia said. "Might take months, but someone's finally pulling the thread.

Brandon scraped the last bits of rice from his plate. "Wait, did anyone officially announce who won the cold case competition?"

Maria snorted. "We won, but the UCLA team is still pushing their cult theory."

Ethan mimicked a dramatic whisper. "'The Mānoa Marauder was just a cover-up for ritual sacrifices. Wake up, sheeple.'"

Diego laughed. "To be fair, it would make a solid Netflix documentary.

Lexi shook her head. "We pieced together four murders. What else do they want, an ancient prophecy?"

"We definitely won," Andrew said. "Morton got best presentation and we had the best evidence."

"Best presentation?" Kalia smirked. "Remember when you tripped over a cable and almost face-planted into the sound system?"

"I call that adding drama," Andrew retorted. "Right, Dr. Sato?"

Cassandra smirked. "If by drama you mean needless mayhem, then sure."

Ivy groaned. "This is why I didn't want us to win."

Andrew sat up, alarmed. "Excuse me. We risked life and limb! We were chased! I was injured!"

"You barely got hit on the head," Lexi deadpanned.

"Brutally hit," Andrew corrected. "And I think that money should go toward Skipper's well-being. A well-deserved retirement, a yacht—"

Maria smirked. "A yacht? For a parrot?"

Andrew gestured dramatically with a French fry. "Excuse me, that parrot was instrumental in solving this case."

Skipper flapped his wings triumphantly. "The family secret!"

Cassandra sighed. "You all are ridiculous."

Kalia cleared her throat, drawing everyone's attention. "All right, Morton College crew, as much as it pains me to say this, you earned it." Kalia hoisted her water bottle with a dramatic sigh. "Congratulations on being slightly less mediocre than I expected."

Cassandra tapped her drink gently against Kalia's. "High praise coming from you."

Kalia waved her hand. "Don't get cocky. My team took home the award for Best Individual Poster Presentation. Remember, our students have *actual* talent. Instead of bumbling into clues by mistake."

"Keep telling yourself that," Lexi shot back.

As the playful jabs flew back and forth, Cassandra leaned toward Kalia. "Why weren't you ever this nice at O'ahu State?"

Kalia's grin widened, her tone dripping with mock innocence. "I've always been this nice. You were just wound too tight to notice."

Cassandra snorted. "That's because you know how to push every button imaginable."

"That's because you're oversensitive," Kalia quipped without missing a beat.

Meg, who had been quietly sipping from a soda can, burst out laughing. "Have you met Cassandra? She doesn't have a sensitive bone in her body."

Connor leaned in with a mischievous grin. "But she does have a few that are easily irritated."

Cassandra rolled her eyes, but a smile tugged at the corners of her mouth. "Well, since we won, we need to decide what to do with the prize money."

Andrew grinned. "I vote Skipper's yacht fund."

Skipper squawked. "The family secret!"

Maria ignored them. "Actually, I was thinking... we don't keep all of it."

Ethan blinked. "I'm sorry, are you feeling okay? Because I distinctly remember you being very invested in the prize money."

Maria shot him a look but didn't take the bait. "I still am. But when we were at the estate, looking through those historical displays and land deeds... I kept thinking about my parents."

She brushed some sand off her shorts. "My father started with nothing when he moved to the U.S. Worked three jobs to put us through school. They taught me education is important, but the real value is what you do with it."

Silence stretched, then Lexi spoke. "You'd give up your winnings?"

Maria shrugged. "Some things are more important than money."

Cassandra watched her for a heartbeat, then nodded. "Maybe we make sure the Morton crew gets their share. But we also give back. Some of it stays local like a scholarship for Hawaiian students. Or something for Maui: recovery funds, student housing, whatever they still need after the wildfires."

A quiet ripple of agreement passed through the group.

Kalia exhaled, then smirked. "Well... I suppose that's not a terrible idea."

Logan snorted. "Wow. Is that the nicest thing Kalia has ever said to us?"

"Don't get used to it," Kalia warned.

Pono glanced at his phone, then cleared his throat. "Well, looks like Angela won't be joining us for a beach bonfire anytime soon."

Cassandra turned. "What do you mean?"

"She cut a deal," he said, scrolling. "Testifying against Nathaniel. They're letting her off with fines."

Ethan scoffed. "Oh sure, let's just let the weird evil assistant walk free."

"Angela might not have personally knocked Andrew on the head," Cassandra said, "but burying evidence and deleting records made her an accessory."

"She still has to face charges," Pono added. "Just... not as many as Mr. Oliver."

Cassandra exhaled, staring at the dark horizon. "I'd like to think this'll be a turning point for her."

"Maybe," Kalia muttered, cracking open a can of soda. "I'll follow up. If Angela's willing to face what she did, maybe there's a way for her to help with the audit. She knows where the bodies are buried, figuratively."

A quiet hum of agreement passed between the group, the waves filling the silence for a breath or two.

Jocelyn nudged Cassandra with her foot. "Eh, you nevah tell me you could still hula!"

Cassandra raised an eyebrow, her accent flipping to local style. "Eh, gotta save my best moves for when the stakes are high. You think I just bust out the pāʻū skirt for any old luau?"

Kalia smiled. "You been hiding, girl."

"No one asked," Cassandra laughed.

The students exchanged wide-eyed glances, clearly enjoying this more relaxed version of their usually buttoned-up mentor.

Lexi leaned over to Diego, whispering loudly, "I think this is the coolest Dr. Sato has ever been."

Logan chuckled, nodding. "Don't tell anyone at Morton, but our chaperone is a total badass."

Cassandra noticed Brandon, normally shy and quiet, deep in conversation with a girl from the Kualoa team.

Lexi elbowed Cassandra. "I did not see that coming."

Cassandra lifted a brow. "Still waters run deep."

Meanwhile, Andrew stood, dramatically. "I'd like to say something!" he announced.

When the voices quieted enough that he could speak over them, he said, "Thanks Dr. Sato, for believing in us even when we didn't believe in ourselves. We couldn't have done this without you."

Cassandra blinked, caught off guard by the sincerity in his voice. For once, Andrew wasn't performing.

"Thank you," she said, her voice softer. "That means a lot coming from you."

Andrew's expression didn't shift. "I mean it. You gave me a chance when no one else would."

Cassandra tilted her head slightly, her gaze steady. "You've changed, Andrew. I'm proud of you." She gave him a small smile. "Still a work in progress. But hey, so am I."

The group's laughter drifted into the night air, but Cassandra's gaze lingered on the horizon.

She turned to Meg, Connor, and Jocelyn. "There's still something that doesn't sit right. I've been piecing it together, and I think the whole setup might've been orchestrated."

Jocelyn raised a brow. "You mean... Nakano?"

Cassandra nodded. "He made the VR competition the centerpiece of the conference. He knew Nathaniel Olivers's connection to the estate. My guess? He saw the outline and needed someone else to fill in the details."

"So we were his pawns," Jocelyn said, arms crossed. "In some weird, academic chess match?"

"Maybe." Cassandra's voice stayed even. "But if it meant exposing what the Olivers covered up then I don't regret it."

Meg tilted her head. "Even if it was part of someone else's agenda?"

Cassandra looked around at the students finally laughing, teasing, free from the tension of the past few days. "I don't care if we were pawns. We honored the victims. We made sure the story didn't die with Linda. That's enough for me."

Andrew glanced up from where he was sculpting a crooked little sandcastle, smoothing the turret with one finger. "We heard in the committee Slack that Dr. Nakano took a leave of absence from Hawai'i Unforgotten."

"Makes sense," Kalia said. "The whole organization's under scrutiny. People want to know what he knew and when."

Lexi exhaled. "It's sad, right? He wanted justice. But he didn't fight clean."

Cassandra murmured, "Not all truths are free. Some come with strings."

Andrew pressed a final shell into one corner, then sat back on his heels. "Guess someone else has to clean up the mess now."

Cassandra glanced at him proudly. He really had grown before her eyes.

She stood, brushing the sand from her skirt. "All right, ya' hooligans. Finish your food and pack up. We've got an early flight, and I'm not dragging anyone through TSA in pajamas."

Logan groaned. "Can't we just sleep on the beach and call it cultural immersion?"

Cassandra arched an eyebrow. "Sure. If you want your parents to bail you out of jail in Honolulu."

Laughter rolled across the beach like the tide, easy and alive. The students shoved leftovers into paper bags, slung backpacks over sunburned shoulders, and kicked sand off their flip-flops with theatrical sighs.

The stars were just beginning to show above the palms, and the warm laughter of her students rose behind her like smoke.

But beneath the joy, something quieter stirred.

Grief. Memory. Questions not solved by cold case files.

Some truths weren't buried, they simply waited. And not every goodbye was finished yet.

Chapter Twenty-Five

C ASSANDRA STOOD ON THE hotel balcony, arms resting on the cool metal railing as she stared out at the darkened ocean. Waikīkī was never truly asleep, but at this hour, the usual hum of tourists had quieted to the rustle of palm fronds and the distant thrum of early morning delivery trucks.

Her phone buzzed in her hand. Marcus Fischer.

She swiped to answer. "I hope you enjoyed your nice, full night of sleep, because I barely got four hours."

Marcus let out a low chuckle. "I was a little surprised you answered me last night. I figured you'd be too busy celebrating your big win to check your messages."

Cassandra tucked her hair into a ponytail. "There was some celebrating. But mostly there was a lot of staring at the ceiling and over-analyzing everything, as usual."

"Ah, classic Sato," Marcus said dryly. "And here I thought a beach vacation might make you relax."

"Beach *work trip*," she corrected, rolling her shoulders. "And it turns out solving a century-old cold case isn't as restful as it sounds."

Marcus sighed. "Well, hopefully, you're still up for one more mystery."

That got her attention. "What do you mean?"

A pause. Then, his tone shifted, more serious. "Fran's making moves. Merging responsibilities."

Cassandra straightened. "Define *moves*."

"She's restructuring leadership," Marcus said. "She's starting with your director, George Hansen. Cutting his hours, shifting his duties."

"That makes sense," Cassandra said. "He naps more than he works."

Marcus sighed. "Yeah, but she's not stopping there. She's also reviewing your role."

Her stomach dropped.

"Me?" Cassandra repeated, her irritation bubbling. "Since when?"

"Since about two days ago," Marcus admitted. "She's been careful about how she's framing it. Talking about 'efficiency' and 'modernizing operations.'"

Cassandra's fingers curled around the railing. "She barely knows me. I've only worked with her for a couple of weeks."

"She knows enough," Marcus said. "She knows you're competent. That you have influence with the faculty. That you're one of the only other women on the leadership team."

Cassandra let out a sharp breath, pushing away from the railing. "So what? She's clearing out anyone who might challenge her?"

Marcus hesitated. "I don't know. But I'd be careful."

In the distance, the first hints of dawn touched the horizon, streaks of gray and indigo brushing the ocean.

Finally, Cassandra asked the question she'd been avoiding. "Does this have anything to do with you?"

A pause. "Not exactly," he said carefully.

Her grip tightened on her phone. "That's not a no."

Marcus sighed. "Look, Fran makes her own decisions. But if she is trying to push you out, I'm not a part of it."

Cassandra wanted to believe him. But she also knew that Marcus had his own career to think about. If Fran was consolidating power, his position wasn't untouchable either.

"Just... don't jump to conclusions," Marcus said. "Talk to Fran when you're back. It might not be what it looks like."

Cassandra wasn't so sure. She exhaled steadying herself. "What else?"

Marcus hesitated. Then, reluctantly, he added, "Fran's pushing through more budget *re-evaluations.* Her word not mine. This time she's looking at cost-saving options for the veterans' program."

She could almost hear the air quotes around "cost-saving." Cassandra stilled. "You're kidding."

"She thinks some of the costs should be covered by external part-ners." Marcus said.

Cassandra snapped. "It's one of the few programs that brings in non-traditional students and federal money. And these are *veterans*. We made a commitment to them."

"She doesn't see it that way," Marcus said. "But she's about to find out that a lot of people disagree with her, including me."

Cassandra inhaled slowly, forcing herself to stay calm.

"I'll deal with it when I get back," she said finally. "But if she's gunning for me, I need to be ready."

Marcus sighed. "Yeah. You do."

Silence stretched between them.

Finally, Marcus said, "Safe travels back. I'll see you soon."

Cassandra hesitated, expecting something more. A flicker of warmth. Anything.

He checked every box: stable, smart, easy to admire. But was that enough? "Yeah... see you soon."

A pause. Then— "Bye, Cassandra."

The line clicked.

She lowered the phone, staring out at the barely-there horizon. She didn't know what was waiting for her in Nebraska.

But for now, she had a sunrise to catch.

By the time Cassandra reached the hotel lobby, Meg was already waiting, clutching two massive coffee cups and looking unusually awake for this hour.

"Here," she said, shoving one into Cassandra's hands. "I'm using caffeine to mimic your chipper morning attitude."

Cassandra took a sip and sighed. "You understand me as only a bestie can."

"Jocelyn's already in the car," Meg added. "She said if we're not out in five, she's reporting us missing and making up dramatic last words for our obituaries."

Ten minutes later, Cassandra sat in the back seat of Meg's rental, her head tilted against the window as they emerged from the tunnel into the Diamond Head parking lot. The ancient volcanic crater loomed ahead in silhouette, its jagged rim outlined faintly against the deepening blue of pre-dawn. Popular with hikers and tourists, the trail to the summit promised postcard views of Honolulu, if you could survive the stairs without questioning all your life choices.

The beauty of the morning didn't do much to lighten the knot in her chest from Marcus's warning.

Her finger hovered over her phone before she typed out a quick message.

Cassandra

Hey, how's Murphy the diva? Still pretending he's tragically abandoned?

The response came almost immediately.

Andy

He's milking it. Took over Buckley's doggie bed and gave me a guilt stare so intense I apologized for you. I think we have a new alpha.

Cassandra

Guilt is his love language. Rookie mistake letting him take over.

Andy

Too late. Buckley's already judging us both. I'm googling 'shared custody agreements.'

Cassandra huffed a quiet laugh, shaking her head as she typed back.

Cassandra

He's still my dog. I'll be home soon.

Andy

Good. I'm running out of emotional support snacks.

She smiled at the screen, her exhaustion softening at the edges.

When she looked up, Meg was watching her quietly. Too observant. Their eyes met for an extra beat. Just enough to let the heat rise in Cassandra's cheeks before Meg returned her gaze to the road.

Cassandra didn't dwell on it. Her thoughts were still tangled with Marcus. She wasn't ready to think about Andy.

Not yet.

The car rumbled to a stop. Cassandra stepped out, stretching as the morning breeze caught the hem of her hoodie. Meg bounded ahead, suspiciously energetic for someone who claimed she hated mornings.

"Meg," Cassandra called, her voice tinged with mock annoyance. "Are you secretly training for a marathon?"

Meg turned, walking backward with a grin. "I'm just trying to keep up with you two! You promised there'd be snacks at the top. I expect full picnic energy."

The trail ahead curved into shadow. The horizon was just starting to shift, deep purple edging toward gold.

Jocelyn swatted at a mosquito. "You know what else has snacks? My living room. This peer pressure is unwelcome."

Cassandra nudged her with an elbow. "You didn't complain this much in college."

"That's because you bribed me with malasadas and caffeine," Jocelyn shot back.

Their laughter drifted up the trail, light against the hush of early morning.

The next half hour passed in a steady rhythm, feet shuffling along the rocky red dirt trail. A few locals breezed past them, earbuds in, already on their second lap like this was their morning coffee run. Jocelyn muttered something about overachievers, while Meg powered ahead like she'd been born on a StairMaster.

They reached the top of the final spiral staircase and squeezed one by one through the narrow opening in the old WWII bunker. Cassandra ducked her head, the concrete walls still faintly smelling of metal and dust.

Outside, the sky had begun to pale. Just a few more steps led them to the summit, where a platform offered sweeping views in every direction. Early risers already lined the railing, phones raised, waiting for the light to break.

Jocelyn groaned, stretching her arms. "That metal staircase always feels like a horror movie."

Meg smirked. "You're so dramatic. It's like a dozen steps."

"Spoken like someone who didn't almost faceplant into a stranger's backpack," Jocelyn said.

Cassandra laid out a towel on a flatter patch of concrete away from the crowd, setting down her bag and pulling out a Tupperware of Spam musubi. "Those last 99 steps didn't used to be this steep. I blame adulthood."

Jocelyn flopped onto a nearby rock, fanning herself. "If another war breaks out, I'm not hiking up here to defend anything. They'll have to send the youth."

Meg shook her head. "Since when are you so fragile?"

"Tell me that's musubi," Jocelyn said, reaching for the container. "I've earned at least three."

Cassandra grinned and passed it over. "Courtesy of my mom."

"Love that woman," Jocelyn said, unwrapping one eagerly.

They ate in comfortable silence for a moment, the breeze carrying the scent of salt and plumeria. Cassandra glanced along the coast, past the harbor and airport, where history was layered in the hills and valleys.

"You know," she said, her tone softening, "this place has seen a lot more than just tourist hikes."

Meg tilted her head. "What do you mean?"

Cassandra traced a finger along the lid of her container. "My great-grandmother grew up in Aiea. On the morning of the Pearl Harbor attack, she was on her front porch, watching the planes fly overhead. She said it was terrifying not just because of the bombing, but because my great-grandfather and his brother were working in the sugar cane fields. She didn't know if they were safe."

Jocelyn's teasing vanished. "She saw it happen?"

Cassandra nodded. "She used to say it felt like watching the end of the world." She hesitated, gripping her water bottle. "It was complicated for her. They were Americans, but she had an uncle back in Japan who served in the Imperial Army. For years, she wondered if he might've been one of the pilots that day."

Meg's eyes widened. "Did she ever find out?"

"Not until much later," Cassandra said. "He wasn't there that day, but the question haunted her. She used to say it felt like being torn in two."

They sat in silence for a moment, the weight of the past settling over them.

Jocelyn finally exhaled. "Your great-grandmother was a force."

"She was," Cassandra said, a faint smile crossing her face. "She taught me a lot about resilience. About finding a way forward when you feel pulled in different directions."

Meg grabbed a musubi, biting into it with a sigh. "So... what did Marcus say?"

Cassandra hesitated, then relayed the conversation. By the time she finished, Meg and Jocelyn exchanged a look that was equal parts knowing and annoyed.

Meg sat up straighter. "Okay, here's the deal. I liked Fran too. But if she's coming for your job, that's a problem."

"I don't even know if that's what's happening," Cassandra admitted. "But I can't ignore the timing. She's barely been there a month, and suddenly she's 'restructuring' my position? Why not just get rid of George entirely and leave me out of it?"

"Because George isn't a threat," Jocelyn said simply. "You are."

Cassandra blinked. "What's that supposed to mean?"

"You're competent," Meg said. "You're ambitious. You're the only other woman on the leadership team. If Fran wants to consolidate power, you're the logical target."

Jocelyn crossed her arms. "And if she's trying to get closer to Marcus..."

Cassandra glared, rubbing her temples. "Stop right there."

Jocelyn held up her hands. "I'm just connecting the dots. Hey, if you shove me off this trail, at least make it look like an accident."

Cassandra waved a hand. "You? You'd haunt me out of spite."

Meg groaned. "Clearly, you both need more coffee. Now focus." She nudged Cassandra. "Whatever's going on, you've got options. Don't let Fran or anyone trap you into thinking you don't."

Cassandra exhaled. "Yeah. I know. But there's more."

They both waited.

Cassandra threw her trash into her pack. "Fran's going after the veterans' program next. Marcus says the cuts are going to backfire."

Jocelyn shook her head. "Veterans? Seriously? That's the last group you want to mess with."

Cassandra shrugged. "He's trying to keep the peace, but he's stuck."

Meg studied her. "So what happens if Morton isn't on your dream path anymore?"

"I... don't know." Cassandra twisted the cap back onto her water bottle. "I always thought I'd climb the ladder. College president. Big mainland university. But solving this case, dancing hula again... it's like remembering a version of me I didn't know I missed."

Jocelyn raised an eyebrow. "Now who's being profound?"

Meg wiped her forehead. "Look, I'm not saying I have it figured out. But chasing success can come with a cost. I've got two kids, a job I like, and most days I still feel like I'm failing at some of it."

Cassandra gave a dry laugh. "You're doing better than me. I've basically been dating my job for six years."

Meg grinned. "Exactly. That's why I'm saying this. If Morton's making you miserable, cut it loose."

Jocelyn leaned back on her elbows. "Just remember, the 'dream job' isn't always the dream life."

Cassandra nodded slowly but didn't reply.

Chapter Twenty-Six

T HE SCENT OF COFFEE mingled with soy sauce and something sweet—probably the mochi her mother always made for goodbye mornings like this one. Cassandra paused in the kitchen doorway, taking in the scene.

Keoni leaned against the counter, sipping coffee while supervising his two boys as they tore into a plate of spam, eggs, and rice. Kathy and Sarah were deep in conversation, their voices overlapping as they teased Rick, who was trying to help Diana open a stubborn yogurt cup. Connor balanced baby Olivia on one leg, dodging tiny, curious hands reaching for his plate.

Meg sat comfortably at the table, sipping tea like she'd been adopted into the ohana years ago. "I think your kitchen is the most efficient place on Earth," she said. "It's like a perfectly run ship."

Mama Sato wiped the counter with a knowing snort. "Of course. I'm the captain."

Keoni raised his mug as Cassandra stepped inside. "Eh, look who finally show up. We thought maybe you passed out on Diamond Head and Meg had to carry you down."

Cassandra smiled, setting her bag down. "Not quite, but my calves are filing a formal complaint. Glad to get some exercise knowing we'll be sitting on a plane for hours."

Kathy rolled her eyes. "Yeah, yeah, we all know you're the sunrise queen. Me, I need two cups of coffee before I can even think straight."

Sarah sipped her coffee. "If Cass sleep past six, must be one apocalypse... or gremlins like you little braddahs."

Keoni's kids gasped in unison. "Gremlins? No way! We're ninja warriors!" They leaped into battle stances, complete with dramatic sound effects.

Keoni chuckled, ruffling his son's hair. "You keep telling yourself that, yah? We see. One day, Daddy goin' sneak up on you."

Meg stretched her arms overhead, sighing. "You know, the early alarm was kind of worth it. The view from the top is my favorite on the island."

Mama Sato, wiping down the counter, gave Cassandra a pointed look. "So that view finally knock some sense into you? Or you still overthinking your whole existence?"

Keoni raised his mug. "If she had one epiphany, we woulda heard already."

Cassandra grabbed a piece of mango off her nephews' plate, popping it into her mouth before replying. "Meg's right, it was a good hike. But true story, I need about three more hours sleep."

The back door swung open, and Leilani walked in, balancing a bakery box. Despite looking a little tired, she wore a satisfied smile.

"Sorry I missed breakfast earlier," she said, setting the box on the counter. "Morning sickness is no joke this time around."

Keoni choked on his coffee mid-sip, his face turning a light shade of pink.

Sarah gasped. "Morning sickness?"

Leilani grinned. "We're having another baby."

The room erupted. Congratulations, teasing, and a whirlwind of laughter swirled around them.

Mama Sato threw up her hands. "Another grandbaby! Ho, you shoulda told me sooner, Leilani. You know how many baby names I get saved up?"

Keoni mumbled something about timing, but his grin betrayed his pride. Cassandra hugged Leilani just as Diana toddled over to tug at her aunt's dress.

"Congratulations," Cassandra said. "And here I thought you were just avoiding my calls."

Leilani laughed. "You know me better than that. I never dodge your calls... for long."

Keoni smirked. "She just puts 'em on silent."

As breakfast wrapped up, Keoni pulled Cassandra aside near the sink, his expression more serious. "So, Cass, this is it? You running back to the mainland?"

"It's not running," she said. "It's a strategic retreat."

Keoni arched a brow. "Strategic retreat? Dats what they calling it now, leaving paradise for snow and cornfields?"

Sarah walked by with Diana on her hip. "Cornfields are exotic to some people."

Mama Sato deadpanned. "Exotic, huh? You goin' miss real food soon enough. So? You stay for the baby, or you really going back to the land of canned soup casseroles and bad weather?"

Meg grinned. "Hey, my mom makes a mean tater tot casserole, thank you very much."

Cassandra shot her mother a look. "You know it's not that simple."

Mama Sato shrugged. "Simple to me. You belong here. But your father say let you chase your dreams, so what do I know?"

Her father, who had been quietly sipping his tea in the corner, looked up with a small smile. "Dreams worth chasing, Cass. Just don't forget where you started."

Keoni leaned in, lowering his voice. "You always do what's right for you. Just don't forget, get plenty right here, too."

Kathy chimed in. "Look, we gonna miss you, but if you miserable here, not worth it. Do what makes you happy."

Sarah smirked. "And if you find one nice Nebraska boy, maybe you stay there forever."

Cassandra groaned. "Can we not make this about my love life?"

Keoni snorted. "Love life? You even get time for that?"

Connor, bouncing Olivia on his knee, grinned. "She'll have plenty of time. Nebraska's thrilling dating scene is just waiting for her."

"Don't knock it," Meg raised an eyebrow. "I found you in Nebraska."

Leilani caught Cassandra at the door as the breakfast bustle shifted into packing up the car.

"You okay?" she asked, voice gentle.

Cassandra hesitated. "I dunno. Hard to leave, yah. But I don't think I'm ready stay, either."

Leilani smiled, squeezing her arm. "Then go. Figure 'em out. No need gotta be forever. We always here when you're ready."

Mama Sato held her shoulders at arm's length, her expression softer than before. "I not goin' say what I tink... 'Cause you already know, my girl. Love you, yeah?"

Cassandra pulled her into a tight hug. "Thanks, Mom."

As they drove away from the house, she glanced back one last time. Her family waved from the carport, their faces bright.

When her gaze met Meg's, they both were glassy-eyed with unshed tears. "Ready or not?"

Cassandra reached over to Olivia's car seat letting the baby grasp her finger. "I guess we'll find out."

By the time they reached the airport, the students were buzzing with energy despite the short night. And apparently, a minor transportation crisis.

"You guys had one job," Cassandra groaned.

Lexi threw up her hands. "How were we supposed to know Honolulu Airport has, like, five different drop-off zones?"

Ethan, still clutching his backpack like it had personally betrayed him, muttered, "Our Uber driver swore this was the right terminal. It wasn't."

Diego sighed, shaking his head. "Bro. He dropped us at the international terminal."

Ivy huffed. "Because—and I quote—'Nebraska sounds foreign.'"

Cassandra blinked. "You're kidding."

Ethan spread his hands. "Nope. Guy legit thought Nebraska was overseas."

Meg covered her mouth, trying not to laugh. "Please tell me you didn't argue."

Logan sighed. "Nah, we just nodded and sprinted for the right terminal like fugitives."

Ivy groaned, shaking her head. "We probably looked like extras in a bad airport rom-com."

Ethan did a big sigh. "And I still didn't get my dramatic reunion with coffee."

Cassandra rolled her eyes but grinned. "Well, congratulations. You officially survived a group trip. Barely."

Once they were through security and on the plane, the students settled into their seats with the ease of travelers who had finally hit their stride.

Cassandra buckled in, but she caught Lexi watching her from across the aisle.

Lexi tilted her head. "So... I gotta ask. You hesitated. Were you thinking about staying?"

Cassandra blinked. "What makes you say that?"

Ethan exchanged a glance with Diego, who was already pulling out his noise-canceling headphones. "You had that far-off 'Maybe I belong here' look in your eyes more than once."

Lexi, leaned against her seat. "Yeah, not gonna lie. We were taking bets on whether you'd actually get on this plane."

Logan, smirked from his seat along the aisle. "I had five bucks on you showing up at the gate last-minute, draped in a lei, giving some big 'I must follow my destiny' speech."

"Wow. Glad to know I'm giving off main character energy." Cassandra groaned. "You really thought I was about to throw my whole life plan out the window at the last second?"

Lexi arched a brow. "You say that like it's a bad thing."

Cassandra sighed, staring out the window as the plane taxied down the runway. "I thought about it," she admitted. "But I'm not done with Nebraska yet."

Logan grinned. "That sounds like an 'until next time' kind of answer."

"Don't make me rethink my life choices mid-flight." Cassandra rested her head against the seat, gazing out the window as the island shrank below them, the familiar tug of home and possibility stretching between two places.

Where she belonged? *That was still up for debate.*

Chapter Twenty–Seven

After ten hours, two in-flight movies, one questionable airline breakfast, and exactly zero hours of real sleep, everything felt muted. Her bed, her dog, even her usual post-trip relief barely registered through the haze.

The group shuffled toward baggage claim, where half of them immediately pulled out their phones like it was a survival instinct.

"We made it," Ethan sighed, stretching. "Barely."

"We thrived under pressure," Logan corrected.

Lexi rolled her eyes. "That's a strong word for what just happened."

Diego smirked. "At least we didn't get off at the wrong stop again."

Cassandra side-eyed them. "I'm never letting you live that down."

Meg, who had Olivia strapped to her chest and was already scanning for their luggage, grinned. "You have to admit, Cass, as far as conference trips go, this one was kind of a win."

Lexi grinned. "You mean because we solved a cold case, made national headlines, and embarrassed half the history department?"

Ethan lifted his phone. "Still can't believe Morton College made the front page of Hawai'i Unforgotten's website. 'Underdog School Cracks Decades-Old Murder Mystery.'" He snorted. "We're famous. Ish."

"We also got prize money," Ivy reminded them.

Logan draped an arm over Ethan's shoulder. "And being the charitable humans that we are, we decided to donate some of it to local Maui students at O'ahu State."

Lexi smirked. "Because we are, in fact, better than the Ivy League snobs."

Cassandra chuckled. "I'm sure they'll be touched by your generous, selfless... bragging."

Lexi grinned. "So now that we've made a name for ourselves, I feel like Morton needs a better mascot. Why is it still the Maples? It's a tree."

Diego shook his head. "Morton College needs a better mascot. Trees don't inspire confidence in times of crisis."

Cassandra scrolled through her messages as the baggage claim belt creaked to life. "You do realize my dog comes to work with me, right? Murphy is already the unofficial office mascot."

"Yeah, but Murphy doesn't interrupt people with ominous one-liners like Skipper the parrot," Ethan pointed out.

Lexi sighed. "That's a loss for all of us."

Cassandra grabbed her bag as it thudded onto the carousel and followed the others through the sliding doors. Nebraska in July wrapped around her like a hot, wet blanket someone had left in the sun."

"And we're back," Ivy groaned, fanning herself with her boarding pass.

"I already miss tradewinds," Brandon muttered.

Lance adjusted his backpack strap and grinned. *You guys realize this means we officially survived a group trip without anyone getting arrested, right?*

Lexi nudged Cassandra. "By the way, did you see the email? Apparently we're getting the full hero treatment when we get back. Panel presentation, press, the whole deal. Guess cold-case fame is trending now. Hope you're ready for your close-up, Dr. S."

Cassandra raised an eyebrow. "Already? We just landed."

Maria, tucking a piece of hair behind her ear, said, "It makes the school look good. They're not gonna waste that."

Brandon stretched. "We'll all be back on campus in a couple of weeks anyway."

Lance nodded. *Good. I'm over this group, but I'm too lazy to make new friends.*

Ethan smirked. "You'll be fine. Just FaceTime Skipper. He'll fill the awkward silences."

Skipper's absence hit Cassandra in a weird, unexpected spot. The parrot had been a feathered wildcard at best but weirdly effective background noise.

Maria groaned. "That bird better not be at our event."

Ivy laughed. "At this rate, they might give him an honorary degree."

Cassandra shook her head. "If Morton College starts handing out diplomas to birds, I'm resigning."

Diego looked around dramatically. "Honestly, it feels suspiciously calm. We're due for one more disaster."

Logan shrugged. "Well, we did get lost at the airport. That's gotta count for something."

Lexi grinned. "Guess we'll see you all in a few weeks, then."

Lance gave Cassandra a pointed look, then signed, *Try not to cause too much chaos while we're gone.*

Cassandra gave him stink eye for the callback to her Queen of Doom nickname, and signed, *No promises.*

A text buzzed from Marcus:

Marcus

> Sorry, I can't pick you up. We've got a mess on campus. Construction crew hit a water main.

She frowned, rereading the message.

Meg hoisted Olivia onto her hip, scanning the curb for their rides, then turned to Cassandra. "I know that face."

Cassandra sighed. "Apparently, my welcome home party is a plumbing emergency."

Connor pulled up with their SUV, parked, and popped the hatch.

When he came around to Meg, she touched his shoulder. "Fischer bailed. Broken pipe on campus."

Connor loaded the luggage. "So much for a peaceful return."

Meg offered, "Need a ride? We're heading out."

They lived in the opposite direction. It wasn't a short detour. Cassandra hesitated.

Before she could answer, a blue campus security sedan pulled to the curb. The window rolled down.

Andy Summers leaned out. "Need a lift?"

Cassandra blinked. "How'd you know I was stranded?"

Andy grinned. "Word travels fast. Leave campus for a week, and everything falls apart."

Meg, buckling Olivia into her car seat, raised an eyebrow, but impressively said nothing.

Connor didn't even try to keep his voice down. "Huh. Almost like you've got a backup boyfriend system."

Cassandra shot him a glare, but Andy just laughed.

"Relax," he said, putting the car in park. "I'm campus security. I get people where they need to go. Safely."

Cassandra tossed her bag in the back. "Fine. But if this turns into a kidnapping, avenge me, Meg."

Meg smirked. "Oh, I don't think you need rescuing."

With the deep sigh of someone too tired to argue, Cassandra climbed in.

As Andy pulled away from the curb, Cassandra stared out the windshield, already bracing for whatever bureaucratic nonsense Morton had waiting.

It wasn't the welcome home she expected.

But it felt like a beginning.

Author's Note

"You never really leave a place you love. Part of it you take with you, leaving a part of you behind."

Before I started high school, my family moved from Connecticut to Nebraska. We left behind cousins, aunts and uncles, lifelong friends, and the only hometown I'd ever known. It felt like the end of the world. When we left, my father gave me a little plaque with those words above, and I've kept it ever since.

They are still true.

Over the years, I've moved many times: chasing jobs, chasing dreams, raising kids. I love to travel. But Nebraska became home in the quiet, faithful way that matters. It's where my family is now. It's where the roots are deep.

But Hawaii is where the tide keeps calling me back.

My husband and I spent our early married life on O'ahu. Our first two sons were born there. We made lifelong friends and fell in love with the food, the culture, and the outrageous beauty of the islands. Those years shaped me. Even after we moved away, I carried the place with me.

This book, like Cassandra herself, is a homecoming. A reckoning with change. A reminder that home isn't simply a location on a map. It's a feeling stitched into memory, anchored in family, culture, history, and heart. It's also about what happens when we dare to go back, and find out who we've become in the process.

And truly, it's a love letter to a place I never really left.

I've said this before, but this time I really mean it: this book might be my favorite yet! Returning to Cassandra's world, to her family, her friends, her secrets and stubborn truths has been a joy. Even the fictional malasadas helped.

As always, these stories don't get written alone. Life is full and chaotic and beautiful: I'm juggling my children's book series, the mysteries, the day job, and most importantly, my amazing family. Since the last book came out, we've added three new grandbabies to the mix, and watching them grow is the sweetest story I get to witness.

Thank you to the writers who walk beside me: my Midwest Mystery Mastermind ladies, the Cozy Zoom Sprints morning crew, my Sisters in Crime chapter family, and the in-real-life friends who keep cheering, even when I'm behind on deadlines. Your encouragement makes the writing not just possible, but joyful.

And to you, dear reader: thank you for coming back to O'ahu with me. I hope Cassandra's journey reminded you, as it did me, that the past isn't gone. It's still speaking through stories, through place, through the people who remember.

Mahalo nui loa, from my heart to yours. ~ Kelly

P.S. Historical note: For clarity, the Mānoa Marauder is entirely fictional. While Hawai'i's history includes many unsolved stories, there are no records of a serial killer on O'ahu around 1910. Early criminal investigations were often informal and inconsistent, with law enforcement evolving over time. In fact, the modern Honolulu Police Department was only formally established in 1932, meaning much of the early twentieth century relied on a sheriff system with limited island-wide authority. I wove this historical backdrop into the story, but the central crime remains invented.

For those interested in diving deeper: exploring Hawaii's land laws and the controversial 1850 Kuleana Act, the story of Queen Lili'uokalani and the illegal 1893 overthrow, and the leadership of Hawaiian wāhine such as Queen Ka'ahumanu and activist-publisher Emma Nāwahī can bring additional perspective to the fictional backdrop of this novel.

Hawaiian Sign Language (HSL) is a distinct and endangered language with deep roots in Hawai'i's Deaf community. Much of what we know about HSL today exists thanks to the tireless work of Linda

Lambrecht, a Deaf educator and historian. Her storytelling and language documentation preserve an essential part of Hawaiian history.

Further Reading

The Overthrow of the Hawaiian Kingdom (KSBE Cultural Vibrancy article) — covers Queen Lili'uokalani, the Bayonet Constitution, and the 1893 coup. https://www.ksbe.edu/assets/pdfs/The_Overthrow_of_the_Hawaiian_Monarchy_PDF.pdf

Hawai'i Sign Language https://w.wiki/EuRnAlso search **Linda Lambrecht Hawaii Sign Language** on YouTube for several helpful videos.

Integrating Kuleana Rights and Land Trust Priorities in Hawaii by Jocelyn B. Garovoy (2019)—on land tenure under the 1850 Kuleana Act. https://journals.law.harvard.edu/elr/wp-content/uploads/sites/79/2019/07/29.2-Garovoy.pdf

Kuleana Act of 1850 (Hawaii)—a clear explanation of Great Māhele and early land documentation. https://w.wiki/EuLW

Emma Nāwahī (1854–1935)—on Hawaiian women's leadership and resistance to overthrow and annexation. https://w.wiki/EuLQ

About the Author

photo credit: Susan Noel

Kelly Brakenhoff is a seasoned American Sign Language Interpreter whose motivation for learning ASL began in high school when she wanted to converse with her Deaf friends. She divides her writing time between the Cassandra Sato Mystery Series and a children's book series featuring Duke the Deaf Dog. In 2025, two of her books were named to the CBC Favorites Award Lists by teachers and librarians nationwide. When she's not writing cozy mysteries or dreaming up adventures for Duke the Deaf Dog, she's likely spoiling her grandkids or her dog.

Sign up for monthly emails with Kelly's special offers, recipes, and book recommendations here:

https://brakenville.myflodesk.com/dbydend

Reach Kelly at her website at kellybrakenhoff.com

Get the latest updates on Facebook: https://www.facebook.com/kellybrakenhoffauthor/

Also By Kelly Brakenhoff

CASSANDRA SATO MYSTERIES
Dead End (Short Story)
Death by Dissertation
Dead Week
Dead of Winter Break
Scavenger Haunt (Short Story)
Death 101: Extra Credit
Halloween Hustle (Novella)
Primary Source (Short Story)
Homecoming Homicide

DUKE THE DEAF DOG ASL SERIES
PICTURE BOOKS
Never Mind
Farts Make Noise
My Dawg Koa
Sometimes I Like the Quiet
Duke the Deaf Dog Workbooks Ages 3-5/Ages 6-9
CHAPTER BOOKS
I Belong Here
It's My Story
Take Your Shot
IEPs R4U and Me / Teacher Guide Workbook